Walls Fall Down

Krys Batts

The Real Ideal, LLC

ISBN: 0996321128

ISBN 13: 9780996321129

Prologue

IT WAS A PALE, mid-June horizon that greeted Cassie on Sunday morning as she sprang from bed. She was grateful for the early rays of light because she had not slept at all, but had instead lain pensively in bed and peered out the window watching the sky change colors from a deep midnight black to the current dusty gray color that so matched her sullen mood. Intermittently during the night, she had also stolen glances at the digital clock on her nightstand and cursed the exceedingly slow passage of time. All she needed was a little sunlight, just a glimmer, and she would get dressed for the power walk that would help clear her mind and relieve the tension that had been building in her body and making her ache. And when the sun finally did peek bravely around the storm clouds that masked the sky, Cassie was quickly out of bed and outside, arms pumping and breath controlled with deep huffs as she rounded a corner to face her first challenge of the day—a street with a steep half-mile incline that usually left her muscles quivering in the aftermath.

Cassie was relieved for the exercise. It was only around six o'clock in the morning, too early for most of her neighbors to be up and about, which meant that she had the sidewalk all to herself. Her mid-length ponytail bobbed back and forth in rhythm with her rapid stride and for a moment Cassie felt at peace for the first time in several hours. The sidewalk was a winding path that circled her apartment complex as well as a nearby subdivision of pricey houses ensconced a mile or so from the Galleria mall. Having never been the type to dwell on extravagant possessions, Cassie instead found more pleasure in the colorful blossoms that lined the sidewalk. Yellow, white, violet, light blue, an array of bright colors that enthralled her eyes despite her inability to name the various flowers. She also admired the tall, beautiful trees that shaded her steps. Even if the sun had been burning brightly, she would have been cooled by the protective tree leaves, which prevented the harshest beams and heat from besetting her. It was one of the many things that Cassie loved about Atlanta's landscaping, and not merely within her own neighborhood. The foliage around many parts of the city was unusually vibrant with color, certainly unlike Chicago, where she had lived for most her life.

Cassie had arrived in Atlanta several years ago, almost immediately after graduating from college and just in time to witness the final stages of a terrific economic boom that had generated thousands of jobs and attracted even more new residents.

Although Atlanta was now settling back down, the city was still a hotspot for African-Americans, who continued pouring in from all over the country. To her complete disappointment, however, a promising career path in the city had not yet revealed itself to Cassie and she had begun to feel stuck in her dead-end job as a pricing analyst for a popular apparel company. Sure, Atlanta had plenty of employment opportunities, but there didn't seem to be the types of jobs that would take Cassie's career in a more interesting, fulfilling direction. She knew she would need to figure out something soon because at age twenty-six, Cassie's window for identifying a specific career track could only be getting smaller, which was a major incentive to take action. But what should that action be? What did she want to do? Some sort of consulting work had always sounded interesting to her, but how could she get her foot in the door with a good company without related work experience? *Oh! It's so frustrating!* She pumped her arms harder and picked up speed as her mind raced with solutions that seemed impossibly out of reach. For a brief moment, Cassie considered using some of the connections and friendships she had developed through her boyfriend, Todd Brody, but then quickly dismissed the idea because she preferred to make her own way.

Todd. He was the reason she needed a power walk this morning. Now that her thoughts had inadvertently traveled to him, Cassie's breath lost its rhythm and she began to feel fatigue, which she adamantly battled against. Why did she always let Todd work her up like this? They had been together for two years now and you would think she would have learned to spot the curve balls before they left the pitcher's grip. *You would think. Why do I even bother?* But then she remembered that the hard decision had been made last night so there was no reason to continue arguing with herself about the man. He would soon be history.

In truth, Cassie should have known from the moment she met Todd that a relationship with him could only prove disastrous. They had met at a club of all places and he had ordered her a martini without even asking what she liked to drink. That should have been the first major clue, but Cassie had naively found his confidence rather appealing as she rarely met men who so naturally took charge of things. She had smiled and drank that martini without one complaint despite the fact that she absolutely hated gin. *Here is a man that I could really go for,* she had thought as she noted his gorgeous looks, the smooth, brown skin, the perfect smile, and his mouthwatering body. And since Cassie hadn't been in a relationship for a while, her mind had quickly wandered to how he must be in the bedroom as the music pulsed around them. It wasn't long before she found out. Surely, it had to be a world record—at least for her—because she had never before met a man and then slept with him within three short days. Without a doubt, the entire situation was a recipe for doom, but Cassie had refused to acknowledge the obvious. Instead, she decided she was in love with Todd and that everything else could be worked out over time, an outlook she would later look back on and fully regret.

Throughout their relationship, Cassie had learned to expect less and less of Todd, who at age twenty-nine worked as a software development manager at TechNet Software and constantly put in long hours to expedite his climb up the corporate ladder. He had a penultimate goal, which he confided to very few people, of someday becoming the company's president, an aspiration that Cassie thought was impossible but nevertheless quite impressive. Although Todd had been raised in a well-to-do family in New Jersey and had never known financial struggles, his parents had instilled in him a healthy regard for hard work as well as a relentless desire for challenges. In Cassie's view, these qualities prompted him to work harder than anyone else she knew and, thus, she had long ago developed a sincere admiration for his intelligence, charisma, and personal goals. She knew that none of his professional success had been merely handed to him. Todd was a self-made man and his sheer determination could only be respected—or so she had once believed.

For the first year, she convinced herself that coming second to everything, including his "boys", was acceptable since the man did after all bear a lot of responsibility at work. She supported his desire to work off steam with basketball until the wee hours of the morning. At least he had never cheated or lied to her, behaviors with which most of her girlfriends were grappling from their own boyfriends. One set of tradeoffs was fair in exchange for a different, more reasonable set of compromises, right? And when he criticized the way she dressed when they went out, she good-naturedly brushed him off since he was only demonstrating his affectionate interest in her appearance. But didn't she also begin to shop for different clothing styles more suited to his tastes to please him? *Hmm...*

After bending and twisting for Todd for a year, Cassie eventually began to resist his controlling behaviors. She stopped allowing him to decide what she would drink or wear when they went out. She stopped accepting his excuses to spend less time with her and more time with his friends. And most recently she stopped sleeping with him, a very difficult but necessary sacrifice—yes, *sacrifice* because Todd was a wonderful lover with a way of making Cassie feel safe and satisfied whenever they were intimate. If these feelings could have flowed into their everyday relations, she would have died before being parted from him. As time had worn on, however, she had begun to feel increasingly slighted and neglected because she clearly was not a priority in Todd's life. Everything and everyone else seemed to come first and the bitterness began to eat away at Cassie even as Todd steadfastly denied the accuracy of her perceptions.

The final straw did not come until last night. Cassie and Todd had made plans to meet at a surprise birthday party for one of her friends and Todd had never shown up. Not only had Cassie been disappointed, but humiliated as well. And she knew exactly where he was—at work as usual. He hadn't even bothered to call her and let her know he wouldn't make it to the party. To say the least, Cassie was perfectly steamed. As she thought about it now, the anger propelled her through the final charge up the concrete hill that had come to represent her early morning nemesis. Once at the top, she stood triumphantly with her hands on her hips and her feet apart in a superwoman stance, wishing that her foolhardy feelings, the senseless love she yet harbored for Todd, could as easily be conquered. *The decision is made. He stood me up last night and now I finally have the courage to do what I should have done one year ago.* Cassie glanced around at the surrounding greenery that shrouded most of the large houses and small shops within the vicinity. She allowed herself only a few moments of restless inner turmoil, heaved a great sigh, and then started back down the hill, not yet headed in the direction of home. Her mind continued to tear into the details of her previous evening and she used the anger to spur her forward with greater momentum.

When Cassie had gotten home from the party, she discovered no messages from Todd on her answering machine and so immediately dialed his office phone number. He picked up after the first ring and announced himself, "Todd Brody," into the phone, but as soon as Cassie had heard his voice, she knew she couldn't talk to him at that moment. The anger inside her threatened to erupt into violence and she would have preferred to throw something at his head rather than rationally discuss his failure to come to the party as planned. Cassie simply hung up the phone and prepared for bed knowing that she would not sleep at all that night.

At around 2:30 a.m., Todd had finally called from his home. Thinking that Cassie was asleep, he left a message on her answering machine as she had lain wide awake and listened, livid with his thoughtlessness.

"Hey, Cass, it's Todd. I'm sure you're asleep now, but I wanted you to have this message when you wake up in the morning. I'm sorry for not making it to the party, but the truth is that I completely forgot. I was so wrapped up in a project at work that I didn't notice the time until it was after midnight. In fact, I'm only now getting home from the office."

Cassie considered picking up the phone, but thought better of it since she knew she couldn't keep her cool. She would only scream at the man because she was so fed up with being unimportant in his overall plans.

"Anyway, let's try to get together tomorrow for lunch and a movie. Call me." And he had hung up. Short, easy, casual, and with the obvious expectation that no difficulties would be forthcoming.

That is it! was the only thing that had run through Cassie's mind for the rest of the night. She had stared out the window and at the clock all night long waiting for a decent hour to call Todd so she could take him up on his offer for lunch and see him in person. Forget the movie.

When Cassie made it back to her apartment from the power walk, the tension that had mounted in her shoulders, stomach, and legs was entirely gone. She felt her heart rate slowing down as she walked into her bathroom, undressed, and stepped into a hot shower.

Cassie held her face under the water, eyes closed, for a few minutes before finally grabbing a shampoo bottle, squeezing a large portion into her hand, and washing her hair. She wanted to be refreshed, but also to purge her entire self of last night and the past two years of various disappointments. She was done with agonizing over Todd's ridiculous hierarchy of priorities and making even the smallest attempts to be physically desirable. Today she would be restored to her true self, pinning her hair back in a bun the way she loved and he hated it, wearing her favorite, beat-up, faded jeans, and shunning all forms of makeup except lip gloss. Todd liked his women to have a glamorous appeal, but Cassie would fall magnificently short of his preferences today.

"Hey, baby," Todd greeted Cassie when she later arrived at his downtown loft at noon sharp. He moved to kiss her, but she turned her head in time to dodge his lips. He didn't seem to notice her attitude. "How was the party last night?"

"It was fine, but I didn't stay for too long so..." She dropped her purse onto one of his chairs and then perched herself on the arm. "I came here because I want to talk to you about last night."

He scratched his head and walked into his kitchen as he talked. "Yeah, like I said on your answering machine, I totally forgot. I'm sorry about that." He washed his hands and threw a dishtowel over his shoulder before pulling out a loaf of French bread. "Do you want anything in particular on your sandwich? I have just about everything here you can name so feel free to be creative." He eyeballed Cassie's clothes and hair critically, but began to slice the bread in preparation for their sandwiches without commenting on her appearance.

"No, thanks. Frankly, I'm really not very hungry." She noted that he looked as scrumptious as ever in a pair of black jogging pants and matching t-shirt. He was around 5'11 with a medium, athletic build, and wonderfully deep brown eyes capable of communicating everything that words could not. Normally, her willpower would have been severely weakened, but not today.

"Oh? Do you want a sandwich or not?"

"Nah, I think I'll pass."

"Okay." He stopped slicing the bread and went to the refrigerator to retrieve the various fixings he wanted.

"Todd, I want you to know that I am extremely hurt and angry with you for blowing off the party last night." Cassie gritted her teeth as she fought to control the tone of her voice.

"I didn't blow off the party, Cass. I told you that I lost track of the time, that's all."

"If you had really wanted to be there, Todd, you would *not* have lost track of the time. As far as I'm concerned, you blew off the party and me."

"And I'm telling you that you're wrong. I'm man enough to tell you if I don't want to be somewhere so let it go, alright?" He began spreading mayonnaise on the bread.

"No, I won't let it go. You know something, Todd? You're the most callous, *selfish* person I've ever known. You don't think about anyone except yourself. I don't know what I ever saw in you because from day *one* you have been a supreme waste of my time."

"Hold up, woman, don't here with all that noise. You know I'm not trying to hear that. If you have something to say, you will say it calmly or you can just keep it to yourself."

To Cassie's surprise, she actually laughed at Todd's cool response. "Uh huh, you're right. I have choices in what I say and what I do." She picked up her purse and walked toward the door. "And right now, I *choose* to leave."

"Do what ya gotta do." He opened a bag of potato chips and poured a healthy portion onto a plate.

"Yeah, I will." She opened the door and looked back over her shoulder. "And Todd?"

"Uh huh?" He looked up as he bit into his sandwich.

"You can take your sorry ass straight to hell." With that, Cassie smiled and strutted out, closing the door very *calmly* behind her. Maybe she could have handled the situation better, but she didn't care anymore. And as she exited Todd's building, she smiled up at the overcast sky, a feeling of lightness overtaking her body and mind. She had never so boldly expressed her displeasure to Todd. Instead, she had always been careful to appear understanding and reasonable. This recent encounter, however, had wholly contradicted her normal desire to demonstrate an agreeable disposition, which had no doubt come as a shock to Todd. Why did women work so hard to treat men with gloves anyway? *Mental note: Be more willing to tell your man when he's pissing you off in the future.* By confronting Todd, Cassie felt she had essentially reclaimed full responsibility for her happiness and she promised herself that no man would ever again provoke her to change herself or to accept less than she deserved in a relationship. And why should she? She was smart, understanding, independent, practical, good-looking, and goal-oriented. Okay, maybe the goals needed some work, but otherwise the most important ingredients were there. *I'm a great catch and Todd should have been grateful that I even gave him a second look.*

As she strode confidently to her car, a silver Nissan Altima, parked at a nearby meter, Cassie actually laughed aloud as she thought of a longstanding joke between her and Todd. Because her complexion was the precise color of coffee with cream while Todd's was a gorgeous, much darker shade, the two had frequently teased each other, with Todd insisting that he liked cream with his coffee while Cassie preferred hers black. She laughed louder, momentarily free of the emotional baggage that had hampered her decision to break up for too long. Yes, he had just lost a real prize in Cassie and there was no going back. Of course, he was so full of himself, he was probably saying the same thing about her at this very moment.

Cassie's relief and joy were short lived. Days had passed since her dramatic exit from Todd's loft and he had not called to reconcile or even to complain. Not once. And only now in the absence of his predetermined futile efforts did Cassie realize she had foolishly expected him to initiate some form of contact after a few "cooling off" days. Meanwhile, both her friends and relatives, particularly her mother, were regularly asking about the relationship and whether Todd had called yet. Of course he would call, everyone said. After all, he and Cassie had been together for two years and nothing that lasted that long could be over so abruptly. But Todd was proving everyone wrong. Rather than hearing about him moping or asking about her through mutual friends, Cassie had instead heard that he started seeing other women, first a young woman he had met at work and then a relatively unknown model that he had once dated while in college. To Cassie's chagrin, people were very generous with sharing information about Todd's personal life and it soon became more than she could stomach. Although she successfully hid her growing hurt at being so quickly forgotten and replaced, she couldn't help crying every night before falling into a miserable sleep. She also began to pick up weight, too depressed to force herself out of bed for the much-needed power walks. Cassie didn't feel powerful. She felt dumb and sorry for herself. For a short time she even forgot exactly why she had dumped Todd in the first place. Why had she broken up with such a sweet, ambitious man?

A few long months passed before Cassie made the decision to leave Atlanta. It was the only way she could regain a realistic perspective and cut the memories of Todd completely out of her life. For heaven's sake, she had started mourning the loss of a man who had treated her like she was insignificant and invisible.

And the loss had been her own decision. The irony of it all was simply ludicrous.

Without bothering to secure employment, Cassie purchased a townhouse in Dallas, Texas, broke her Atlanta apartment lease, and gave notice at her current job. She remained burdened, however, by her lingering emotions for Todd despite the excitement of making so many new changes in her life. Not until she boarded her one-way flight to Dallas did she really begin to feel a sense of comfort, exhaling some sorrow and inhaling reprieve, thankful to be en route to the clean slate that she needed, the new start that would be Todd-free.

Chapter 1

THE BRISK, WARM WIND brazenly blew through Cassie's dark brown hair, abruptly whipping her shoulder-length curls into a whirlwind that briefly circled her head before dropping back down to frame her heart-shaped face. Ignoring the gusty breeze, Cassie walked hurriedly to the street corner and peered at the Coney Island diner on the other side of the street. Having only minutes earlier wrapped up a meeting with her boss, she was over ten minutes late for her lunch date and anticipated a playful scorning from Johnson, her first steady significant other—a more formal term had not yet been established—since moving to Dallas, Texas, nearly a year ago. As of last week, the two had been dating for four months.

After only a few moments, Cassie spotted Johnson, who had taken refuge from the sun, and was sitting at a table beneath one of the blue and white Coney Island umbrellas. The scene was almost comical because he appeared so relaxed, even reposed, beneath the umbrella, which flapped wildly above him in the wind. But that was Johnson—always in control, even when everything around him seemed on the brink of collapse. And in a steel gray suit, minus the coat that was surely hanging neatly in his office, the man looked meticulously groomed, pleasant, and somehow formidable.

Johnson lifted an arm and waved at Cassie, who was waiting amid a bustling, hungry crowd for the traffic light to signal pedestrians to cross. Smiling, Cassie waved back and shrugged her shoulders to indicate how helpless she was to being tardy. In return, Johnson wagged his finger at her with a grin, stood up, and walked over to the corner at which she would soon arrive. It had become a game with them because one of them was always late. As a result, they had agreed to allow fifteen-minute windows from their designated meeting times. If one of them failed to arrive within that time span, they would simply meet later for dinner or exchange their latest adventures on the phone. As they became more comfortable with each other, however, the phone had quickly become a disdainful form of communication.

"Well, it's about time." Johnson laughed when Cassie finally reached him. He then pointedly looked at his watch before adding, "Lady, you had exactly five more minutes and the clock was ticking. You always keep me waiting."

"Don't even try it." Cassie rapidly hugged Johnson and kissed him lightly on the cheek. Since they were both only footsteps from their offices, they were very reserved in public. "Your building is right next door, which already gives you an advantage. Shoot, I have to walk all the way down to the corner and *then* cross the street. Not to mention that I have to wear these heels, which aren't exactly made for long hikes, sir."

Johnson wasn't going to let her off that easy. "Baby, I would hardly call a few paces to the corner a long hike." He placed his hand on her waist, pulled her in front of him, and guided her through the crowd into the diner, gently pressing his hand against the small of her back. "No," he was saying as they approached the long, ordering line, "I don't accept that business about heels slowing you down. You wanna know what I really think?"

Still facing forward and unable to see Johnson's face, Cassie began to laugh. She knew that Johnson was setting her up for some absurd observation. "What, baby? What do you really think? You know how I just love a man with a brain."

Johnson lowered his mouth to Cassie's ear and began whispering while holding her shoulders. "I think that you enjoy making me wait for you because you know how sexy you look crossing the street with the wind blowing through your beautiful hair. I think you know that I'll sit in that damn seat all day just to watch you walk your fine self over to the corner in one of your Ms. Woman-of-the-World business suits. Furthermore, I think you like seeing me struggle to keep my facial expression under control as I check you out and wish I could get you in private *now* instead of later. That's what I think."

Cassie clapped her hand over her mouth to prevent the threatening, thunderous laughter from escaping into the already noisy atmosphere. Her freckled, almond-colored complexion turned a fiery scarlet before finally calming down to a rosy blush on her cheeks. Several moments passed before Cassie had regained her composure well enough to face Johnson without giving in to the stifled giggles. "You are so full of it." She turned to look directly into his eyes, which danced with merriment.

"Uh, baby, the line is moving. Walk up a little." Again his hand circled her waist and guided her closer to the cashier taking orders.

Deciding not to turn back around, Cassie ended up taking a few steps backwards, relying on Johnson's hand to stop her when necessary.

"You know, Mr. Hughes, I believe that I may be cracking your usually controlled posture. You'd better watch it or I'll think that I'm actually getting under your skin, that I just might have a little hold on you." Cassie's eyes challenged Johnson's as mirth tickled her curved lips. The line moved forward again.

"Well, I think you're gonna see a lot of cracked postures if you don't turn around and order. You're holding up the line." As usual, Johnson had expertly dodged a response about his feelings for Cassie.

Undaunted, Cassie stood her ground until she heard the cashier behind her.

"Ma'am, may I take your order?"

A smug grin crossed Johnson's mouth.

Realizing her momentary defeat, Cassie nevertheless allowed her gaze to linger on Johnson's face. "Okay, buster, you got off easy this time, but don't count your chickens yet because the day is still young."

"Yeah, yeah, yeah...Just order already. Women always hold people up, I swear. You take six hours to get dressed for any occasion, five hours to get excited enough for your man to handle his *most serious* business, if you know what I mean. Ha! Ha! Four hours to eat a salad, three hours to get out of the bathroom. And *now* you're holding up a crowd of potentially violent, hungry folks, unnecessarily depriving them of their long-awaited meals." At six-foot one in height, Johnson was tall enough to see directly over Cassie's head. He winked at the cashier, placed his hands on Cassie's shoulders, and turned her around to order. "Tell the lady what you want, and for God's sake hurry up!"

Cassie turned her head back around, but Johnson held a finger to his lips to discourage her from immediately returning the insults. Complying and once again scarlet red, she turned once more to the waiting cashier, this time with a burst of laughter that she could no longer contain.

"Hey, Johnson," a male voice boomed from a table at least ten feet away. "Wanna sit with us? Looks like all the other tables inside are taken."

Still chuckling as she ordered, Cassie heard Johnson decline the offer. Without looking, she knew that a firm nod of his head had accompanied the refusal and precluded any further discussion. More than anything he ever said, it was Johnson's quietly decisive body language that asserted his governance. Among other qualities, his innate confidence would assure a thirty-year-old Johnson a quick rise in his advertising field.

After receiving their lunch orders, Cassie and Johnson walked back outside the diner. They could always count on a few empty tables since the typically one-hundred-degree temperature sent most people racing for the nearest air-conditioned building. The heat didn't bother them, though, since they could speak more freely outside. It was a concession they had accepted when the Texas summer imposed itself on their amiable lunches.

Johnson picked up his hotdog and took a large bite as Cassie fumbled with a fork and knife. She was wearing a cream-colored suit and was unwilling to risk a drop of chili smudging her skirt, especially with more meetings lying ahead in the afternoon. Slowly and awkwardly, she sliced her hotdog and bun into bite-size pieces while Johnson polished off his hotdog and began working on his French fries.

"So Mitchell held you up as usual?" He picked up two fries and dumped them into catsup.

"Yeah, you know how he is. We have to make sure every 'T' is crossed before we submit this proposal. It's worth over twenty-million dollars, you know." Now at age twenty-seven, Cassie was a process engineer for Pinnacle Consulting and spent many late nights at the office scrutinizing department structures, her missions to implement faster processes and to lower operating costs. She loved the job, but hated the ridiculous amount of time it took to do it well. And now her manager, Mitchell, had asked her to assist with a contract proposal that could either make or break her career.

"I have to say that I'm proud of you, Cass. Pretty soon you'll be able to write your own ticket. I know it's hard right now, but within another year you'll have more time to spend doing whatever you want. I'm telling you, I see it coming. Just hang in there and stay positive."

"I know, I know. I just want that time to come *now*. I've got other goals I would like to begin pursuing and this job is killing me." Cassie carefully placed food in her mouth while using her other hand to counter the breeze's assault on her napkin. Meanwhile, the wind had also again taken control of her hair, blowing it up into the air and backward from her face.

Cassie and Johnson were silent as they became lost in their own thoughts. Dismissing her current job issues, Cassie turned her thoughts to Johnson, who was staring at but not seeing a stray, mangy dog sniffing for scraps on the perimeters of their dining area.

Since she had begun dating him, Cassie had not completely figured out exactly *what* had attracted her to Johnson. He was a very average looking man, his skin the exact shade of a brown Crayola, full lips, thick eyebrows, his physique a little too thin for her liking. But Cassie had a high degree of respect for Johnson's intelligence. He was a man that people listened to with an expectant regard, which Cassie liked. And there was no denying that he was on a fast track to success at his firm. Within the past month alone, Johnson had won coveted praises from clients who were amazed at the ad campaigns he had formulated. Still, she wondered what had attracted her when they initially met. You certainly couldn't look at him and know he had a brilliant business mind. And it definitely was not his outward appearance that had caught her attention. For the hundredth time, Cassie puzzled over this phenomenon.

"Earth to Cassie, come in Cassie." Johnson seemed to be speaking from a great distance rather than from across the table. "Baby, come back to our dimension. Hello? What are you thinking about? You haven't even finished your hotdog and the lunch hour is nearly over."

Cassie looked down at her now cold hotdog and realized that she no longer had an appetite. Suddenly she was eager to get the workday behind her and to go home.

"What time is it?"

"It's 12:51 and our duties are calling. We'd better head back to work." Johnson stood up and collected his empty paper plate and Cassie's uneaten food.

"Thanks, baby." She, too, stood up, though with more reluctance than enthusiasm. "Work, work, work," Cassie mumbled to herself. "Meetings, reports, data collections, reorganizing—every day's the same." Already at a nearby garbage can, Johnson didn't hear the resigned breath that Cassie heaved. "Duties indeed..."

When Cassie returned to her office, the message light on her phone was blinking. Groaning, she closed her door and dropped heavily into her chair. Should she check the messages or claim a lack of time and wait until tomorrow? She *did* have a meeting in thirty minutes for which she needed to review a few documents and market statistics. As she toyed with the idea of waiting, she heard Johnson's voice echoing in her mind: *Our duties are calling*. And Cassie knew that Johnson, rather than sit and debate whether to do his job efficiently, would answer the call no matter how much he would prefer to take a break. At the moment, Johnson's mysterious appeal was becoming dubious.

Deciding to obey her nagging conscience, Cassie took out a pen and writing pad to record the names and purposes for the callers' voicemail messages. She hoped she wouldn't need to do any research before returning the calls. A late night at the office was simply more than she could bear today.

To her pleasure, the first message was a no-brainer: a client was calling to confirm a meeting date. No problem. Cassie wrote down the client's name and phone number and then moved on to the next message.

Feeling somehow redeemed from calamity, Cassie was tapping her pen on the writing pad when the second message began to play back. As the electronic operator broadcast the date and time the message was received, Cassie preoccupied herself with ideas of an evening of rapture with Johnson, who was now regaining his appeal. She pondered doing something different that would thrill and surprise him. Perhaps answering her door in only a bath towel when he arrived that evening. Or maybe she would soak in candlelight until he arrived and then let him dry her off. Nothing fancy, but enough to keep him guessing. Cassie smiled wickedly to herself, still tapping the pen and enjoying the anticipation.

It wasn't until Cassie heard the familiar voice on the message that her smile faded.

"Hello, Cassie," came that voice, *his* voice. And suddenly, with the pronouncement of two words, Cassie was a castaway, both repulsed by and drawn to the ensuing emotions, the pure passion that touched her, the memories of love. After the first two words, she had heard nothing else and was soon forced to replay the message. She inhaled deeply before commanding the service to repeat.

"Hello, Cassie. This is Todd Brody. Uh, I'm in town for a few days visiting some friends and I was hoping that you and I could get together for lunch. I've been thinking about you and… uh…would like to hear about all the good things you've been up to since you moved to Dallas. I don't doubt that everything has been going well for you. If you can, please call me at 972-555-3613. I hope to hear from you soon. Bye."

The voice was so smooth and mellow. Goosebumps jumped from Cassie's skin. Todd. The name alone washed over her, the memories became murky waters and she was rapidly pulled under in a current that was too deep for a clean stroke, a break and getaway. So long ago she had resolved never to speak to him again. Now, after a year of ignoring their painful past, a lone phone call from him had melted her constitution. When she had lived in Atlanta, Cassie had believed that Todd was the love of her life. Now it seemed a lifetime had come and gone since she had heard that beautiful, tempting voice. God! She realized how much she had missed hearing his voice. She also realized that she was still vulnerable to a man who had hurt her more than any other.

Chapter 2

WHEN CASSIE GOT HOME that evening, she was still debating whether or not to return Todd's call. She changed out of her suit and put on a pair of red shorts, an old Hands on Atlanta t-shirt, and a pair of new tennis shoes. She had no intention of jogging in the heat, but a power walk might help clear her mind. Before she could exit her townhome, however, the phone rang.

"Oh, no. I hope that's not Todd or Johnson." Cassie walked to the phone and checked out the caller ID while biting her lower lip. She was relieved to see it was her friend, Monique, a recruiter she had met before being hired at Pinnacle Consulting.

Cassie picked up the phone. "Hello?"

"Hey, girl! What's up?"

"Monique, you are not going to believe the day I've had." Cassie dropped onto her large, comfortable sofa and turned on the lamp beside the phone.

"Really? Sounds like we both have some news to exchange. Wanna meet for dinner at Ruth's Chris Steak House?"

"I don't think so. I'm feeling a little disoriented. I think I need to stay in tonight."

"Are you disoriented or expecting some company?" Monique was referring to Johnson, of course.

Cassie smiled into the phone. "No, I'm not expecting company tonight, thank you. I just don't feel like going anywhere."

"Wow! You sound like crap."

"I feel like crap."

"Okay, don't say one more word until I get there. I want to hear all about it and then I have something to show you."

Before Cassie could object to Monique inviting herself over, the phone line was released. Cassie shook her head with a smile and put her phone down. What would she do without Monique's unrelenting energy to pick her up? It seemed like Monique was always excited about something. She wondered what her friend's news could be.

With the prospect of company and conversation on the way, Cassie no longer felt the need for a power walk. She walked into the kitchen and opened the refrigerator in search of a cheesecake snack bar. She loved cheesecake, but hated knowing that the fat took up residence on her round hips.

The phone rang again. A quick glance at the caller ID revealed that Johnson was the caller and he was still at work.

"Baby, what are you wearing?" Johnson got right to the point with his favorite question.

Cassie couldn't help teasing the man. "I was just about to soak in the bathtub so I'm not wearing anything." She smiled while biting into the cheesecake bar.

"Ooh, sounds like you need some company. I'm still at the office, but I'll be leaving in around ten minutes. Got room for two in that tub?"

"Not tonight, baby. Monique is coming over. She's got some sort of exciting news to share."

"When does Monique *not* have something exciting to talk about?"

Cassie laughed since Johnson's observation mirrored her own.

He lowered his voice. "So when is Monique leaving? We can still get together later, can't we?"

The question was ripe with the intended seductive message, but Cassie was not going for it tonight. "I'm going to bed after she leaves, sweetie. I've had a really hectic day and I don't think tomorrow will be much better. You know how Mitchell is riding me about these market stats. Why don't we plan on tomorrow night? I promise I'll be rested up for you."

Johnson paused before responding. His disappointment was obvious. "Okay, baby, I understand. You get some sleep tonight."

"I will."

They were both silent. At this time, most couples would exchange *I love you* and end the call. But for Cassie and Johnson the moment was awkward. Either Johnson wasn't ready for an emotional commitment or he simply did not have deep feelings for Cassie. She couldn't tell so she refused to go out on the limb by herself.

Finally, "Goodnight, Cass. I'll talk to you tomorrow."

"Okay, goodnight."

Cassie disconnected and wondered if Johnson loved her. They had met nearly six months ago when Cassie had blindly bumped into him and spilled her entire lunch on the same Coney Island floor where they had eaten today. Quite unexpectedly, Johnson had laughed and leaned down with her to help clean up the mess, at which point his head had collided with hers. While rubbing the clobbered spot that would surely develop into a bruise on her own head, Cassie had shared in his laughter and apologized for being such a klutz. Even then she had not been able to identify the *something* about Johnson that had peaked her interest, but *something* had immediately electrified her heart despite the learned skepticism now speckling her soul. Still, Cassie would not again be seduced by the unrealistic notion of love at first sight, leaping without first carefully looking after the painful disappointments she had known with Todd. Without realizing it, Johnson had made everything so easy and yet so difficult for her, never pressuring her for anything more than friendship, but nevertheless drawing her into the allure and beauty of his mind and spirit. It had not been a physical attraction for Cassie, but rather something much deeper, something that transcended skin, bone, and flesh. And that as yet unidentified *something* had caused her to appreciate Johnson's conversation, his companionship, and his dreams long before their relationship had integrated the soft mysteries of romance. She and Johnson had just seemed to click in every possible way, conversing about everything that happened in their lives, eventually restoring each other so lovingly in the night, and leaning on each other for fortitude and encouragement. They had become inseparable friends and for the past four months they had been lovers as well. And oh how rapidly the months had passed. How rapidly they had passed without Johnson feeling compelled to express any serious emotions that would solidify their relationship as something more involved than sheer friendship. What were they anyway? Bed buddies? Maybe Johnson would prove to be just another mistake to add to a growing list after all. Maybe Johnson was another Todd.

Once again, Cassie somberly dropped onto her sofa. Rather than dwell on Johnson, she picked up the remote control and turned on the television, opting for the evening news on ABC. Tonight, David Muir was reporting on a shooting in a predominantly black neighborhood. The authorities were puzzled about the senselessness of black-on-black crime. Today, a twelve-year-old boy had been shot because he refused to hand over his Air Jordan tennis shoes to another kid with a gun. Cassie was disgusted with the coverage. It seemed that the media portrayed young black children as intellectually challenged. Then, when white children gunned down several classmates in a single shooting incident, the public needed to understand that bullying and gun accessibility were the real problems, not the white children. Cassie changed the channel to BET news.

After a half hour, Cassie heard Monique's car in the driveway. When her friend finally entered the townhouse, she was practically breathless.

"Girl, the traffic coming over was a nightmare. A cop pulled over someone on highway 635 and everybody must have been driving five miles per hour just to get a look at him writing the ticket. Can you believe that? Some people are too damned nosy." Monique was understandably in a huff. As she spoke, she stood before Cassie with her hands on her hips and shifted her weight to one side.

Monique was a beautiful woman who seemed miraculously unaware of her looks. Today, her black hair was pulled back into a smooth, tight bun that accentuated her stunning African features. She had mahogany skin, well-shaped lips, deeply set eyes, and a figure that most women would kill for.

"I know," Cassie agreed about the ridiculous traffic that had set off her friend. "There you are stuck on the freeway, *creeping*, absolutely sure that someone must be dead up ahead. Then, when you finally reach the problem, it's either someone has pulled over to fix a flat tire or a cop has stopped someone during rush hour. I get so mad when I'm late for work because people rubberneck down the highway. It's so irritating."

The two walked into the kitchen.

"Well, I'm glad you finally made it here. Do you want something to drink? I've got orange juice, milk, and ginger ale." Cassie opened the refrigerator as she talked.

"No, thanks, Cass. I had a cheeseburger and a huge Coke during the drive over." Monique's frustration was subsiding as her normal exuberance returned. She was almost ready to get down to the purpose for the visit. "I'm going to use the bathroom and then we've got to talk. Is the bathroom in your hall fixed yet?"

"Yeah. I'll be in the den." Cassie poured a tall glass of orange juice as Monique went down the hall. Once again, she wondered what Monique's news could be. There was no way to guess, but Cassie was sure it was good since it had necessitated the showing of something.

With her orange juice in hand, she walked back into the den and made herself comfortable on the sofa. Before long, Monique was rushing into the room. "Okay, Cass, you go first. What's going on that has you feeling so bad?" She practically leapt onto the sofa and landed so that she was facing her friend. She then placed one leg on the sofa and one arm on top of the back cushions.

Cassie wasn't sure she wanted to talk about Todd's call so she attempted to shift the conversation to Monique's news. "You go first. You sound so excited about something. I can't wait to hear about it."

"No, Cass, my news can wait." Monique was firm although her voice was warm with affection and friendship. She reached over and lightly tapped Cassie's shoulder. "Tell me what's going on, girl. Is it Johnson?"

Cassie looked down at her orange juice and was silent for a few moments. If only it were that simple. Since Monique knew about Cassie's history with Todd, she would also know when she heard about the call that an ugly problem had presented itself. There was no way to hide it.

Monique was silent as Cassie heaved a long breath and spilled the story. To her surprise, she was relieved to talk to someone about it. She realized how much she needed an objective opinion and Monique certainly had solid judgment. Cassie trusted her to weigh all the facts, both past and present, before suggesting any moves.

"So anyway," Cassie was finishing, "I really don't know what to do. I mean, I have deliberately cut Todd out of my life for all this time and then, pow, he knocks me over the head with an unexpected phone call and that smooth voice." She rolled her eyes up and looked back at her friend. "I had forgotten how good he sounds, Monique. I felt like putty just listening to the message. I really don't think I can handle talking to him. And I certainly don't want to see him. That would be asking for trouble that I don't need stirred up."

Monique had not moved, had not shifted her position or her facial expression one inch throughout Cassie's revelation. She was absorbing and now reflecting on every word, skills she used daily when interviewing job candidates. After several moments, Monique finally said, "Cass, it's pretty obvious to me that you still have feelings for Todd."

"No, I don't—" Cassie started before being cut off by Monique's hand in the air, the palm facing Cassie in the halt position.

"Be quiet and let me finish." Her voice was still calm yet firm. "Like I said, it is obvious that you still have feelings for Todd. Now, what those feelings are only you can say. But if just a phone call has got you all worked up, that suggests to me that your emotions are still heavy whether or not you want to admit it to yourself." Monique paused for effect, her eyes never wavering from Cassie's face. "I think you should return Todd's call."

"No, I can't—"

Monique again cut off Cassie's statement. "I'm not finished yet. I'm going to tell you why I believe you should return Todd's call."

Cassie fell silent, but was clearly edgy about whatever Monique might say next.

"You should return Todd's call for two reasons. Number one, he may slip up and prove that he's still the same jerk you left behind a year ago. If that happens, you won't have so many unresolved feelings and questions about what might have been. Number two, if he's not the same jerk and you're still attracted to him, now is the time to make sure you'll never have regrets about being stubborn at the wrong time. Yes, Todd was an asshole while you dated in Atlanta. Based on everything you told me, he needed to be dropped, I'd say even *thrown* out the picture. But all that aside, he must have done more things right than wrong because you're still hung up on the guy. So I say give him a call and give him a chance to hang himself."

Cassie released a long breath and shook her head. "I'm telling you that I just don't think I can do it. I feel so guilty about even thinking about calling Todd. I keep asking myself how would I feel if one of Johnson's old girlfriends called him out of the blue like this. I would be really pissed off if he started talking to an old flame that he had loved before me."

"Okay, so Johnson has finally said the 'L' word to you?"

"Well, no." It was embarrassing for Cassie to admit.

"Are you two in a committed relationship?" Monique didn't miss a beat.

Again, this time with a weak shrug, "No, I don't think so."

"So then what's the problem? It sounds to me as if you're feeling guilty about calling a man even though you don't have one. Am I missing something here?"

Broken down to such a basic level, the answer was, "No, I guess not. Know something? I'm beginning to think that *I'm* the one who's missing something. Not once has Johnson indicated that he wants a serious relationship and yet I'm worrying about him as if I've got something to lose. And anyway, I'm not planning to sleep with Todd. It's not like I'm thinking about meeting him at a hotel or something."

"That's right. And even if you were planning to meet Todd at a hotel, it wouldn't be Johnson's business. I'm sure he doesn't tell you everything he does when you're not around."

"Yeah, but I don't think Johnson is seeing anyone else." Small stings of guilt again pierced Cassie's conscience.

"I'm not saying he's seeing anyone else. I'm just saying that you owe it to yourself to be sure you're with the right man. And you shouldn't feel guilty about wanting that for yourself. Call Todd and find out what he has to say. It may be something. It may be nothing. Either way, you should at least find out."

"Alright, alright...I'll think about it." Another long sigh.

"I hope you do. Personally, I'm just dying to know why Todd is calling you after all this time. All kinds of ideas are running through my mind. If you don't call him for yourself, then call for me because I'm on pins and needles, girl!"

As usual, Monique had found a thought provoking twist that caused Cassie to rethink her initial reaction. She still wasn't sure whether she should return Todd's call, but she was grateful for Monique's objective perspective, which differed so greatly from her own.

"Okay, Monique, now you have to share *your* news." Cassie was ready to change the subject. "What is so exciting that you had to rush all the way over here?"

Although Monique's face lit up with glee, she seemed reluctant to fess up. "Um, it's something that will shock you. You're not going to believe it."

Cassie did not like being held in suspense. "What? *What?* Tell me!"

Monique was all teeth and clearly on the verge of exploding with the news. "I *am* going to tell you. Just hold your horses." Still nothing but teeth, Monique grabbed her purse from the coffee table and thrust both hands into it. From Cassie's view, her friend was yanking and tugging on something, but she couldn't see what. When Monique's hands finally emerged from the purse, she held one out for Cassie to inspect. There was a huge diamond on the ring finger.

Cassie's eyes immediately grew to the size of walnuts. "Oh my God! Is that what I think it is? Hold on, girl, let me get a better look." Cassie grabbed Monique's extended hand and stared at the shining object that had to be the largest diamond she'd ever seen outside of a display case. "Oh my God!" She repeated and looked up at Monique, who was still smiling deliriously. "Are you and Rodney engaged?"

Monique threw her head back with delight. "Yes! He proposed this morning. Can you believe it?" Monique retrieved her hand and gazed at the diamond, probably for the millionth time, while gushing about how Rodney had proposed. "He brought breakfast to me in bed and the ring was on top of an omelet. I didn't even see it because I didn't have my contacts in. So I'm slicing the omelet and he's watching me cut it into these small pieces." Now she laughed, remembering the moment. "Right before I could place the knife on top of the ring, he caught my wrist and said 'Nicky, you are as blind as a bat.' And that's when he took the ring off the omelet, held it up to my eyes, and proposed. I know it sounds corny, but it was so *sweet*." Monique's eyes were as bright as the diamond. "Okay, it was funny, too." More laughter as she again envisioned the breakfast proposal.

Cassie only smiled as she struggled with her concerns and emotions. "But you've only been seeing each other for, what, eight, nine months?" She was not only stunned by the news, but also mildly jealous.

"We've been seeing each other now for almost nine months. Long enough to have a baby." Monique was already deciding on and shaping a picture of her future with Rodney. She was nearly thirty-four and very much ready to have a family, but she had steadfastly held out for someone she considered Mr. Right. According to her, she had turned down at least three men before meeting Rodney.

Monique's overwhelming happiness caused Cassie's selfish thoughts to evaporate. Her friend deserved to be happy and Rodney had certainly been spoiling her since they met. There was no reason for Monique to question the integrity of the man or his feelings for her. And Cassie realized that her jealousy was rooted in her confusion about her own personal life, which was on the verge of a catastrophe rather than harmony. She leaned forward and hugged her ecstatic friend. "I'm so happy for you, Monique. I really am. I hope I marry a man who makes me as happy as Rodney obviously makes you."

Monique hugged her friend back. "You will, Cass. You will. You just have to be very picky. Look at me. It took me thirty-four years to finally find that jewel, but it was worth it because Rodney is the best lover, best friend, best man I have ever met in my whole life. I feel like the luckiest woman on the planet!" Monique and Cassie released each other and now Monique studied her friend's face. She was an expert at reading people's expressions. "Cassie, I hope you do decide to call Todd."

"Don't start on that again." Cassie slumped backward and stared at the ceiling. "I don't know what I'm going to do. I mean, you and Rodney knew it was right from the day you met. You both just *knew* there was something strong and powerful that drew you to each other. I've never had that with anyone. Doesn't that say something? Doesn't that tell me that I haven't met the right man yet?"

"Cassie, it's different for everybody. We can never know how or when we're going to meet our best partners. Frankly, I don't know if you *haven't* already met Mr. Right, but I do know one thing."

"What?"

"You sure as hell won't find out who Mr. Right is if you're afraid of your emotions. Take Todd, for example..."

Cassie grabbed a small sofa pillow and threw it at Monique, who quickly ducked while laughing. The pillow hit the wall and fell harmlessly to the floor as both women laughed together.

Chapter 3

WHEN CASSIE WALKED TOWARD her office at seven-thirty the following morning, her boss, Mitchell, was already standing in the doorway as though expecting to see her. Although approaching age forty, Mitchell's youthful looks frequently caused him to be mistaken for around thirty-two. The gravity of his demeanor, however, put his audience and employees on alert. He had dark red hair that was always perfectly groomed and sharp blue eyes that missed nothing. Cassie enjoyed working with him immensely because he possessed an impeccable business sense. She regarded him as both a mentor and friend, always making sure to exceed his demands as a manager. As a result, Cassie and Mitchell enjoyed a relaxed working relationship that was founded on mutual respect.

Because Mitchell's back was turned to her, Cassie called out to him as she approached while also speeding up her pace. "Good morning, Mitchell."

Mitchell looked over his shoulder, his brow furrowed. The expression on his face communicated the question before it was asked. "Cassie, I'm glad you're here. I was just stopping by to ask about those market statistics. I promised ColaCorp that we'd get something to them by tomorrow. What's the status?"

Cassie breezed past Mitchell and strode into her office as he followed. "I've got the drafts prepared, but I'm waiting to see how Philadelphia responds to the new wireless solutions before finalizing a recommendation. I should know something by this afternoon."

"What kind of numbers do you expect?" Mitchell was fishing for news he could pass along to his own boss.

Cassie sat down and turned on her computer while continuing to talk. "Well, based on the responses in New York and St. Louis, I'm expecting that the number of employees required to maintain the manufacturing equipment can be reduced significantly. So far, there haven't been any major disasters without one-hundred percent continual manpower and monitoring in either of these markets. As you know, the wireless technology enables machines to communicate shutdowns and mechanical problems to anyone and everyone who needs to know within two minutes. I'd say that ColaCorp stands to save millions of dollars by implementing these methods internationally. And the really good news is that they can do so with minimal risk."

"But you still aren't giving me hard numbers."

"And I'm not going to until I get Philadelphia's data this afternoon. I'd hate to commit to something and then renege later. If you can wait a few more hours, I'll have numbers that you can take to the bank."

Mitchell stood in silence before saying, "Cassie, you're doing great work. I'll expect that final report along with the cost and benefit analysis on my desk by two o'clock today so we can discuss it."

"You got it, Mitchell." Cassie began tapping on her computer keyboard as Mitchell exited toward his own office.

As Cassie was pulling up her corporate e-mail on the computer, one of her coworkers, Judy, popped her head in the door.

"Cass, are you coming to Humperdink's with everyone after work today?"

Cassie was scanning the e-mail inbox to decide which message should receive priority attention. She responded distractedly, "I don't know. What's going on at Humperdink's?"

"What do you mean, 'What's going on?' It's Carl's last day and we're taking him out. Did you forget?"

Now Cassie looked up. "Shoot. Yes, I forgot. It totally slipped my mind." She quickly scanned the piles of paper scattered across her desk. "There's no way I can make it. Is Carl in yet?"

"Are you kidding? I just told you it's his last day. He'll probably show up long enough to collect his final check and then head out with everyone to celebrate the new job. I think he's going to be a manager at this other company."

"You're right. He's really excited about the move up." Cassie began looking at her computer screen again. "I'll be sure to catch up with him before y'all head out today."

Taking the cue, Judy moved to exit the office before turning back around. "By the way, did Carolyn leave a message for you this morning?"

"No. Why?" Once more, Cassie was forced to divert her attention from the computer, this time to look quizzically at Judy.

"Someone came by to see you yesterday, a client or something. Anyway, Carolyn tried to call you, but I told her you were already gone for the day. You may want to ask her about it when she gets in." Judy left the office before Cassie could ask more questions.

Now feeling extremely disconcerted, Cassie rapidly examined the calendar screen on her computer to determine if she had forgotten a client meeting. Had she been so preoccupied and absent-minded? She could have sworn that no one was scheduled. In her job, neglecting clients could translate into a pink slip so she was prepared to phone over an immediate, heartfelt apology.

Cassie quickly reviewed yesterday's schedule and was relieved to confirm that no client meeting had been set up. Thank God. Now that left the million-dollar question: Who had stopped by to see her? The question rocketed upward in her mind, but quickly lost fuel and plummeted back down. Cassie simply did not have time right now for such distractions. Once again, she forced her attention back to the computer and to the e-mail that demanded her immediate feedback. She also decided to finalize her ColaCorp report to Mitchell by one o'clock to ensure she beat his deadline.

By late afternoon, Cassie was completely exhausted. For more than three solid hours, she and Mitchell had thoroughly discussed every period and comma in her ColaCorp analysis until he knew all the details as well as she did. Not only had he reviewed and interrogated her on all the market results, but he had also questioned the final analysis from every possible angle, ensuring that all bases were covered. In the end, a few minor adjustments were made and Cassie had received high praises for her work. She was further pleased to detect a promotion on the way. She began to hum as she walked back to her office to plan the presentation of her analysis and recommendations to Co-laCorp. Mitchell was going to let her run the entire finalization stage, another promising sign of a promotion.

Before Cassie reached her office, she remembered Judy's comments about an unknown visitor dropping by yesterday. She stopped short and changed direction for Carolyn's office, which was near the reception area. Hopefully, Carolyn was working late. Since she and her husband traded days for picking up their young children from daycare, Cassie had a fifty-fifty chance of catching Carolyn at work after four-thirty in the afternoon.

Cassie rounded the corner and knocked on Carolyn's door, which was slightly cracked open. "Come in," came Carolyn's voice, clearly not pleased with the interruption. As a customer service supervisor, Carolyn rarely found moments of solitude during which time she could weed through the multiple issues that confronted her and her staff. Cassie had also heard through the grapevine that her marriage was on the rocks. Although Cassie was glad to find Carolyn still at work, she was also mindful that the woman probably had frayed nerves. Cassie almost timidly stepped into the office.

"Oh, hi, Cassie." Carolyn showed no enthusiasm. "Do you need something?"

When Carolyn looked up at her visitor, Cassie could see dark circles beneath her eyes. Despite the shadows, however, Carolyn had an attractive face along with blond hair that she kept shoulder length, and long eyelashes that normally made her large eyes appear deep and inquisitive. Today, however, she appeared annoyed. Cassie would make it fast.

"I'm sorry to interrupt you, Carolyn. I realize how busy you are. This morning, Judy mentioned that someone had stopped by to see me yesterday after I'd left. She also said that you had talked to the person. I was hoping you could tell me who it was that had come by."

Carolyn exhaled and shook her head apologetically. "Gosh, I'm sorry, Cassie. I was planning to leave a message about that for you this morning, but I completely forgot."

"That's okay."

Carolyn again exhaled deeply, now shaking her head while using her fingers to twist her wedding band. "There's really not much to tell. I was walking through the reception area late yesterday afternoon and there was a young man who needed assistance. He asked to see you, but Judy walked by and said you had left for the day. I'm sure that neither one of us got his name, though. Once he learned that you weren't here, he just said he'd get in touch with you later. I'm sorry, but I don't have more concrete information for you."

Cassie was sorry, too. "Can you tell me how he looked? Did he appear to be a client?"

"I really don't know if he was a client or not. He seemed very professional, nice looking, African-American, sort of tall. I haven't seen him around before so that's all I can tell you." Though apologetic, Carolyn's tone was rapidly becoming one of dismissal. "Can I help you with anything else?"

Disappointed, Cassie moved toward the door. "No thanks. I'll get out of your way."

"You're not in the way. And, hey, I apologize again for not leaving a message for you this morning. That was really thoughtless of me."

"I understand. Sounds like it wasn't urgent so..." Cassie shrugged her shoulders to say *I'm not worried about it*. She exited the office and grabbed the doorknob. "Don't work too late Carolyn," she said while closing the door behind her.

Before the door was entirely shut, she heard Carolyn respond, "Look who's talking."

❧

After sitting in her office for around forty-five minutes, Cassie decided to pack up her ColaCorp presentation project and work on it at home. It was nearly six-thirty and her creative juices just weren't flowing. Admittedly, she was still feeling disappointed that Carolyn had not been able to provide more details about the visitor. It could have been anybody.

Cassie placed all the documents she needed into her leather satchel, turned off the computer and stared at her desk for a moment. She felt like she was forgetting something. What was it? Finally, she remembered. Johnson. They had planned on getting together that evening. Good Lord, where was her mind going? She unpacked her satchel and left the ColaCorp data on her desk. For once, the work could wait until tomorrow.

Now heading for the lobby, Cassie's thoughts turned toward Johnson. When she had cancelled their normal lunch date earlier that day, he had immediately known that Mitchell was the reason. He had also known that Cassie was in a hurry and did not have time for one of their usual conversations. Without a word of objection, Johnson had reminded her of their evening plans, wished her luck with her project, and shooed her off the phone. As she now reflected on the phone call, Cassie liked the fact that Johnson was becoming so familiar with her work and her moods. Furthermore, because he had been so supportive, Cassie felt he deserved a reward. He would receive it tonight.

"Cassie."

That voice. She had not seen him, but she knew the voice *so* well. She immediately felt sick to her stomach as she stopped and glanced around the lobby. And then she saw him walking toward her. Apparently, Todd had been sitting on one of the corner sofa chairs, visible only to someone entering the reception area. Undoubtedly, it had also been him who had come to the office yesterday. Without intending to, Cassie quickly noted that he was still exceedingly *fine* and her breath shortened. Surely his eyes could see inside her.

"I'm glad I finally caught you," he continued while approaching her.

Feeling confused, exhilarated and tense all at once, Cassie paused before saying, "Hiii." The word escaped her as one long breath and she hated herself. *Get a grip*, her mind coached as the rest of her body went limp. She wondered how she must be looking and grappled with fixing a noncommittal expression on her face. It wasn't working.

"Did you get my messages?" He was still crossing the lobby toward her, smiling broadly. His smile was perfect, inviting.

"Uh, yeah," she stammered and watched his smooth stroll. Was everything about him so smooth? "I received one yesterday, but I haven't had a chance to call you back. This is really an unexpected surprise. I mean, I'm surprised that you're actually here in this lobby."

As Todd drew closer, Cassie began gesturing with her free hand, trying to decide whether or not to extend it for a formal handshake in greeting. Finally, believing her hand must appear to be jerking spastically in the air, she ran her fingers through her hair before allowing it to fall casually—she hoped—to her side.

She then stood deathly still, concentrating on not trembling and watching him draw still closer. The seconds played out in slow motion and Cassie didn't know if she was thrilled or frightened to see Todd. She soon realized she was both.

Todd was finally close enough to circle his arms around her for a long embrace. "It's so good to see you." As he spoke, his arms tightened and pressed her closer to him. As always, he smelled like soap and cologne.

Cassie closed her eyes and soaked him up, reflexively returning his hug with the one free arm. Not only did he still look and smell good, he felt wonderful against her. He was all man.

"Cass, you are still so beautiful," he whispered into her ear before pressing his warm lips against the same lobe.

You're still beautiful, too, Cassie thought, but was unable to verbalize. For a few moments, she simply couldn't speak. For a few moments, she was back in Atlanta and Todd was both her love and her lover. *Umm...*She remembered the lover all too well.

With Todd so close to her, Cassie found it impossible to remember what had driven her from him while living in Atlanta. When she finally pulled away from him, she stepped back a few paces and looked him over curiously, struggling to collect her thoughts. It all seemed so unreal. "So what brings you to Dallas?" she managed, her mind clouded.

Todd placed his hands in his pants pockets, but remained stationary. "Some friends of mine invited me down for the week and it seemed like a good time for a change of scenery. And I admit I knew you were here so I wanted to see you. I hope you're not upset that I came to your office unannounced."

"No, I'm not upset, just surprised." Cassie was also confused. She tilted her head slightly before asking, "Why did you want to see me?"

This time, Todd stepped forward to close the gap Cassie had placed between them. "I was hoping we could talk about that over dinner. I thought maybe we could leave here and catch up on each other over chardonnay and perhaps some seafood?" That gorgeous smile again.

Cassie wondered if he knew how disarming he was at that moment. If she were not already committed to see Johnson that evening, the offer would have been tempting.

Reality began to seep back in and Cassie was mildly flustered as she looked at her watch. She would have to cut this reunion short as Johnson would be at her home in less than thirty minutes. "I'm sorry, Todd, but I already have plans tonight. In fact, I need to get home." She moved toward the lobby exit. "Do you want to walk with me to my car? I'm sort of in a hurry. We can talk and walk at the same time."

Todd seemed somewhat surprised by Cassie's refusal, but quickly saved face. "Sure. Lead the way."

He waved his hand in a "ladies first" gesture and fell into stride immediately behind Cassie. If offered a wager, she would bet money he was using the opportunity to stare at her derriere.

The two exited the building and began walking toward the parking lot. It was a couple of blocks away since the Pinnacle

Consulting building consisted only of offices. For the first time, Cassie was glad for the trek because it afforded her and Todd more time to talk. Maybe she could figure out why he was suddenly so eager to see her. As they walked, the nervousness she had felt was rapidly evaporating and her emotions, though initially stronger than she could have anticipated, were now in check.

Todd could hardly wait to ask the obvious question. "I don't want to seem nosy, but I can't help wondering about your evening plans. Do you mind my asking if you're seeing someone?"

He looked at the sidewalk, preventing Cassie from seeing what may be lurking in his eyes.

"Actually, yes, I am seeing someone."

"He's a lucky man, and if he's smart, he knows it." Todd gazed at Cassie's profile. "Do you love him?"

"Why do you want to know?"

"Hey, I'm just asking, that's all. Just making conversation."

"Yeah, right. Well, let's make conversation about you. Are *you* seeing anyone? And, if so, do *you* love *her*?"

Todd chuckled. "You're still the same, Cass. Anyway, to answer your question, no, I'm not seeing anyone right now."

"That's too bad. Then again, that's probably a good thing. If memory serves me correctly, you never had time for a relationship."

"I guess I deserve that. I know I didn't give you the attention I should have when we were together. I was too caught up in my job and everything that was going on at the time. You probably think I only cared about making money and getting promoted."

"No, you cared about other things, too. You cared about playing basketball and clubbing with your friends and—oh yeah—making sure I knew my insignificant place." Cassie had meant for the comment to be playful, but the sarcasm and scorn nevertheless came through.

"Is that what you think?"

Todd seemed appalled, but Cassie reacted only with a sideways roll of her eyes to say *You already knew that.*

"Cassie, you were never insignificant to me. I know my priorities were messed up, but that was never about you or us. I was just trying to get ahead in the corporate rat race. I wanted to make something of myself that people respect and not be just another black man that gets treated like a company token."

Bitterness had begun to creep into Todd's voice, but Cassie made no comment. She'd heard it all before. They walked silently for a few moments as Todd stared into the distance, beyond anything Cassie would ever see.

"I did make time for you, Cassie. I knew it wasn't as much as I should have, but I did the best I could at the time."

"Your best could have been better."

"What do you mean by that?"

"Forget it. It's old news and not worth rehashing after all this time."

"No, I don't want to forget it. I want to know what you mean."

Cassie looked at Todd and pursed her lips. She really did not want to elaborate since she had deliberately buried her frustrations so long ago. Plus, as far as she was concerned, there simply was no point now. But she knew that Todd would not willingly let the subject go without some form of an explanation.

"Todd, for the entire two years that we were together, we probably saw each other an average of once each week. But I could have lived with that if you weren't constantly criticizing me whenever we *did* see each other. I don't know what kind of relationship you remember, but I remember everything—the good, the bad, and the ugly. And sometimes it was very ugly." Cassie's memory was suddenly quite vivid and the hurt she had experienced a heartbeat away. Her car was now just across the street and Todd was steadfastly keeping up with her rapid pace.

"Cass, I'm sorry. I really am. There's no way I should have let you leave the city with that impression."

"It wasn't an impression, Todd. It was reality. But guess what. It's also the past so let's not dwell on it." They finally approached Cassie's car and she reached into her purse to hunt for the keys.

With his hands pushed deeper into his pockets, Todd soberly watched Cassie dig through her purse. "Cass, can we get together tomorrow for dinner? I'm in town for only a few more days and I'd really hate for us to part again on such a sour note. Or do you already have plans with that mysterious man of yours?" The last question was a failed attempt at humor.

Cassie pulled her keys from the purse and looked up at Todd. "I don't know, Todd. I've got a major project to work on tomorrow and, to be honest with you, I was thinking about working late." As she spoke, she pressed a button on her key chain to unlock the car doors. She then turned to grab the door handle, but Todd beat her to it and opened the door for her.

"So now *you're* the one who's wrapped up in a job and unavailable. That's an interesting turn of events."

Before lowering herself into her car, Cassie turned to look at Todd. "I'm not wrapped up in my job. I'm just busy. I'm sure you can relate to that." She got into her car and shut the door. The heat in the vehicle was stifling so she quickly turned the ignition and let the windows down.

Todd leaned over to peer at Cassie through the window. "Cass, I'd really like it if we could meet for dinner tomorrow. What do I have to do for you to show up?"

Now Cassie could see the earnest emotions in his eyes and something inside her melted against her will. She hated herself again for the weakness and released a long breath. "Alright, Todd. Where and when tomorrow?"

The smile instantly appeared again. "I don't know. I'm just a visitor in the city, remember?"

"Do you want me to pick a place?"

"No, I'll handle it. I'll call you tomorrow to finalize everything, okay?" He looked as though he wanted to kiss her, but he instead stood straight up and stepped away from the car. "I'll see you tomorrow, Cass."

Cassie wondered if she would be entering the lion's den tomorrow night. "Yeah, okay, I'll see you tomorrow."

If Todd heard or saw the wariness that Cassie was feeling, he ignored it and continued to smile. As she drove away from the parking lot, she glanced in her rearview mirror several times and saw Todd watching her car until she turned a corner and was out of sight.

Chapter 4

"You're late as usual," Johnson noted as Cassie unlocked the door to her home. She had pulled into the driveway only minutes earlier and found him sitting in his air-conditioned Toyota 4Runner reading a newspaper as he awaited her arrival. "What time does your watch say? It must be running slow."

"Give me a break, Johnson. I got here as fast as I could." Still feeling uneasy after seeing Todd, Cassie opened the door and stepped inside with Johnson following behind her.

"Sounds like somebody had a rough day. Mitchell again?"

Cassie decided not to mention Todd. "Something like that. I was trying to get some work done for this ColaCorp presentation, but I kept drawing blanks. I'm pretty frustrated about it right now."

"The ColaCorp presentation?"

"Yeah. Mitchell has decided to let me run the final meeting and present our proposals." Cassie was too mentally exhausted to feel any enthusiasm right now. She walked into her living room, sat down, and removed her shoes. Her mind was still on Todd so she was barely listening to Johnson.

"That's great! You didn't tell me when we spoke this afternoon."

"What? I'm sorry, what did you say?"

"I said that you didn't tell me when we spoke this afternoon." Johnson came around and sat beside Cassie on the sofa.

"I didn't know. Mitchell told me today after literally dissecting my analysis. It was nerve-racking, too, but at the end of the day he seemed happy with it. I think I may even get a promotion when this is all done."

"For someone who just scored major points, you sure don't sound excited about it. What's wrong?"

"I already told you. I'm having a hard time coming up with ideas for the presentation." It wasn't Johnson's fault, but he was really working Cassie's nerves. She wished he wasn't there so she could call Monique with the Todd update.

"Need some help? Presentations are my specialty, you know."

"I appreciate that, but I don't know. If I keep drawing blanks next week, though, I'll definitely be begging for your expertise."

"Baby, you won't have to beg. Just say the word and we'll get it done."

Surprised and warmed by Johnson's willingness to help, Cassie leaned forward and kissed his lips. "Thanks, sweetie." *Sometimes you make me feel so special.* For a moment, she wanted to speak the words, but she quickly let it pass. The cloud of confusion was already large and dark enough. Cassie stood up and began walking toward her bedroom. "I'm going to get out of these clothes."

Johnson also stood up and began to follow her.

Upon realizing that he was on her heels, Cassie stopped. "Where are you going?"

"I thought I'd help you get out of your clothes."

The reason for *this* offer of help was obviously self-serving and Cassie smiled while shaking her head. "I don't think so."

"You sure? You seem a little tired so you might find me handy."

"I have no doubt that you would be handy." Cassie laughed at the transparent motives. "A hand over here, a hand over there…"

"Okay, guilty as charged. You can't blame a man for trying." He smiled and leaned against the display table placed immediately behind the sofa. "Well, before you disappear into your private chambers for three hours, I have something to tell you."

"Okay. What's up?" All at once, Cassie's curiosity was peaked. She wondered if he was finally going to confess meaningful emotions, which would be right on time with Todd in town stirring up old feelings. She almost held her breath.

"I'll tell you what's up. *I'm* up!" Johnson could no longer contain his excitement as the cloud of confusion loomed yet more densely over Cassie.

"What do you mean?"

"Do you remember that position I told you about a few months ago? The manager opening."

"Yeah, sort of." Now she shook her head as understanding came to her. "Are you saying that you got the promotion?"

"Yep. It's official as of today. Baby, you are talking to the new manager of pharmaceutical promotions." Todd touched both sides of his shirt collar and pretended to make much ado about stiffening his shoulders and raising his head with a pompous air. "Madam, I am now running the show."

Cassie clapped her hands and laughed, briefly forgetting her need to know his emotional status. She could not have been happier for Johnson. "My dear sir, I believe what you are running is your mouth. But I applaud you anyway. And now I bow to your esteemed presence." She curtsied as though standing before royalty. When she straightened back up, Johnson was standing directly in front of her. "I am so proud of you. I believe that congratulations are in order."

"So how are you going to congratulate me?" He placed his hands around her waist and pulled her closer.

"Something tells me that you already have a few ideas." Cassie was still laughing as he kissed her neck and began rubbing her back.

"You better believe it." He kissed her lips now and began trying to undo the buttons of her blouse, but Cassie gently pulled away.

"Wait, baby. I really want to get out of these clothes and relax." *I need to switch gears and get my head together.*

Johnson was now kissing her neck and ears. "Me, too. Let's both get out of our clothes and help each other relax."

Cassie smiled, but still pushed Johnson away. "That's not what I had in mind. I've had a long day and it's hot as all get-out. I want to take a shower and cool off." She traced his lips with one of her fingers. "Then I will give you the royal treatment."

Johnson's smile could not have been larger. "You will, baby? Umm..." He kissed her expectantly.

Cassie paused, taking a moment to verily look into his eyes. "I really am proud of you, ya know."

"Thank you, baby." He was still smiling, unable to conceal his own pride. He kissed her cheek and pulled her back to him for a long embrace.

Although truly happy for Johnson, Cassie found her thoughts returning to Todd and to how it felt when he held her in the lobby a short time ago. The closer Johnson held her, the more she thought about Todd and she began to feel an overwhelming need to escape both the room and Johnson.

Frazzled, Cassie released him and attempted a playful air. "I suggest that you help yourself to something in the fridge while I'm in the shower. You may need the energy later." She began walking toward her bedroom, grateful to get away.

"Woman, what I want to help myself to ain't in no fridge."

She smirked as she closed the bedroom door. Relieved to be alone, Cassie fell back against the door and closed her eyes. She just couldn't stop thinking about the conversation with Todd, the way he looked and smelled, how he had walked toward her in the lobby. It was all messing with her mind. And now Johnson was here expecting her to celebrate his promotion with him. The world seemed mad and Cassie's head spun from the effort at composing her emotions. Once again, she wished that Johnson wasn't there so she could call Monique and run the latest developments by her friend. With Johnson in the other room, a conversation with Monique was definitely impossible.

To help calm her frenzied state of mind, Cassie walked over to her CD player and selected the Roberta Flack greatest hits disk. Music usually worked when she needed help relaxing. One of her favorite songs, *Feel Like Makin' Love*, began to play and Cassie again closed her eyes. She had always loved the simplicity of this song. As she listened to the lyrics, her mind began to wander. *I remember how it felt to make love with Todd.* He had large hands that seemed to hold her entire body at once and she had felt so safe in those moments. But Cassie had to acknowledge feeling safer with Johnson despite the question of their ambiguous relationship. Unlike Todd, Johnson communicated with her about his life and desires. He shared his plans and valued her opinions about them, something Todd had never done. How ironic that the very thing that Cassie adored about Johnson would also be his greatest downfall: *communication*. He communicated everything that really mattered except his feelings for her.

For the time being, Cassie purposefully reopened her eyes and shut the troubling thoughts and comparisons out of her mind. She then walked into the bathroom and turned on the shower. As the water heated up, she lit scented candles all around the bedroom and undressed. By the time she stepped into the shower, the steam was drifting into the bedroom only to be burned off by the candles' flames.

Cassie stood beneath the hot water and let the streams massage her skin for several minutes. She briefly thought again about Todd holding her tightly in the lobby. Then she willed her thoughts back to Johnson and how excited he was about being promoted. Certainly, he deserved the recognition and the boost up. As she lathered her body with peach scented soap, Cassie consciously blocked any more thoughts of Todd and decided to make tonight a memorable evening for Johnson. She began to hum *Feel Like Makin' Love*, forcing the day's confusing events out of her mind. With each passing minute, Cassie's previous desire to be alone was slowly replaced by a stronger desire to act on the song she was beginning to hear so clearly in her mind.

Johnson, who was lying comfortably on the sofa watching TV, could smell the wafts of peaches, honey, and perfume before he saw her. He sat up just as Cassie came to stand in front of him wearing a black lace teddy with a matching lace robe that stopped at her smooth thighs. Based on his facial expression, she knew he was pleased with the view.

He placed his hands around her waist and pulled her midsection to his nose and lips, kissing her stomach through the negligee. Then he looked up at her face, seemingly enamored by the combination of lingerie and perfumes.

Cassie took a step back and held her hand out to Johnson. "Come with me, honey."

Johnson was wordlessly led to the bedroom, which was lit only by the candles and smelled like vanilla, peaches, and oranges. Cassie had also switched the music to Marvin Gaye, who was now crooning about a distant lover. The effect was that most of Johnson's primary senses were engulfed with delights, promoting a very willing pliability. Enjoying the moment, Cassie took him near the bed, but didn't let him sit down. She removed her robe as he watched it fall carelessly to the floor, giving him a full view of the teddy, which accentuated her flat stomach and covered practically none of her body. Before he could touch her, however, she shook her head *no*. Anticipation was part of the pleasure.

Cassie unbuttoned Johnson's shirt, removed it, and dropped it on the floor. As she worked on the buttons and zipper on his slacks, he quickly removed the t-shirt he had been wearing beneath the business shirt, his eyes glued to Cassie's face. He was obeying her silent commands not to touch her, but she knew it was becoming more difficult for him. When he was completely undressed, Cassie kissed him softly, but again refused to allow him to remove her teddy. Now she gently pushed him down on the bed and then crouched on top of him without touching him. Using only her lips for contact, she again kissed him, this time slowly covering his entire body. The stereo began playing *Sexual Healing* and Cassie felt herself forgetting everything except her need for Johnson. As though reading her mind, he grabbed Cassie by her waist and back so he could flip himself on top of her. He kissed her deeply while working off the lingerie that was now a hindrance to both of their needs. Cassie stroked his face with her hands and for one long moment they looked at each other, their souls almost touching. When he finally entered her, the rest of the world had already disappeared, both of them long ago lost in one desire.

At around 2:00 a.m., Cassie was jolted from sleep by a nightmare that a ferocious, brown bear was chasing her through a dark forest. In her dream, she had just fallen and the wild bear was leaping toward her, the sharp teeth soon to rip through her flesh. Screaming with terror, Cassie abruptly awakened covered in sweat and clutched the bedcovers. To her acute dismay, however, the vicious growling was still quite audible, the source only inches away. After a few shaky breaths, she realized it was Johnson, deeply asleep and snoring loud enough to wake the dead. Apparently, she had incorporated the snoring into her nightmare. *It's amazing that I slept at all.*

Thirsty, Cassie rose from the bed, slipped on her lace robe, and walked into the kitchen. As she drank a glass of water, her mind wandered to her dinner plans with Todd. Admittedly, she was still experiencing mixed feelings about seeing him. There was no disputing the facts that the man was gorgeous and Cassie was yet vulnerable in some ways to the magnetism he naturally emitted. He was like some kind of walking pheromone that caused her to ignore her instincts. But maybe she was being too hard on herself. It wasn't like she had fallen all over the man—even though she had wanted to. And, like Monique had said, she should at least find out why Todd wanted to see her. She owed that to herself. Cassie also had to remember the bottom line: she was not committed to Johnson. Repeat: *You are not committed to Johnson.* The last reality check was hard to swallow, particularly in light of the strong connection they had seemed to share earlier in bed. Cassie again struggled with the internal conflicts and exhaled a long breath.

When she returned to bed, Johnson was still snoring deeply. Wide awake, Cassie rested her elbow on a pillow, propped her head on her hand, and silently studied his face. Even in the shadowy darkness, there was nothing exceptional about his looks. Quite to the contrary, his head appeared thinner and his lips looked larger to a disproportionate degree. Compared to Todd, Johnson's appearance left much to be desired.

Cassie was struck by memories of Todd and his still perfect physique. When they had been dating in Atlanta, she had often watched him sleep and marveled at his flawless form. Of course, she had never told him of her admiration since he already possessed some arrogant qualities. If only his treatment of her had been as perfect as his body. If only his treatment had been more like Johnson's. Then again, Johnson didn't seem to want a serious relationship so that wouldn't solve anything. The circle of confusion was endless and as perfect as Todd's body.

Cassie now lowered her head to the pillow and began to silently reassure herself that Todd had no idea that he had affected her so greatly in the lobby. She resolved to keep it that way, which meant that her defenses absolutely had to be fully operable when they met for dinner that evening. Otherwise, she could have a real problem on her hands. Why had Todd decided to show up *now*?

Cassie's thoughts returned to the nightmare that had earlier awakened her. The wild, ferocious bear had already pounced before she could save herself and, in her dream, she knew she was about to die an excruciatingly painful death. Now she wondered if that bear had actually been either Todd or Johnson.

Chapter 5

A PERSON MUST RESPECT and admire ants. Yes, ants. They each have a purpose and go about it with copasetic singularity. They know their individual missions. They effectively communicate danger and safety to each other. They know their enemies and defend themselves and their hearths as one unit. Everything is black and white, consummately without the gray tinges that provoke flirtations with imminent disasters. If you are an ant born of the same queen, then you are a fellow soldier and your loyalties-slash-intentions need not be questioned. If you are an enemy—whether or not also an ant—you are unfailingly recognized and summarily attacked. There are no secrets or disguises among ants. No emotions and no confusion.

What Cassie wouldn't give to be an ant right now. As the tiny soldiers marched in a single file line across the sidewalk, she yearned to share such clarity of mind and motion. Instead, she identified more with the prey they hoisted: a fat, green caterpillar that had long since surrendered and died. Poor thing.

It was mid-afternoon and Cassie was sitting alone outside the office on an empty bench beneath a large shade tree. As usual, the heat was oppressive and relentless, but she endured it because she needed time alone to think.

She peered down the walkway at a couple standing in the sunlight holding hands. The woman looked familiar, but Cassie couldn't quite make her out from the bench. She seemed to be laughing, throwing her head back as the sunlight caused her reddish hair to glow like an auburn fire. The man then reached for her shoulder and drew her beside him so that they walked side by side as though joined at the hip. It was obvious that they were lovers.

As she gazed at the couple, Cassie reflected on a conversation she and her mother had had a short time ago. It was this conversation, which they repeated a few times each year, that had knocked her, arms flailing, into the emotional dumpster. Even though Cassie knew what to expect from her mother, she still fell victim to the woman, who knew all her weaknesses and mercilessly pushed her daughter's buttons. She was constantly pressuring Cassie to do two things immediately: get a man and get married. Today, Cassie had been concentrating on the Cola-Corp presentation and making good progress when her mother called.

"I thought I'd check on you since we haven't talked in a few weeks," her mother had started off with her usual comment.

Currently, her parents lived in New Orleans, where Cassie's mother worked as a career counselor at Dillard University and her retired father spent most days playing golf. They had moved there last year after Cassie's only sibling, Maven, had graduated from college and gotten her own place. "So what's going on with you? Anything new?"

"No, not really, Mama. I've just been staying busy here at work. You know how it is." Cassie wheeled her chair around to face the large office window, which offered an uninspiring view of the busy street below.

"Is that all you do? Work? What's going on with that young man you were seeing?"

"You mean Johnson?"

"Yeah, Johnson. I like him. He sounds like he's got things on the ball. What's going on with him these days?"

"Not much more than when you asked the last time we talked. He's just as busy as I am."

There was a marked pause before, "I hope you're not sleeping with him, Cassie. You know what they say about loose women. No need to buy the cow when you're getting the milk for free."

"What in the *world* made you say that?" Cassie was immediately annoyed.

"I don't know. I just thought I'd remind you. Johnson seems like a nice young man, but he's still a man just the same. And men don't respect loose women."

"Mama, you've been telling me that all my life and the message has been received, alright?" Cassie's mental focus began to crumble and she knew nothing else would get done that day. Instead she'd spend the rest of the day beating herself up for sleeping with Johnson. She was the cow and he was definitely milking her. After last night, he probably even had a lactose hangover.

"Don't get mad, dear. I'm just telling you like it is. Men will toy with women who let them, but then they turn around and *marry* the women who make men *work* for their attention."

"Mama, why do we always have the same conversation over and over again? Why don't you ever ask me about my job or my goals or something unrelated to men?" As usual, Cassie was now exasperated and defensive.

"Because I worry about you. A woman your age should be married, not dating. Sometimes I wonder if you just don't *want* to get married. Don't you want children? Cuz if you do, you'd better get on the ball and find somebody who wants to marry you. Pretty soon, you'll be too old and *nobody* will want you."

"Honestly, Mama, I don't even *know* if I want children."

Her mother gasped at the other end of the line. "You don't want children? Chile, what is wrong with you? Every woman who is blessed to be able to have children should want them."

"Well, Mama, there's a lot of women out there who are older than me, unmarried, and happy without children. Believe it or not, there's nothing unusual about me. This is not the year 1800 and women aren't automatically expected to give birth nowadays just because we have uteruses."

"All I can say is that I hope you *do* have children. You should have at least one—after you get married, of course."

Cassie didn't respond. There was no point beating a dead horse.

"Cassie, are you still there?"

"Yes, Mama, I'm here."

Silence. Cassie continued staring out the window. Before her mother had unwittingly called her a cow, Cassie had intended to tell her about Todd's recent appearance. Despite all the grief he had caused Cassie, Mama had somehow managed to remain open-minded about him, stressing that both Todd *and* Cassie were *equally* responsible for their failed relationship. Somehow, despite Todd's worst shenanigans, Mama had always found a way to forgive him while also advising Cassie to please, please marry him if asked. In truth, Cassie sometimes believed the woman would willingly compromise almost anything for the sake of being married. Goals, true love, passion, personal needs, ambition—it all meant nothing to Mama if a man and marriage would consequently be sacrificed. The woman was definitely old school. Cassie wondered what her mother had compromised to be with her father and if she ever regretted those decisions. She also wondered if her mother would happily see Cassie and her younger sister in similar situations since they would *at least* be married and socially redeemed. She already wanted to end this conversation.

Realizing that Cassie was not offering up anything to discuss, her mother broke the prolonged silence. "I have some vacation time coming up and I'd like to come visit you for a few days. Do you have any plans around Labor Day weekend?"

"Um, I don't know offhand. I'll have to let you know later." Cassie spoke quickly to indicate that she needed to get back to work.

Her mother unhurriedly continued. "That's fine. When I come, I'd like for you to introduce me to Johnson."

"We'll see. Let me look at my calendar and get back to you in a few days." Again, Cassie spoke with some impatience while simultaneously turning her chair back around to face her cluttered desk. The piles of paper just kept getting bigger.

"Alright, I'll wait to hear from you."

More silence as Cassie began to audibly type on her keyboard.

Finally, her mother gave up. "I know you're busy, sweetheart, so I'll let you go. Make sure you call me this weekend."

"I will, Mama. Give Daddy my love and tell him I'll talk to him soon."

"And *you* be careful. Remember what I said about Johnson."

"Yeees, Mama." Cassie barely suppressed the sarcasm. She hated being treated like a ten-year-old, but she knew her mother meant well. "I love you."

"I love you, too."

When Cassie finally hung up the phone, depression swooped down and perched on her shoulder. She could still hear her mother's voice urging her to avoid sex and being construed as loose. Cassie reluctantly admitted to herself that there was probably some truth to the warning since men didn't seem to change with the times, a lesson that history taught all too well. If she briefly reflected on the multitude of history classes everyone took in grade school and college, there was one pervasive bottom line fact to them all: men had always been consumed with the need to conquer, both in ancient and modern history. Hundreds of wars over thousands of years had erupted solely because one man or a group of men had possessed something that another man wanted. Obtaining that thing, whatever it was, then became a quest. Vast empires, treasures—to men, these things had been worth pursuing, maybe even dying for. And nowadays, expensive cars, top jobs, and large bank accounts had become the bounty, the quests. Take Todd and Johnson, for example. Both men had an innate drive to be the best in their chosen fields as well as to enjoy the choicest fruits of their successes. For these things, they also were willing to work hard, essentially chasing dreams that with elusion became yet more desirable. But Cassie believed they both *preferred* this elusion because neither could truly be satisfied with success if it came too easily, if it were merely handed to them. Somehow the rewards would be damaged goods. Didn't it then make sense that men would also prefer to pursue women? And perhaps they also sought to conquer women, but then conquered women would not be their chosen mates for life. Men ultimately wanted women who continued to challenge them in some way. Was that why Todd had shown back up after so much time? Because Cassie had refused to be conquered? And was that why Johnson didn't seem interested in a serious relationship? Because she was too easy?

Confused, Cassie stared blankly at the stacks of paper on her desk before deciding to take a break outside. Once seated on the bench, her attention was eventually drawn to the ants and the order with which they carried out their day. No confusion. No what-ifs. No emotions. The green caterpillar was nearly inside the ant bed now and she watched with fascination as the ants determinedly stuffed the blubbery bug into a dark, narrow passageway.

"Did you drop something on the ground?"

The question startled Cassie, who caught her breath and looked up. To her surprise, Charles, a manager within the Pinnacle Consulting accounting department, was sitting on the bench beside her. Cassie had been so involved with the plight of the ants that she had not realized she was no longer alone. She smiled at him, hoping the encroaching sadness wasn't obvious.

"Charles, I haven't seen you in weeks. Where have you been?"

"I've been on vacation." He leaned back comfortably and stretched his legs out straight before him. "Me and the wife went to see our oldest son in Kansas City for a couple of weeks. He made us grandparents a few months ago and we finally got a good look at the little rascal."

"Congratulations! So is the baby a boy or a girl?"

"A boy." He chuckled and placed his left arm on the back of the bench. "He sure is cute, too. He already favors his grandpa."

Now Cassie laughed. She had met Charles within days of joining the company and had instantly liked him. Since he was African-American, he made it his business to meet and greet all incoming sistahs and brothuhs, letting them know that a "friend" was in management. Cassie wasn't sure of Charles's age, but she guessed he must be in his mid-fifties since most of his hair was gray. His skin, however, was still unwrinkled.

"Charles, you are too much."

"I know. My wife tells me that all the time." He chuckled again and looked upward. "It sure is a beautiful day. Get a look at that sky."

Cassie also looked upward and noticed for the first time that it *was* a spectacular day. The white clouds looked like cotton balls against a bright blue canvas. She nodded her head in agreement. "It *is* gorgeous today. We need more days like this one."

"Are you kidding me? Almost every day is like this one. You need to get out more. Before you know it, winter will be here."

"Yeah, I need to stop working so many late hours. Sometimes I forget that daylight even exists." Smiling, Cassie looked over at Charles. In many ways he was like her father, sort of laid back with the expectation that life would be good to him.

"So how are things going, kiddo? Have you been promoted yet?" Just as Charles expected good things in his life, he expected good things for others.

"No, not yet, but I'm working on it."

"Make sure you play a little, too. All work and no play makes for a pretty dull life."

Cassie snorted at the cliché. "The way things are going right now, I'd kill for a little dullness."

"Oh yeah? What's going on? Or would you rather not talk about it?"

"No, I don't mind." She shook her head and looked back at the ground. The caterpillar had now disappeared entirely, leaving behind only a trail of soldiers still in a single file line. "There's this guy—"

"I knew it."

"Knew what?" Once again, Cassie looked at Charles, now with bewilderment.

Charles only smiled. "I knew it had to be a guy. You're out here moping, staring at the ground like your best friend died. Usually men bring that out of a woman."

"Oh." Her attention was restored to the ants as she thought about his comment. "Yeah, I guess you're right about that," she sullenly concurred.

"I'm sorry. I shouldn't have interrupted. So tell me about this guy. Is he your boyfriend?"

"No...he's not my boyfriend and, to tell you the truth, I really don't know *what* he is. We've been seeing each other for around four months now and...and I guess that's all I know."

"Is this the guy that you've been having lunch with? I think I've seen you together a few times."

"It was more than likely him. Kind of tall, brown skin, wearing a suit?"

"Yeah, that sounds right."

Cassie nodded and squeezed the edges of the bench with both hands. "That was him. His name is Johnson"

"Okay." Now Charles nodded while recalling Johnson. "So you've been seeing each other for a few months. What's the problem? Is he seeing someone else?"

"Not that I know of." The idea of Johnson going out with another woman provoked immediate jealousy within Cassie.

"Whoa, calm down. It was just a question." Charles moved his hand in a downward motion.

Cassie ignored his gestures, the jealousy still flaring. "Why? Have you seen him with other women during lunch?"

"No, so don't get upset about nothing. Just calm down." Again the downward hand gestures. "Boy, I sure won't ask that again."

"I'm sorry, Charles. I wasn't trying to snap at you or anything." Now Cassie was beyond depressed. She was morose. Her already lowered shoulders sank even lower.

Charles smiled quietly for a few moments. "I will say one thing. For someone who isn't your boyfriend, he sure has got your nose wide open."

"Yeah...maybe so." *But that's only half the problem.* Cassie thought for a minute before asking, "Charles, do you mind if I ask you a question?"

"No, go right ahead."

"It's sort of personal."

"Okay. Ask."

Cassie turned and fixed her eyes on the man's face. "When you met your wife, how long did it take you to figure out that she was the one? Did y'all date for a few years or did you just know right off the bat?"

Charles fell silent, his expression more thoughtful as he pondered the question. "Well, now, let's see here...I met Brenda almost thirty years ago. At the time, she was the lead singer in the church choir and I have to say that I thought she was the prettiest woman I'd ever seen. And she sang like a *bird*." As the memories flooded his mind, Charles drifted away, seeming to forget that Cassie was there. He smiled as though seeing his wife for the first time again. "I think I knew from the moment I saw her that she was something special. Of course, I didn't think that she'd want a man like me. I thought Brenda was out of my league."

"Why did you think that?" Cassie couldn't imagine Charles thinking he wasn't good enough for anything or anyone.

"Because she was so perfect; everything about her that I could see was perfect. And, anyway, I could take a quick look around the church and pick out several other fellas who could *really* take care of her, way better than I could. I'm talking about finances now." He looked over at Cassie. "Things were different back then. I was raised to believe a man should be able to provide for his wife. Oh sure, I had graduated from college and had a job, but I didn't have much to offer at the time." Charles again stared forward into the sky, reliving the church scene and seeing the men that he once believed would be better matches for his wife.

"She could have been with any of those guys and they would've been happy to have her."

Cassie smiled, imagining that she was also there at the church to see his wife and how Charles reacted upon first seeing her. "So how did y'all finally hook up?"

He immediately snickered mischievously. "Now that's the funny part. I joined the choir so I would have a reason to see her more often than just on Sundays. I couldn't sing a lick. I don't think I was *ever* on key. I mean I was so bad that one day the choir director pulled me off to the side and said 'I'm glad that you love the Lord, Charles, but from now on, please just sing His praises in your heart. Believe me, the Lord will understand.'"

Both he and Cassie laughed at this anecdote for a couple of minutes.

"It became our little secret that I only mouthed the words to the songs after that." He paused for a long moment before continuing. "Anyway, I introduced myself to Brenda on the first night that I went to choir practice. That woman, she's a sharp one. No sooner had I said my name than Brenda saw right through me. And I remember how she smiled knowingly. She wasn't fooled for one minute." As though trying to enter the memory, Charles now leaned forward. "Wanna hear something weird? After we were married, she told me that when we met she *knew* I would be her husband. She even told her family when she got home that night."

Cassie thought about Monique, who had made similar comments about Rodney throughout their relationship. "How do people *know* like that, Charles? What is it?"

"Cassie, the truth is *I* don't know. I really don't." As Charles released images of the past, he slowly leaned back against the bench, the physical commute simultaneously marking the mental one. "I have no idea. But, as you know, we did get married. I don't think we dated more than a year."

They were both quiet for a few minutes as Charles reflected on his history and Cassie tried to make sense of her present. Finally he asked, "Do you think this guy Johnson is the one for you?"

The very question had been on Cassie's mind lately. "I wish I knew, but...It just seems like things are more complicated than they would be if he *were*, ya know? I keep thinking I should be *sure* like your wife was." She huffed dispassionately. "It probably doesn't matter anyway. I don't think he wants a serious relationship."

"Have you ever asked him?"

"No."

"Why not?"

"Because I don't think I should *have* to."

"So he's supposed to read your mind?" Charles' tone was patient and reasonable as he sought an understanding of Cassie's point of view.

"No, I just think it's common sense that he should tell me what he wants by now."

"Have you told him what you want?"

"No."

"Why not?"

This was getting redundant. "Because he should know how I feel based on the way I treat him. Charles, I'm really good to this guy."

"Is he good to you?"

"Yeah, I guess so."

"Then why don't you know how he feels or what he wants?"

"Because he hasn't told me." Now Cassie was beginning to lose patience, but refrained from any hints that would indicate as much.

"Why should he have to *tell* you when he's good to you? Shouldn't you already know based on that?"

Cassie half-smiled at the sheer logic of Charles's line of questioning. He had just trapped her with her own words before she could see it coming. "Alright, Charles, I see where you're going with this."

He laughed. "Good, because it's pretty cut and dry to me. Talk to Johnson the next time you see him. Tell him how you feel and ask him what he wants out of the relationship before it goes any further. If he's worth his salt, he'll step up to the batter's plate." More chuckles. "You may even find out he's been there swinging like crazy all along."

"That's easy for you to say." The depression found a perch on Cassie's shoulders once more. "I just wish it was easy for me, too."

"Cassie I'm going to tell you like I always tell my children: It is your responsibility to take the bull by the horns. Don't just sit back in life and let things happen *to* you. Be proactive and make things happen *for* you. Master your own destiny rather than allowing circumstances or others to master *you*." He stood up to return to the office while going on to say, "As much as possible, don't watch the world go by like a spectator. Don't be afraid to take risks and, while you're at it, keep your chin up. You've got too much going for you to let anyone get you down."

Charles's words caused tears to sting Cassie's eyes. "Thanks, Charles. I appreciate that."

"I'm sure things will work out, kiddo. But if you need to talk again, give me a call, okay?" He patted her shoulder lightly.

"I will."

Charles walked back to the office, leaving Cassie to contemplate his advice. *Tell him how you feel.* Definitely easier said than done. What was purely logical to Charles was like asking her to break an unspoken, personal code of conduct. In past relationships, Cassie had seen men undergo dramatic, unpleasant changes if she initiated expressions of deep feelings. Therefore, she had adopted a rule to never discuss her emotions with a man—unless he did so first. It was the only way she could protect herself on that front. If she broke that rule with Johnson, would the results be different than they had been with other men? She'd have to think about it.

In the meantime, she needed to get her concentration together and focus on the ColaCorp presentation. The finalization meeting was scheduled for Wednesday and she was not on target for the deadline. Plus, she was already being asked to participate on other projects and had meetings with new clients next week, which amounted to more big chunks of time down the tube. Organization was the key to her getting everything done and keeping Mitchell happy.

Cassie inhaled a deep breath, held it in for a few seconds, and then exhaled slowly. She promised herself that she would at least complete a draft of her presentation today and then tweak it over the weekend. By Tuesday morning, the graphics department would need to begin assembling the color layouts that would help illustrate the significance of her recommendations. Of course, Mitchell would be asking for a status first thing Monday morning, thus making the weekend tweaking all the more crucial.

She finally stood up to return to work. It was already approaching three o'clock, but she felt that her afternoon draft goal was doable since Todd didn't expect her at Lawry's Prime Rib restaurant until seven-thirty that evening. As promised, he had called earlier to finalize their dinner plans. During the call, he had been disappointed to learn that Cassie intended to work late, which meant that she would need to meet him at the restaurant as opposed to him picking her up from home. Cassie considered the arrangement ideal because the *last* thing she wanted was Todd in her personal space. Her defenses were still as solid as brick walls and she was determined to keep things as impersonal as possible.

As she walked back to her office, she counseled herself: *I'm going to complete this draft and keep my cool tonight with Todd. And, by the way,* she told herself indignantly, *you're not a cow.*

Chapter 6

WITH THE SUN STILL glowing dully at 7:30 p.m., Lawry's looked fairly plain and understated on the outside. The building was made of cream-colored stucco and the windows were framed with large, reddish-brown shutters that appeared to be highly polished wood. At night, however, strategic lighting lent the restaurant a much more elegant aura. Both the roof above the entrance and the pathway below were glamorously illuminated so that guests almost felt as though they were attending a gala affair.

Grappling with nervous tension, Cassie handed her car keys to the valet and walked inside the restaurant. Unlike the building's exterior, the décor within was quite charming. The combination of hardwood floors and colorful artwork lining the taupe walls was beautiful while at the same time relaxing. Upon entering, Cassie was besieged by the aromatic food being served and was surprised to discover that she was absolutely ravenous.

Todd was seated facing the doorway and, having seen Cassie's entrance, was already standing when the host led her to the table. Seemingly without much effort, the man was wonderfully good-looking wearing navy blue slacks and a casual, white business shirt that had maroon, forest green and navy blue pinstripes. The affection on his face was practically palpable.

"Cass, you look great. I'm glad you're here."

"Thank you."

The host pulled out a table chair for Cassie and Todd waited until she was seated across from him before also sitting back down.

"Would you like for me to bring the wine now, sir?" The waiter had instantly appeared at the table as the host departed.

"Yes, thank you." Todd quickly restored his full attention to Cassie. "I took the liberty of ordering a bottle of white wine to celebrate the occasion." The perfect smile appeared.

"How long have you been here?" Cassie's eyebrow was raised as she folded her tablecloth neatly on her lap.

"Not too long, maybe ten minutes. I wanted to be sure I found the place on time so I left a little early." The smile again.

"Where are you staying anyway? I didn't know you had friends in Dallas." *I'm keeping my cool. Stay cool. Cool.*

"I'm staying in Plano with my friend, Lawrence, and his wife. We all went to college together."

The waiter now returned with the wine and began to fill their glasses. He then recited from memory the evening's specially prepared dishes before asking, "Would you like to begin with an appetizer while you look at the menus?"

Todd deferred to Cassie, who shook her head *no*. Following her lead, he also declined.

"Very well. I'll return shortly to take your orders."

"Great, thanks." Todd looked back to Cassie and held up his glass of wine. "Before we do anything else, I'd like to propose a toast."

Once again, Cassie's eyebrow was raised. "A toast to what?"

"You'll find out in a second," he coaxed playfully. "Now just pick your glass up, raise it in the air, and stop being difficult."

Cassie smiled. As with their previous encounter, her nervousness was dissipating and the feelings of old times began to set in. She picked up her glass and held it up. "Okay, I'll go along. What are we toasting?"

"We are toasting friendship. May we always recognize the value of our true friends for they are rare and hard to find."

"Here, here." They lightly tapped their glasses together and then drank from them. Though Cassie was intrigued by the toast, Todd shifted the conversation before she could inquire about it.

"How is your family doing?"

Cassie hesitated for a quick second, preferring to probe the suggestive toast, but decided to let it go for now. "They're all doing fine. Maven graduated from college in May and my parents have moved to New Orleans." She picked up her menu and opened it. Almost immediately, the lobster tails caught her attention. She really was hungry!

Now also reviewing the menu, Todd continued talking. "New Orleans. That's a long way from Chicago. Why'd they move there?"

"To get away from the cold. They're both getting older and want to live in a more hospitable climate. That's the word my mother uses: 'hospitable.' Only, when she says it, it sounds more like hospital. You know how she talks with that weird accent." *The lobster tails. Definitely the lobster tails.*

"Yeah, I remember." He chuckled for a moment. "Mrs. Stewart used to crack me up. She has so much *energy* for her age. You know, you're a lot like her."

"That's a scary thought." *Downright chilling.* Cassie set down her menu and took another sip of wine. "What makes you think that?"

"Because both of you have this, I don't know, *fire* inside you. It's like you won't let anything get in the way of what you want. You make a decision and you see it through. That's one of the things I admire about you."

"If I didn't know better, I'd think you were talking about yourself."

"Well, maybe I am. Maybe you and I are also alike in a lot of ways." He placed his menu down and the waiter appeared out of nowhere.

"Are you ready to order?"

"Yes, I think we are." He motioned for Cassie to place her order and then he placed his own. Surprisingly, they had both decided on the same dish. "I told you we're a lot alike," Todd commented after the waiter was gone.

"Puh-lease. We have almost nothing in common." Cassie was only half-joking, but rolled her eyes with pronounced jest.

"Now see, I disagree with you about that." He began using one hand to count fingers on the other while listing his points. "For one, we're both ambitious. We also share similar views about the importance and role of our families. But at the same time we're both independent thinkers and neither of us clings to our relatives." He was on the fourth finger now. "Our educational backgrounds are almost identical and, most importantly, we're both very spiritual people. What more is there?"

"Hmm. You've put a lot of thought into it. My question is *why* have you put so much thought into it?" Cassie was riddled with suspicion and distrust. *What are you after?*

Todd leaned back in his chair and silently studied Cassie's face as though trying to decide whether or not to answer her question. "Why do you think I have?"

"I really don't know. That's why I'm asking." She returned his steady stare, trying not to betray the nervousness that was creeping back on her. She was beginning to think that she didn't want to hear the answer.

Still watching her closely, he asked, "Cass, why do you think I'm here? Seriously, why do you think I'm in Dallas?"

"You tell me. Why *are* you in Dallas? And what's so important that you had to see me after a year of no conversation or any other contact?" Butterflies took flight in her stomach. She wasn't feeling as confident as she sounded.

Todd's eyes never wavered from hers. As far as she could tell, he was still very much controlled and relaxed. His simply stated answer was, "I came for you."

In the midst of the restaurant bustle, the laughter around her, the clinking of dishes and silverware, Cassie's mind went numb. Unable to think of a reasonable response, she merely looked at him, still returning his unmitigated gaze, though now without the strength or resolve that had previously propped her up.

"I see I have your attention." Smooth. And the smile had reappeared. Todd finally broke his gaze from Cassie's and briefly looked down. "Cass, I know you think I'm an insensitive, unworthy jerk. Remember what you told me last year? 'You're the most callous, *selfish* person I've ever known. You don't think about anyone except yourself.'"

He paused, again looking down, composed and clearly contemplating his next words while Cassie remained mute and increasingly disconcerted.

"When you walked out that day, I thought you were just too damned *needy*. I was *not* selfish. No way. *Me? Selfish?* And *callous* on top of that?? No, uh-uh. Not *me*." He shook his head. "I was furious with you for saying that. So I decided to make a list of *all* the times I had been there for you or stopped *everything* to spend time with you that really counted. I was even going to write down every compliment, every gift, anything and everything I could think of that proved you wrong. But I wasn't going to stop there. I was going to *email* that list to you because I wanted you to *know* that you had really messed up with a good man."

Although Todd's body language was quite poised, his eyes communicated the emotions that came with the memories. For the first time, Cassie realized that she had wounded him with carps viciously sneered when they last saw each other in Atlanta. She had wanted to hurt him that day. She had wanted him to feel if even for the briefest second a *fraction* of the pain he had caused her throughout their relationship. Until now, Cassie had mistakenly believed that she had never punctured his stoic veneer. Not only was she now surprised by the truth, but she was also astonished by his sensitivity to their grievous past.

"I worked on that list for a few days off and on," Todd continued. "I'd write something down and then scribble it out because it wasn't good enough to make you feel as lousy as I wanted you to. Then I'd make up my mind to come back to the list later after I'd had more time to think of all those great things I had done for you. But after three days of racking my brain, my great list had just one thing on it. Know what that was?"

Cassie silently shook her head.

"It's so pathetic that I'm ashamed to even say it. The one noteworthy event was when I helped you move from one apartment to another on the same apartment grounds. That's the best I could do. And that was when it hit me: I deserved to be dumped."

"Maybe so, but it was still a difficult decision for me." Hearing Todd's self-recriminations softened Cassie's defenses enough for her to share her own feelings about the breakup. Nevertheless, she avoided getting too close to the faded emotions.

"Well, it shouldn't have been difficult for you. I couldn't even get my *mother* to take my side. When I told her you had quit me, she said she didn't blame you." He laughed at this admission.

"Really?" Cassie was incredulous because she'd always thought his mother didn't like her. The one time they had met, his mother had appeared excessively protective of Todd and given Cassie the impression that no one was good enough for him. "She actually defended me?"

"She sure did. She also told me that I owed you an apology."

"Really?"

"Yeah, she did. She thought you had a lot of spunk and she respected that. You're the only woman who's ever told her son where to get off."

"And she told you that right after we broke up?"

Todd nodded an affirmative.

"So why didn't you ever apologize?"

"I guess I had several reasons, the first one being pride. I didn't want you to think I was going to *beg* you to forgive me." He shrugged his shoulders as he recalled his stubbornness.

"Then I heard you were moving to Dallas so I figured it didn't matter anymore."

"If it didn't matter anymore, why are you here?" Cassie almost whispered the question. The emotions she had strenuously avoided had suddenly leapt into her throat and the knot was beginning to hurt. Part of her was inexplicably anguished by their history as though the breakup had happened yesterday and that part was yet asking the same question: *What are you after?*

His intense gaze was once again bestowed on Cassie's face. "Because after I started going out with other women again, I realized that I was comparing everyone to you and no one else was stacking up. No one else had your particular combination of beauty and brains. There was usually more *beauty* than brain and that got old. No one else understood me or looked at me the way you did. And I missed it. I missed *you*." He toyed with the fine neck of the wine glass before finally looking back up into her eyes. "Most of the women I've met over the last year were looking for men to take care of them. They don't have any real goals and they don't think they *should* have any goals beyond getting married and making babies. And although I definitely want kids of my own one day, I don't want to be with a woman who thinks of nothing else as if that's the only contribution she can make to the world. Hell, anybody can do that. And then I'd think of you, how you were always trying to find your niche so you could make something of yourself. I can't remember how many times I heard you complain about wanting to succeed in your career, but I was too caught up in my own thing to really appreciate how similar we are. And now look at you. You're on your way to doing exactly what you've always wanted and I think that's awesome. I also realize how rare and special you are. You spoiled me, Cass, and I know now that I took you for granted. I also know that I don't deserve your forgiveness but I'm here asking for it anyway. You've got to believe that if I had it to do all over again, I would do *everything* differently."

It was Cassie's turn to look away. The raw emotions had resurfaced and she knew it was in her eyes. Although somehow gratified by his confession, she was more afraid of the feelings that began to well up within her. As she battled with herself, her face flushed to a pale red and her skin began to burn.

"Are you okay?" Todd moved to the edge of his chair as though prepared to stand up and walk around the table to her.

"Yes, I'm fine." *Keep your cool.* She drank some wine, using the seconds to corral her disordered emotions. In the process, her face slowly returned to its normal, honey color. She'd probably kick herself later, but, "I feel like I should make a confession of my own. This is going to sound silly, but for the longest time, I just *knew* you were going to call and we would work everything out. I just *knew* it. But the phone never rang. After a while, I thought it was for the best. I mean, we had already wasted two years and couldn't get the relationship together so there was really nothing to work out. Then I got mad because I had tolerated so much crap from you. And for what? To be treated like *that*?"

"I'm sorry, Cass."

Cassie didn't hear him. She was more focused on her need to purge the frustrations that had eroded into such jagged edges over the years. She had to face them and Todd head-on tonight. "It was hard, Todd. It really was. It was hard to accept that so much had gone wrong and that we didn't make it. But when I finally *did* accept it, I knew I couldn't live in the same city with you. We know all the same people and they were constantly telling me about you or asking how you were doing. I couldn't move on with my life while carrying all of that baggage."

"I'm sorry. I can't tell you how much I regret the way things happened. The way I *let* things happen."

The sadness was now laid bare on Todd's face and the heaviness reached out to Cassie, issuing away the remaining bitterness she had carried for so long.

"I know you're sorry. I know. I just wish you had told me before I moved away." She made an effort at smiling, but it never reached her eyes. Cassie was now also saddened by the regrets and love lost. There was a time when the future was unimaginable without Todd in it. But life without him *had* gone on and she had moved forward with the lesson that to love him was to ask for a terrific, unbearable heartache.

Todd could scarcely look at her now and Cassie guessed that he was struggling with his own emotions, whatever they were.

When he finally raised his eyes to hers once more, he said, "I know what you mean about people making it difficult to move on. Some of your friends still ask me about you to this day. Actually, that's how I found out you work at Pinnacle Consulting. Do you remember Linda? She used to date Thomas Lopez."

"Yeah, I remember her." Cassie took another sip of wine while trying to reel back in the emotions still lodged in her throat. Perhaps the bittersweet liquid would wash them down.

"She's the one that told me how to get in touch with you."

"But how would she know? I haven't even talked to Linda since I moved." Yet another wonderment this evening.

"Apparently, she's seeing Rudy Orion now and he told her. She thought I already knew and just mentioned how well you're doing on the new job."

"I shouldn't be surprised. That just goes to show you why I had to leave. The circle was too small."

"If it weren't for that circle, though, I wouldn't be sitting here with you tonight."

Todd seemed to be searching for a way to approach something on his mind, but Cassie didn't respond or encourage him. Instead, she nodded slightly, drank more wine and then casually glanced around the restaurant. So much laughter around her. So much happiness. How many of these people already knew the secrets of making love and relationships work in this mixed up world?

"Cass, I'm going to ask you something, but you don't have to give me an answer tonight." Todd's manner was subdued, obviously reluctant and unsure of whether or not to ask, uncertain of the timing.

Oh God. She eyeballed him warily and stiffened, but responded, "Okay." *If he asks me to marry him, I'm walking out.*

Before he could utter another word, however, the waiter walked to their table and set their dinners down in front of them. The lobsters were huge and smelled delicious, but Cassie's appetite had waned to nothing.

"Will there be anything else, sir?"

"No, this is great. Cass?"

"Uh, no, thank you."

They were both caught off guard by the interruption. Although polite, Todd was clearly eager for the waiter to leave.

"Very well. Enjoy your meal." He smiled and then efficiently rushed to another table to check on the customers.

Both Todd and Cassie examined their dinners. He picked up a fork and poked the steamed vegetables that were also on the plate, but soon put the utensil back down. "You know, it's funny, but I don't have much of an appetite. When I got here I was starving, but now...I don't know. I think I'll need a carryout bag."

"I was just thinking the same thing." Cassie could barely swallow the wine, much less lobster or any other food. The moment was extremely awkward. "Everything looks really good, though."

"Yeah, it does." Todd looked at Cassie as she distractedly gazed around the restaurant. "I still have something to ask you, but, like I said a minute ago, you don't have to answer me tonight, okay?"

"Okay." She faced him again and fidgeted nervously with the tablecloth in her lap.

Todd hesitated briefly before, "I'd really like for you to come visit me in Atlanta for a weekend. I'd like to spend time with you, *quality* time, and show you how much I've changed."

Cassie moved to respond, but he cut her off.

"I know you're seeing that other guy, but I don't care. I'm just asking you to spend a weekend with me. No strings attached."

The earnest emotions swam in his eyes and Cassie fought against getting caught up in them, already shaking her head *no*. Beneath the table, she was now jerking the tablecloth around, wrenching it with two fists.

"Todd, I can't do that. Not only am I seeing someone else, but I just don't think it's a good idea. You and I are like oil and water. We've already proven that."

"That's not true, Cass. I've changed. I'm not the same man you knew in Atlanta."

"I'm sure you really believe that, but I don't. People don't change so easily."

"They do when they have to." Todd leaned forward. "Cassie, whether you believe or not, I still love you. You were the best thing that ever happened to me and I shit all over it. Ever since I realized what I had done, I've been trying to figure out a way to get you back and I don't care what it takes. All that pride I used to have is gone." He shook his head adamantly and repeated, "It's gone. Cass, I need you. I need a chance to *be* with you. Will you give me that chance?"

"Stop it, Todd. Stop doing this." Her defenses had abruptly disappeared and her emotions were doing flip-flops. The vulnerability she was feeling was more than she was prepared to handle tonight.

"Stop doing what? Stop telling you how I feel? If that's what you want, I can't do it."

Her face began to flush again and she bit her lower lip. "Todd, I'm not coming to Atlanta. I don't know what you expected, but I have a life here now and I'm happy. I'm sorry, I don't want to hurt you, but that's the way it is."

He stared at her, the mixture of pain and disappointment smoldering in his eyes. "I know you have a life here. I just..." He faltered. "I guess I just wanted to know if *we* could have a life."

Cassie only looked at him, once again not knowing how to respond and, thus, electing to remain silent. Watching Todd grapple with his emotions disturbed her, but there was nothing she could do.

Thankfully, she was spared the uncomfortable silence when her cell phone rang. Initially relieved by the distraction, she pulled the small device from her purse, looked at the caller ID, and then frowned. It was Johnson and his timing couldn't be worse. She considered turning off the phone so that this and all calls would be routed to the voicemail box.

"Are you going to answer it?" Todd had seen her displeasure and was immediately interested in the reason for it.

She barely glanced up at him, currently more preoccupied with weighing her options. "Uh, yeah." If she didn't answer the call, Johnson, who believed Cassie was having dinner with Monique, would have a million questions later. He knew that Cassie faithfully carried her phone and left it turned on so she could be reached in case of emergencies. She pressed a button to answer the call. "Hello?"

"Hey, baby. Where are you?" Johnson had music playing softly in the background and Cassie guessed he was in his car.

Not wanting Todd to hear her conversation, she turned side-ways and lowered her voice. "I'm at the restaurant. We just got our food so we're about to eat."

"Oh yeah? Well, I was thinking about stopping by since I haven't eaten yet. Would you and Monique mind? I'm only a few minutes away."

Cassie cut her eyes in Todd's direction. He had clearly guessed who her caller was and now glared at her from across the table. She hunched slightly over and turned further to the side in hopes of preventing him from hearing her response. "Yes, we would mind. This is a girls' night out, which means that no men are allowed." She tried to put a smile in her voice and stole another quick glance at Todd, who was now staring tensely at a wall in a different direction.

"I figured you'd say that." Johnson laughed good-naturedly. "Okay, then put Monique on the phone for a second. I want to congratulate her on getting engaged."

Cassie's heart pounded in her chest as she hunted for a logical response. "I can't. She's in the bathroom right now."

"Aw, too bad. Well, I'll catch her another time."

"Okay. Look, I've got to go. My food is getting cold." She again glanced at Todd. He didn't meet her eyes, but rather picked up his glass of wine and took a large swallow.

"Alright. We're still on for tomorrow night?"

"Of course." Cassie began to straighten back up, but remained turned sideways. Only after she and Johnson said their goodbyes did she finally resituate herself such that she was again facing Todd. Oddly, the anger she had seen on his face a moment ago had vanished and been replaced by defeat and resignation.

"I'm sure I already know who that was. Does he know you're out with another man tonight?"

"I hate to appear rude, but that's really none of your business." Cassie placed the phone back in her purse as she responded.

"Why are you being so defensive? I just asked a simple question."

"You asked a question about something that's none of your business. I don't have to explain myself or anything else to you." Though her heart wasn't in it, she pretended annoyance only to discourage his queries, which *would* have been simple if she had not lied to Johnson about who she was with.

Todd tapped the edge of the table with his fingertips. "Okay, I think I've made a big enough fool of myself for one night." He attempted his usual smile, but it came off as more of a grimace.

Sympathetic and guilty, Cassie dropped her eyes to her lap. "Todd, I'm sorry, but I can't tell you what you want to hear. Things are different now."

"Well, I have no one to blame except myself, right? Hindsight is always twenty-twenty." He again tapped the table edge before glancing around for the waiter. Upon making eye contact with him, he waived him over. "Can we get carryout packages please?"

"I'm sorry, sir, are you dissatisfied with the meal?" Seeing the untouched dinners, the waiter was graciously concerned.

Todd looked at Cassie and mumbled, "I'm dissatisfied with something, but it's not the food."

She squirmed uncomfortably under his crestfallen eye.

"Excuse me, sir?"

He looked at the waiter. "Everything is fine. The lady and I simply weren't as hungry as we thought." The dazzling smile appeared for the waiter's benefit. Relieved, he took their plates to prepare individual carryout bags and, upon his departure, Todd allowed his chagrin to be unveiled. "I hope that this guy you're seeing is worth it. I hope he knows what he has."

False pride puffed up Cassie and she resolutely responded, "He does know." Then she broke eye contact, ashamed of now lying to Todd. Or was it a lie? She had no idea.

"Good, because you deserve that. You deserve to be happy."

"Thanks." Now she faltered, searching for the right words. "I hope you find happiness, too, Todd. I really do."

He reached into his pocket and pulled out his wallet. "Yeah." Anticipating the bill, he pulled a credit card from his wallet. "Even though you've turned me down, I want you to know that the invitation still stands. If you ever change your mind about coming to Atlanta, just call and I'll handle everything else."

"I won't change my mind, but I appreciate the invitation." *This is for the best.* Cassie's eyes roamed Todd's face as he looked in the direction the waiter had gone a short time ago. There had always been something about the man that made her heart do cartwheels even now. Still, she was also afraid to love him like she had in Atlanta. The painful memories had sustained her tonight and Cassie knew she would never visit him in Atlanta. Never.

The waiter finally returned and Todd paid for the dinners, which were now packaged neatly for them.

"Do you want mine?" Todd held his package out to her once they were outside waiting for the valets to bring their cars. "I'm flying out tomorrow so it will just go to waste."

"Sure." Cassie placed his package on top of her own even though she really didn't want it. She obliged Todd only because she felt awful about the evening, especially Johnson's inopportune phone call. "Thanks for dinner tonight, even though we never actually ate it." It was a lame attempt at humor.

"You're certainly welcome." He looked at her meaningfully and touched her arm. "Lady, I'll be talking to you soon. In fact, you'll be hearing from me every chance I get now that I have your phone number."

Cassie had given Todd her unlisted home number before they exited the restaurant.

She smiled, still feeling guilty and sympathetic. "I'd like that. Take care of yourself."

The valet brought Todd's rental car first. Before walking to the car, he hugged Cassie, crushing her body against his. "Don't forget, Cass. The invitation stands."

"I won't forget. Goodnight." As he walked to his car and got in, the valet parked her car beside the curb. Soon they were both turning out of the parking lot and heading in opposite directions, the irony of which struck Cassie as prophetic. Traffic was fairly heavy this evening so within a few seconds she could no longer see his car in her rearview mirror. For a brief moment, she wondered if she had made the right decision about Todd. He seemed different somehow, although Cassie had been unwilling to admit it in the restaurant. Something else was there now that she had not ever glimpsed in Atlanta, something endearing and surprisingly vulnerable. Perhaps she should not have been so quick to dismiss him before determining whether or not the changes were genuine. She wouldn't have had much to lose for exploring.

"Oh well." Cassie turned on the radio and tuned it to a contemporary jazz station. *Better to leave well enough alone*, she told herself while glancing in the rearview mirror again. Of course, Todd's car was long gone by this time. *Goodnight and goodbye, Todd. Goodbye.*

Chapter 7

"WELL, AT LEAST NOW you know what he wants!" Monique bit into a large blueberry muffin.

She, Cassie, and their friend, Dana, had met at Le Peep for breakfast, a Saturday morning tradition for the three women. It was the only way they could work group girl-talk sessions into their busy weeks. As a general rule, they all wore shorts, t-shirts, and absolutely no makeup.

"Girl, this is high drama." Monique was trying to talk with her mouth full of food.

Having failed to eat anything last night, Cassie was beyond famished this morning. She scooped up a fork full of eggs, stuffed them in her mouth, and nodded emphatically. "I know," she eventually managed.

"So what are you going to do?" Dana tossed her long, dark hair back from her face. She had radiant, olive-colored skin and hazel eyes that reflected her Mediterranean roots. Having been raised in a military family, she also had lived in Spain for several years and so had a mild accent that lent her speech a rhapsodic quality. Unlike Cassie and Monique, Dana was married and had recently given birth to her second child. Now determined to lose the extra weight she had gained while pregnant, Dana had only a bran muffin and a glass of orange juice while Cassie and Monique unabashedly gorged themselves.

"I'll tell you what she's going to do," Monique announced. "She's going to call Todd and accept his invitation." She now dug into the hashbrowns on her plate as Dana looked on with disbelief.

"Monique, how can you eat like a pig and stay so thin?"

"Easy. I work out three or four days a week." Now talking with her mouth full, she used her hand to cover her mouth.

Cassie interjected. "Girl, stop lying. You haven't gone to the gym one time since I've known you."

"Who said anything about a gym?" Still chewing, Monique began to spread butter on the blueberry muffin.

"But you just said you work out. Do you have equipment at your home?" Dana was determined to learn the secret.

Before answering, Monique again bit into the muffin. "You could say that."

Cassie and Dana exchanged looks. Neither of them had ever seen any sort of workout equipment in Monique's house.

"Is it the sort of equipment you can store beneath your bed or something?" Cassie ate more eggs and sliced her pancakes while chewing.

"No, it's the sort of equipment you place *on* your bed."

"Monique, what kind of exercise equipment is used on *top* of a bed?" Dana again looked at Cassie, her incredulity evident.

Monique stopped chewing and looked at her friends. "Come on! You should already know." She rolled her eyes and shook her head. "A man, of course. Jees."

"Good God!"

"One track mind."

"I should have known."

Cassie and Dana began giggling like teenagers.

"What's so funny? I'm being serious." Monique pointed a finger at them both. "I will have you know that sex is the best workout you can get. You burn two-thousand calories just kissing."

"That's because you're not married yet." Dana again tossed her hair back, still smiling. "I'd like to hear your story when you've been with the same man for five or ten years and have kids. Believe me, sex will be the last thing on your mind. When he nudges you in the middle of the night, you won't be thinking '*How romantic.*' You'll be thinking '*Go find a tree hole and leave me alone.*'"

All three women nearly fell out of their chairs with laughter. Cassie grabbed her stomach, which began to ache from the prolonged, vigorous laughter, and tears streamed down Monique's face.

"God, I hope not," Monique finally said between giggles. "I really hope that's not true. I hope I enjoy sex in all its splendor until I'm dead and in my grave, kids or no kids."

Dana's knowing facial expression silently advised of a more dubious reality, but she said nothing more.

"Anyway, we're not here to talk about me. The problem child this morning is Cassie and the question is what should she do about Todd and Johnson. Or should I say, who should she *choose*? Todd *or* Johnson?" Monique raised her hands in the air, palms up, and pretended as though weights were in each hand, one representing Todd, the other representing Johnson. "Todd?" Hand up. "Johnson?" Hand down. "Todd?" Hand down. "Or Johnson?" Hand up. "Umph. I don't know, girl, this is a tough one." She placed a forkful of hashbrowns in her mouth, looked at Cassie, and shook her head with dismay.

Dana got to the heart of the matter with the simplest question. "Tell me, Cassie, do you love either of these men?"

Cassie swallowed her food and wiped her mouth with a napkin before speaking. "I used to love Todd, but I don't think I do anymore. I won't let myself. And if I love Johnson, I don't think I even *want* to know."

"But why not? Johnson seems like a nice guy."

"Yeah, he so nice that he's milking me." She drank some milk.

Monique almost choked. "*Milking* you? What the—? Girl, what are you talking about?"

"According to my mother, he's milking me. She practically called me a cow yesterday!"

Dana looked from one woman to the other. "I'm sorry, but I don't get it. How can a man milk a woman?"

Flustered, Cassie explained. "Haven't you ever heard that saying 'Why buy the cow when you can get the milk for free?'"

As Dana answered *no*, a look of understanding crossed Monique's face, but she let Cassie continue uninterrupted.

"It means that men have no reason to marry women that they're already having sex with."

"Ohhh." Now Dana understood. "But your saying doesn't make any sense. Everyone has sex before they get married. At least, everyone *I* know."

"Are you kidding? You *have* to have sex before you get married." Monique interjected. "You wouldn't buy a pair of *shoes* without trying them on first, would you? You don't want to get *corns* all over your feet because the shoes are too tight or don't fit. And by then, it's too late. You're stuck with duds. So I say, think of *men* like shoes. Try them on before you buy them. You'll save yourself a lot of trouble that way."

As Monique polished off her breakfast, Cassie and Dana laughed at her crude comparison.

"But what if having sex *does* make some men inclined to avoid marriage? Aren't you preventing the relationship from maturing when you get that involved without a commitment?" Cassie pushed her plate away, now more interested in the conversation than the food.

"No." Dana patted Cassie back like a mother soothing a child. "Dear Cassie, you have so much to learn. Having sex is not what causes men to avoid marriage."

Monique again piped in. "That's right, because if it did, rest assured that Rodney and I would *never* get married."

Dana shook her head at Monique and turned back to Cassie. "If you really want to know what turns men off, I'll tell you what I think based on conversations I've had with my husband. One of the reasons that Alan and I get along so well is that we don't *need* each other. We both have good jobs and make good money. He doesn't need my salary to have the things he wants and I don't need his. We also have a few independent hobbies and respect one another's need for space. Neither of us believes that being married means we've forfeited our rights to time alone, even away from each other every now and then." She crossed her arms and rested them on the table. "That's where I think women get into trouble a lot of times. We find it difficult to let our men do things that don't involve us. For some reason, we feel threatened by it. But I always tell my friends, 'Let him go do his thing and find something that is yours and yours alone.' Men respect that because they don't want to feel trapped. When they start feeling trapped, that's when they dodge commitment and become restless."

"You know, Todd told me last night that he thought I was needy when I lived in Atlanta, but I don't agree with him. I didn't *see* him enough to be needy. So even if we're not clingy or needy, men imagine that we are. There's no way to win."

"You weren't needy, Cassie. Todd was just an asshole." Monique sipped her coffee with a very matter-of-fact expression on her face.

"That's true. And he knows that now." She paused long enough to look from Dana to Monique. "But it doesn't matter because I have no intention of starting up anything with Todd. My mind is made up."

Monique looked at Cassie over the top of her coffee mug. "I think you're making a big mistake."

"Well, I don't because, personally, I like Johnson. Todd already had his chance and he blew it."

"If it were *me*," Monique chimed in again, "I'd be on the phone right now accepting Todd's invitation to fly up to Atlanta because the fact remains that Johnson hasn't told you what he wants. I don't care how nice he seems to be. Facts are facts and you have to look out for yourself."

"Well, Monique, you're not me so don't worry about it. Anyway, I think I'm going to take Charles's advice and talk to Johnson about our relationship."

"Oh really? And what exactly does Charles think you should say?" Monique didn't seem pleased with this development. Like Cassie, she preferred to let men go out on a limb emotionally before she followed, the operative word being *followed*.

"He just thinks I should ask Johnson what he wants, that's all."

Dana's brow furrowed slightly. "Cass, why are you in such a hurry to be in a relationship? Don't you enjoy your freedom?"

"I don't think I'm in a hurry. I just don't like feeling as though I'm wasting my time." She frowned as she considered Dana's questions. "What makes you think I'm in a hurry?"

Dana again tossed her hair back and Cassie wondered why her friend didn't just cut it all off since she always seemed to want it out of the way.

"Maybe *hurry* is the wrong word. Sometimes I think you're much too concerned with defining your relationship with Johnson. Things have been going along very well for the two of you up till now. And you've got a very demanding job, a bright career ahead...Why isn't that enough for the moment? Why must you pin the man down instead of just enjoying the relationship for whatever it is?"

Both Monique and Cassie were dumbfounded by Dana's comments.

Still frowning, Cassie subconsciously scratched her head. "Dana, I don't get what you're trying to say."

"Yeah, me neither," Monique agreed. "I mean, here you are, the queen of marital bliss, and yet you seem to be suggesting that the single life is preferable. What's up with that?" She sipped her coffee without taking her eyes off Dana.

"I'm not saying that being single is better. I'm saying that being single is okay and that Cassie can have fun with Johnson without feeling pressured to have a serious relationship."

"Oh, you're saying that I can let him *milk* me without feeling like a cow." In addition to feeling confused, Cassie was also mortified by the notion.

"No, no, no. That's not what I'm saying." Dana tossed her hair back for the hundredth time as Cassie and Monique quietly awaited her explanation. "By the time I was your age, Cassie, I had already been married for nearly five years and had a baby. There was a lot of pressure on me to be the perfect mother and wife and some kind of marketing guru at work. As you both know, I've always wanted it all—a career, kids, and marriage—and I wouldn't have it any other way." She paused in reflection. "It's just that sometimes I wish I had waited for the kids and marriage. I wish that I had spent my twenties living just for me. I look at you and Monique and wonder where I would be and what I would be doing if I had not married so young. And I envy your freedom to do what you want *when* you want most of the time. But please don't misunderstand me. I do love my husband and I know that I'm fortunate. Still, I would do many things differently if I could and that is why I think you shouldn't be so concerned with Johnson or any other man. If I were you, I would relish having so much freedom at my fingertips for as long as it lasts."

"Dana, I never knew you felt that way." Cassie was truly surprised by her advice.

"I never knew either until I had my second child. Now that I know what's in store, I've been somewhat saddened that I will again be forced to base many decisions and plans on when the baby sleeps, when she eats, when she cries, what time to pick her up from daycare. That sounds horrible, doesn't it? I'm a horrible mother for saying that."

Monique softly patted Dana's back. "No, that doesn't sound horrible. Don't be so hard on yourself."

Dana merely sighed. "I was just so relieved when Gregory could talk and tell me what he wants and feed himself without spilling food everywhere. And now I'm back at square one with another baby. My freedoms are again being held hostage by my beloved child, who I would die for." She grabbed Cassie's hand and squeezed it. "Take your time, Cassie. Take your time and enjoy yourself."

"She has a point, Cass, which is why you should go to Atlanta and see Todd. I'm sure you'd *really* enjoy yourself." Monique winked and then giggled when both Cassie and Dana playfully jabbed her on each arm. "Alright, alright, I'll give it a rest."

"Good, because I've already told you that it won't happen." Cassie was immovable on this point.

Dana looked at her watch and reached for her purse. "Well, you two, I have to be going. Alan is waiting for me so we can take Gregory to his soccer game." She placed a five-dollar bill on the table and stood up.

"Okay, girl." Cassie also stood and hugged her friend. "Thanks for all the advice."

"Anytime."

"Hey, give me a call next week. Let's try to have lunch." Monique also stood up and hugged Dana. Since they worked for the same corporation, they were sometimes able to schedule lunches together.

"I will. And you make sure to update Cassie on the wedding plans we've discussed so far." She turned, walked toward the door, and exited the restaurant.

"So what wedding plans have you made?" Cassie looked at Monique expectantly.

Immediately enthused, Monique told Cassie her ideas for colors, flowers, and the location, which was particularly important since at least three-hundred guests were expected. But, of course, the most important detail of the wedding was her dress and she desperately needed help to choose one. Monique had already combed fruitlessly through several bridal magazines and was ready to pull her hair out so Cassie agreed to accompany her on shop visits until she found the perfect gown.

After settling this issue, the two women exchanged similar opinions that weddings seemed more stressful than joyful. Why didn't everyone simply elope?

Despite Dana's and Monique's advice, Cassie decided to do as Charles had recommended and find out what, if anything, Johnson wanted from her. But finding the right time to talk to him about their relationship proved easier said than done. For the next four weeks, Cassie was bogged down with multiple projects at work and Johnson was settling into his new manager position. Each day brought with it a new challenge that required special, exhaustive attention, leaving the two little time for each other. Although they continued to meet for lunch each workday, there was never an appropriate occasion for conversations beyond the latest disasters or ridiculous demands they confronted on their jobs. And they were both pulling long work hours in the evenings as well as on weekends. Still, Cassie and Johnson were invigorated by the pressures they complained about, recognizing that pressure symbolized their employers' faith in their abilities. If handled correctly, this faith would ultimately lead to yet more opportunities for both of them.

So much was happening at once that Cassie eventually lost her sense of urgency to question Johnson about their relationship. The ColaCorp deal was sealed without a hitch and afterward she was promoted to a project lead in her department. The step up meant that she would be overseeing consultant teams on process improvement contracts with various corporations. It also meant that she would sometimes travel with the teams to meet with clients, walk through their organizations, talk with their staff, and collect information about their current processes. To say the least, the challenges would sometimes seem insurmountable, but Cassie was thrilled to take them on.

Meanwhile, throughout the weeks that literally flew by, Todd called for one reason or another, slowly trying to reinstate himself as a normal part of Cassie's life. When she was promoted, he sent two dozen long stem white roses to her office along with a bottle of champagne. *Wishing I was there to paint the town red with you! Congratulations, Todd*, the card had read. After calling to thank him for such thoughtfulness, Cassie had immediately given the unopened champagne to Mitchell and let the roses die in her new, larger office.

Although truly excited about her promotion, Cassie was even more excited about the things she could now afford. One of her first priorities became replacing her dining room table, which she'd had for nearly five years. Having received a great bargain on the table, she had regretted the selection almost immediately after buying it because it just didn't blend well with her other furniture. When she finally had a free weekend, Cassie's mission became finding the perfect table regardless of the price—and dragging Johnson along against his will to help with the hunt. At this moment, they were at a Haverty's Furniture Showroom, the third stop of the day.

"What do you think about this one?" Cassie stood beside a very elegant, cherry oak dining room table that seated eight guests.

Johnson did a quick once over and shrugged nonchalantly. "It's alright, I guess. Looks like the one we saw at Robb & Stucky Furniture."

"Yeah, you're right." She placed one finger beneath her chin and shifted her hips as she continued to study the table. "I really do like this table, but I don't think it will fit in my dining room area. It may be too large."

Johnson had walked away while she scrutinized the table and picked out a slightly smaller one made from glass and marble. "Cass, come here. Check out this table."

As soon as she saw it, she turned her nose up. It looked nothing like anything she had complimented or picked out so far. Couldn't he see this table didn't match her taste? "No, it's too overstated. I'd be afraid to eat on it." Cassie noticed another cherry oak table slightly smaller than the previous one. "Hey, look at this one." She speedily walked over to it as Johnson loped behind. "This is gorgeous." She ran her hand along the top and then found her reflection in the sheen. "Johnson, I think this might be the one."

"Thank God." He fell onto a burgundy leather recliner placed near the table.

"Aren't you going to look at it? I want your opinion."

"I'm looking at it. I can see it from here."

"No, I want you to *really* look at it. See how the wood is carved on the chairs? Don't you think it's nice?" She looked from Johnson to the table and then back at Johnson.

He bobbed his head indifferently. "Yeah, it's nice."

Cassie crossed her arms and walked over to Johnson. "What's the deal with you?"

"What do you mean?"

"I mean you're not being much help."

"You asked me if I liked it and I said yes. What else am I supposed to do?"

"Well, you could start by actually *looking* at it."

"Cass, we've gone to three stores today and you keep picking out the same table so just buy it already."

Now irritated, Cassie placed her hands on her hips. "I do *not* keep picking out the same table. If you were paying any attention, you'd see that there's something different about all of them."

He threw his hands up. "Whatever. It's *your* table so it really doesn't matter what I think."

"Yes it *does* matter. That's why I wanted you to help me choose one."

"No, Cass, my opinion does not matter. The table is for *you*, not me, and *you're* the one who's going to look at it every day." He made himself more comfortable in the chair.

For some reason she couldn't quite pinpoint, Johnson's lack of interest bothered Cassie and she began to feel dejected. "But I want you to like it, too," was all she could think of to say.

"Why, Cassie? What's the big deal?"

"I don't know. I mean, whatever I buy might someday be a family heirloom or something. Who knows? Maybe I'll have kids that sit down to dinner at the table in few years."

"Yeah, but what does that have to do with me?"

"Well, don't you think you'd be around if I had kids?" Cassie was grasping for a delicate way to word the question without implying that she was proposing a future marriage.

"I don't know. I'm not even thinking that far ahead." His facial expression lost all emotional suggestion.

Cassie was stung by the implication of Johnson's response. "So what *are* you thinking about?" She made every effort to remain calm, but she felt as though her face had been slapped.

"Nothing. I'm just taking everything one day at a time."

A list of possible reactions ran through Cassie's mind as she and Johnson looked at each other. *Are you wasting my time? You sorry son-of-a——! So Mama was right. What are we doing?* In the end, however, she walked away under the guise of taking a second look at a table she had already admired a few minutes earlier. She walked away because she realized that whatever she said to Johnson couldn't possibly convey the broad range of emotions she was feeling at the moment. On one hand she wanted to strangle him for his audacity. How *dare* he make their relationship sound so trivial, like a way to merely pass the time. But on the other hand she wanted to cry and release the frustration at being made to feel like an incidental frivolity. Since neither reaction was acceptable to Cassie, she left him sitting on the sofa. Johnson never saw the angry tears that rolled freely from her eyes.

After leaving Haverty's, the drive back to Cassie's home was a tense one, at least for Cassie. She didn't know what Johnson was thinking about or if he even knew how upset she was. He made a few attempts at drawing her out into conversations, but was equally as happy to sing along with the radio upon recognizing her preoccupation. He truly wasn't concerned or apparently cognizant of what had transpired at the furniture store. *Men can be so dense sometimes!* Cassie suspected that he pretended ignorance in order to avoid the issue, which continued to weigh heavily on her mind.

When they finally arrived at her townhouse, Cassie went into the kitchen as Johnson went into the living room.

"Baby, can you get me a glass of water while you're in there?" He sat on the couch and used the remote control to turn on the television.

Get it yourself, she thought, but then answered, "Okay, sure." *Jerk*. She got two glasses of water, went into the living room, and sat beside Johnson after handing him his water.

"Thanks." His eyes were glued to the television, which was showing the movie *Predator* with Arnold Schwarzenegger. Meanwhile, Cassie's eyes were glued to his face as she sipped her water. They sat in this manner for several minutes and Cassie wondered again if he was purposefully ignoring her in hopes of dodging the issues that boiled inside her. Regardless, she decided that it was time she knew the truth about Johnson's intentions. She decided to ignore that small voice she had allowed to convince her that it wasn't really necessary since things were going relatively smoothly. That small voice, she now realized, had actually been the voice of fear. Somewhere deep down, she had not *wanted* to ask Johnson because she feared the answer. She also had feared jeopardizing their relationship—such as it was—by cornering him with something he obviously didn't want to talk about. Maybe he would bring it up without her intervention, she had wanted to believe. Or maybe he had assumed that it was understood, that the nature and significance of their relationship was already known. Now, however, she knew better and there was no easy way to approach the matter so Cassie would have to just spit it out. She reached over, grabbed the remote control, and turned the television off.

"Hey, hey! What are you doing? I was watching that."

Johnson attempted to retrieve the remote control from Cassie, but she set it down on an end table out of his reach.

"I know you were, but I want to talk to you."

"Can it wait? The movie was getting to one of my favorite parts."

"No, it can't wait. And anyway, if you've seen the movie enough times to have favorite parts, then it won't kill you to miss it this one time." She wasn't going to budge.

He heaved a great breath as though resigning himself to some form of inevitable torture. "Alright, Cass. What do you want to talk about?"

"Us. I want to know what we're doing." She scooted closer to Johnson and rested her hand on his arm to signal the intimacy she desired of their conversation. She also spoke softly to better mask her emotions as well as to lower the risk of sounding confrontational.

"I don't understand."

"I need to know what this is between us. What is it to you?"

Johnson appeared helplessly confused. "It is what it is. What am I supposed to say?"

"Why do you keep asking me what you're supposed to say or do? Stop answering my questions with *more* questions."

He placed his hands palms down on his knees and studied them as Cassie sat and waited.

"Well?" she finally broke the silence after a few long seconds.

"Well what?"

The blank expression on Johnson's face provoked the impatience she had barely held at bay and she could feel the mixture of anger and fear churning in her stomach.

"Well, what do you have to say? What are we doing? Are we just bed buddies or what?"

"Cass, why do we have to label it? Everything is cool so why can't we leave it at that?"

Outrage at his response replaced the uncertainty that Cassie had been battling for the past two months. She sprang angrily from the sofa and stormed to the center of the living room and faced him while standing there. "See, that's where you've got it wrong. Everything is *not* cool. What do you think I am? Some kind of slut that you can just use to get your rocks off on whenever you want to? Is that what you think I'm about?"

"No, I don't think that. If I did, I wouldn't be here." Johnson's tone remained emotionless, wholly failing to offer a significant reaction to Cassie's outburst.

"So what *do* you think, Johnson? Because it's been nearly *six months* and you have never *once* told me how you feel about me or what you want."

"What are you talking about? I tell you how I feel about you all the time. I'm always telling you how proud I am of you and how much I like spending time with you."

Cassie walked back over to the sofa and sat back down. She once again lowered her voice as the painful longing to know if he loved her swelled and extended inside her. "Yes, you do tell me those things, Johnson, but I need to know if it's more than that. I need to know if our relationship, if *I'm* important to you."

Now it was Johnson's turn to rise from the sofa as though fleeing Cassie. His body language evidenced the agitation he was feeling. "Cass, you know that you're important to me, but if you're looking for some kind of commitment I can't give you that right now."

"I'm not asking you to *marry* me, Johnson. I'm asking if you consider me..." She had nearly said *your girl*, but stopped short because it sounded so juvenile to her. "Are we a *couple* or are we just *dating*."

"What's the difference?"

"If we're a couple, then we agree that neither of us will date other people. If we're dating, then we're still free to see others when we want to."

Johnson placed one hand on his hip and used the other to rub his jaw while turning the question over in his mind. "Okay, then I guess we're dating."

"*Dating?*" Cassie was stunned.

"Yeah, dating."

"So do you *sleep* with everyone that you *date*?"

"I'm not even answering that."

"Are you *dating* anyone else?"

"Okay, well, it's time for me to go. I'm not making time for all this drama." He walked over to the coffee table and grabbed his car keys.

Both amazed and confounded, Cassie watched without moving, still struggling with the fact that he had viewed her as only a *date* for so many months.

"I deserve an answer to my question, Johnson. I want to know if you're seeing someone else."

He was almost to the door now. As he reached for the door-knob, he looked at her long enough to say, "Call me when you calm down and can talk like you have some sense."

"What? Johnson!" Cassie leapt to her feet as he opened the door and walked out. Before the door closed, she caught it and yanked it back open to discover that he was already unlocking his car. "Johnson, I'm not finished talking to you!"

Ignoring Cassie entirely, he got into his car and turned the ignition.

"Johnson!" He backed out of the driveway as the tears welled up and finally erupted from Cassie's eyes. Everything blurred as his car roared away. He obviously could not have cared less about the emotional devastation and humiliation that he was causing her. Had his affection for her been all in her head? Maybe her imagination had been working overtime because she had wanted to believe she was special to him.

Overcome with anguish as well as feeling like a fool, Cassie closed the door, threw her hands over her face, and sobbed miserably. Never in her life had she allowed a man to treat her with such flagrant disregard. She would never have thought Johnson was even capable of being so cold. Mama had been right after all. He was still a man.

But the further truth was that Cassie had played a hand in her own undoing by not clarifying their relationship sooner. She should have raised the questions long before today, long before it mattered as much as it did now. The more she thought about it, the angrier she became with herself. Hadn't she learned *anything* from her past relationships? If nothing else, hadn't she learned to shield herself, to protect her emotions? She had mistakenly thought so before today. What a rude awakening she was now suffering.

Cassie sank to a squatting position on the floor and cried until no more tears would come. She wasn't crying over Johnson now. She was crying because of her own stupidity. Eventually, however, anger and resentment took hold and Cassie felt her emotions harden toward Johnson. After the way he had treated her today, she vowed that he would never again have the upper hand or be in a position to hurt her. She would be sure of that.

Chapter 8

THE FOLLOWING MONDAY, CASSIE was in her office preparing a meeting agenda for her project team. It had been two days since she and Johnson had fallen out and neither of them had made the first move to call the other. From time to time, Cassie glanced at her phone thinking that he would call to confirm their usual lunch date, which she was eager to decline indefinitely, but the phone never complied with her premonitions. *Lucky for him*, she sneered contemptuously to herself. *If he never calls, that's fine.*

Someone knocked on her open door and she looked up to find Mitchell walking toward her. "Good morning, Cassie."

"Hey, Mitchell. Good morning."

He seated himself in one of the chairs set in front of her desk. "You sound a little glum. Tough weekend?"

"Oh, you know, same ole same ole." She wheeled her chair around to face him and rested her arms on her desk. "What's up?"

"Well, we've secured another new client and I've decided to put you on the job. How does your schedule look?"

"Actually, it's pretty tight right now. My team and I have already booked flights to Puerto Rico next week for a walk-through of the BookMart order processing center. Then we're going to spend a few weeks strategizing the efficiency analysis. I've already pulled Jennifer on board from Pat's group to help out with systems and automation designs because I can see this job is going to be a whopper."

"Okay. What have you got after that job?"

"I think we've been slated for another beverage company project. Word got out about our ColaCorp success and another company wants to find out what we can do for them."

"I haven't heard about that one. Who scheduled you without talking to me?"

"Sarah did a couple of weeks ago. I would have told you, but she was supposed to give you a heads up on the same day she talked to me so I assumed you already knew."

Mitchell frowned. Sarah was his boss and she had a bad habit of assigning work to his employees without his involvement or knowledge. "Fine. I'll speak with Sarah today about that because I think we'll need to pass that job to another team. I want you on this new client and I'm sure she'll agree."

"Oh really? Who is the client? I'm intrigued."

"It's a company called Pilot Software. Apparently, they're a fairly new operation, but business is booming. Since the company took off so quickly, the CEO wasn't quite prepared to focus on administrative efficiency so now he needs someone to come in and recommend aggressive process improvements before things get out of hand."

"Sounds interesting. Where are they based?"

"In Atlanta. Say, aren't you from there?"

"Sort of. I moved to Dallas from Atlanta." *In fact, I fled the city to escape this really obnoxious guy I stopped seeing shortly before moving.*

"Great! That will make the job more fun for you."

Cassie was sure that the smile that she gave him was the phoniest in her repertoire, but it was the best she could muster. "Yeah, lots of fun for me. Good ole *Hot*lanta."

"Awesome." He clasped his hands and placed them on the desk. "So when can you calendar this company in and catch a flight there? I'm assuming that you'll be available after getting your group off and running on the job in Puerto Rico."

"Wait a minute. Are you asking me to do this job in Atlanta *by myself*?"

"I sure am. I also want it on your calendar this month. The company is less than a year old and only has around twenty employees, most of which are programmers. Since they're only requesting administrative improvements, you should be able to knock out the job in two weeks or less."

Now Cassie was extremely flustered and put out by the abrupt schedule changes that Mitchell was imposing on her. "But I've already made plans for the Puerto Rico job. I've got several ideas I wanted to experiment with during the process improvement stage."

"Then make sure you communicate them to your group. That's what they're there for and I'm sure they can handle the job without you for a couple of weeks. You've got a strong team." Mitchell rose from the chair and moved toward the door.

"Mitchell, with all due respect, would you please tell me why this job is so important? There are other employees here who are capable of taking on the Pilot project. Why do I have to stop everything for it?" She couldn't be more upset with him for pulling the rug out from under her with absolutely no warning.

Without breaking stride, he looked over his shoulder and said, "Because you're the best I've got and this is easy money. When we get this extra revenue on the books, we're all going to look really good and that's reason enough for me."

Annoyed, Cassie tossed her pen on her desk when he was gone and stared blindly at her computer screen. When it rained it poured.

By the end of the week, Cassie still had not heard from Johnson and her pride was mildly injured. Although she had no intention on calling him, she fervently wanted *him* to call *her*—so she could slam the phone down in his face. It was all about pride right now.

"Girl, do *not* worry about Johnson's sorry ass." Monique picked up a gorgeous white gown with pearls lining the bodice and held it against her body. She and Cassie were currently at a bridal boutique in the Galleria. "This is cute, but not sexy enough. I want Rodney to *drool* when I walk down the aisle." She replaced the gown on the rack and moved on.

Meanwhile, Cassie disinterestedly scrutinized a few other dresses, but her mind was hardly on the task at hand. "I'm not *worried* about him like that. I just want him to call, that's all."

"He'll call. They always do. But if I were you, I wouldn't give him the time of day. I'm telling you, that man would have to do some serious begging just for me to look at my watch and *tell* him the time."

"I know. I feel the same way." Cassie selected an off-white dress with a straighter design that was meant to hug the bride's body. Monique certainly had the figure for it. "How do you like this one?"

She looked up intending to do a quick once over but instead did a double-take. "Girl, that's the most beautiful dress I've ever seen." She slowly walked toward Cassie and the gown, her mouth agape. When she was close enough, she touched the gown and felt the fabric. "It's so *soft*, like satin. I love it! I'm definitely trying this one on." Monique checked out the dress size and then carried it to the fitting rooms, dismissing the attendant from any obligatory customer care.

As Monique undressed, Cassie sat on a bench outside in the waiting area. There were mirrors all around the room so that brides could view themselves in their gowns from every angle. Cassie stood up and checked herself out in the mirrors. In a pair of very faded blue jeans and a white t-shirt, she thought she looked tired. Her butt also appeared to be spreading, which was never a good thing. She sat back down before she could get depressed about it.

"Hey," Monique called out from the dressing room. "When are you going to Atlanta for that project?"

"In two weeks. And against my will, I might add." Just thinking about the trip was irritating.

Monique carelessly slung her jeans over the fitting room door behind which she was changing. "That sure is a wild coincidence, you having a project in Atlanta. Do you think God is trying to tell you something?"

"Something like what?" Cassie already knew where Monique was going with the question, but she wasn't going to help her get there.

"You know what, girl. Like Todd might be the one."

"No, I do not think God is trying to tell me that. If Todd were the one, I would have known a long time ago."

"Hmph. Well, I still say that it's just too coincidental that of *all* the cities in this country, you're being sent to Atlanta. I'd keep my eyes peeled for something off the wall to happen while you're there."

"Monique, you are way too superstitious for me." Cassie laughed in spite of her agitation about the trip. "Todd won't even know I'm in the city. I've decided not to tell him about the job so you can just forget about anything 'off the wall' going on."

"Okay, I hear you." Her blouse and brazier were now on top of the door and a rustling sound came from the tiny room as Monique removed the dress from the hanger. "Sometimes you are too stubborn for your own good."

"What you call being stubborn I call being smart. I don't need to travel down that rocky road with Todd again." Cassie smiled to herself and shook her head. "Do you need any help in there?"

"As a matter of fact, I do." Monique emerged from the dressing room in the gown with an expression on her face that clearly signaled her proclivity toward the dress. Now she was searching Cassie's face for confirmation, which Cassie immediately supplied.

"You are going to be such a beautiful bride! That dress was made for you." Awestruck by her friend's radiance, Cassie placed her hand over her mouth and took a few steps backward to get a better look.

"You think so?" Monique went to stand before the mirrors and gazed at herself in the dress. "Cass, would you help me with this zipper? I can't get it all the way up."

She pointed to her back and Cassie realized that the zipper was only halfway done.

"Of course." She rushed over and zipped the gown and then returned to her spot a few paces back. While some minor alterations would certainly be needed to make the fit perfect, the dress nevertheless flattered Monique's enviable figure wonderfully. Entirely sleeveless, the bodice very elegantly framed her torso and flowed into a skirt that not many women could successfully pull off since it accentuated every curve of the wearer's body. The back of the gown was equally as exquisite, cut into a "V" shape that revealed just enough of Monique's mahogany skin. "Girlfriend, I think you're going to have to buy this one. This is definitely *your* dress."

Monique touched the lace that lined the gown's trail. She was also pleased with the way she looked in the dress. "Maybe, but I'm going to ask the attendant to hold the dress for twenty-four hours. I want to look around a little more before making a final decision."

"Okay, but I think this is the one." She eyeballed the dress for a few more moments before remembering a question that had crossed her mind earlier. "You never told me the wedding date. Have you set one yet?"

"Yeah. We've decided to get married on Valentine's Day. Cheesy, huh?" Monique used the mirrors to look at Cassie while talking. She was also pinching a few places on the dress that would need to be taken in if she bought it.

"Valentine's Day? But that's only six or seven months away."

"I know, but I don't want to wait a *year* to marry Rodney." Monique turned and stepped off the small pedestal set in the center of the mirrors. When she reached Cassie, she turned around so the zipper could be undone and continued talking. "Cass, for the first time in my life, I've met a man that I love as much as he loves me. You know, I never thought I'd hear myself say this, but he adds something really incredible to my life that just wasn't there before and I feel complete when we're together. Why should I wait a whole year to feel that way every day?"

"When you put it like that, I see your point." Cassie had already unzipped the dress and Monique now headed back into the small dressing room. Every time she and Monique had these types of conversations, Cassie wondered if she would ever share such strong feelings with her own prince charming. And, more importantly, *who* was her prince charming? "That's great, Monique. You're both lucky to have found each other."

"We sure are lucky." Monique closed the door to the fitting room and began to remove the dress. "Some people go through their whole lives and never find what Rodney and I have."

And right now I'm shaping up to be one of those people. Cassie thought about Johnson and how easily he had disengaged himself when she was at her most vulnerable last Saturday. If he had loved her, he wouldn't have been able to simply walk out that way. And the fact that he hadn't called since then was yet more testimony to his emotional detachment. Undoubtedly, he had turned out to be just another mistake, something else to regret whenever she was alone and introspective.

Finally dressed in her blue jeans and blouse once more, Monique opened the dressing room door. She was carrying the wedding gown like a very fragile treasure and Cassie felt certain that she would be back for the dress tomorrow.

After they left the boutique, the friends stopped through a few more stores, but Monique was clearly not as enamored with the gown selections. "Let's go get something to eat and catch a movie. I've had enough shopping for one day."

"Does that mean you've decided to get the dress you tried on earlier?" Cassie wanted Monique to be absolutely sure.

"Not quite. I want my mother to see the dress first and give me her opinion. Then I'll probably take her with me to a few other places tomorrow, but I don't want to look at *one more dress* today." She linked her arm in Cassie's as they walked through the mall passed a host of vendors and crowded shops. "Thanks for coming with me today. I'm really glad to have you for a friend."

"Girl, you don't have to thank me for coming with you. I wouldn't have it any other way." Cassie gave her friend a strange look to say, *That's what friends do. What planet are you from?*

Monique got the message and laughed at Cassie's facial expression. "Too bad you can't make money for contorting your face that way. It's priceless."

Cassie responded by more tightly linking their arms. "Friends forever."

"That's right. Friends forever. Let no man come between us."

"No man, no children, no jobs, no nothing!"

"No *nothing!*"

They continued walking through the mall in this manner, paying no heed to the curious looks people gave them. Rather, they reveled in their friendship and the invincibility it gave them. *We are toasting friendship. May we always recognize the value of our true friends for they are rare and hard to find.* If ever Cassie had known a true friend, there had been no one better than Monique. Thank God for her.

When Cassie got home that evening, she was thoroughly exhausted. After she and Monique had caught a movie, they had talked nonstop over dinner and drinks until midnight. It had seemed that they would never run out of things to say about Rodney, Johnson, the upcoming wedding, Cassie's mother, and the list went on. As usual, Monique had come through with clever perspectives to share and Cassie's outlook had dramatically improved compared to how she had felt earlier. She knew she would sleep like a rock tonight.

She went into her bedroom and turned on the lamp beside her bed. The answering machine was on the nightstand beside the lamp and she noticed the light was blinking. Cassie pressed the "play new messages" button and began to undress absentmindedly while waiting to hear the first message.

"Hey, Sis. What's up?" It was Maven calling to check in. "Mama told me that she's coming to see you during the Labor Day weekend and I want to come, too. I've already done some research on the internet and there are a lot of cheap flights out of Chicago as long as I book one this weekend. Call me back by tomorrow and let me know if it's okay for me to fly out there. Love you. Bye."

Now she knows better than to ask me if it's okay, Cassie thought as she hung up her jeans. She and her sister had always been close and Cassie really missed having her around. For many good reasons, Cassie viewed their relationship as the catalyst for much of her life and habits. Maven's high regard for Cassie placed a lot of pressure on her to be strong and independent. Just knowing that Maven's eyes were always watching motivated Cassie to be better and more thoughtful than she might otherwise be. Cassie felt that she was setting the example for her little sister and so far Maven was following in her tracks much to her mother's dismay. Mama would probably be frustrated while trying to deal with them both during the Labor Day weekend. Like Cassie, Maven didn't have a prospective husband to speak of at the moment, which was reason enough for Mama to spend all three days lecturing about loose women and predatory men.

As Cassie thought about her mother's and Maven's upcoming visit, her answering machine began to play back the next message. Cassie halted all movement until she could catch the callers' voice, but the next two messages were only hang-ups. Somewhat disappointed and at the same time very curious, she searched the caller ID history for the calls. One was an unavailable phone number, which probably meant it had been a telemarketer. The other call had been placed from Johnson's office. It could be none other than the man himself.

"So you finally decided to call," Cassie spoke aloud to the device as though it were Johnson. "Brothuh, you have a *lot* of nerve." She whipped her t-shirt over her head in one swift movement and threw it on a wooden rocking chair in a corner of the room. "You don't want to talk to me," she continued scolding the device before walking into her bathroom and turning on the shower. "Oh no. You *definitely* don't want to talk to *me* because I will really hurt your feelings right now. If you have *half* a brain, you'll wait a while before you call again." She stepped into the shower thinking, *Apparently, he doesn't know who he's dealing with. I'm not the sort of woman who's going to just say, 'Okay, baby,' and let everything go back to the way it was. He'd better get real. The sorry sucka!*

Cassie was feeling much more indignant than she had a few scant hours earlier. Just knowing that Johnson was getting off his high horse and making efforts to get in touch with her was enough to provoke her rage and resentment anew. Clearly, he had been waiting all this time for Cassie to be the one that caved in, but she had held her ground. She'd rather *die* than give him that satisfaction. And anyway, the truth was she really had nothing to say to him; therefore, she had no reason to call him. Only one thing was certain: she would never expose her soft belly again. Dogs did that to demonstrate submission to their owners or to stronger canines. Well, Cassie wasn't a dog and she would be damned if she was going to be treated like one.

Johnson would soon be meeting a side of her that Todd was sorry to have met before they broke up. It was the side of Cassie that she used to barricade her emotions like a steel wall, making it impossible for the perceived threat—always a man—to get close to her. Up until recently, Johnson had never known her to be anything but cooperative, fun, and easygoing. Now that he had been identified as a threat, however, he would discover that he had burned both his bridges and his drawers.

Chapter 9

THAT FOLLOWING SUNDAY MORNING, Cassie awakened with the desire to do absolutely nothing. She didn't want to go anywhere, do anything, or talk to anyone. Instead, she decided to spend the day in her pajamas and reading a good book, a luxury she rarely allowed herself. Since the day promised to be rainy and dreary anyway, spending it at home was all the more appealing. She got out of bed, brushed her teeth, and pulled her hair up into an uncombed ponytail. Then, wearing green boxer shorts and a yellow tank top, she shuffled into the kitchen to make a pot of coffee.

Minutes later with coffee in hand, she was sitting outside on her patio and taking in the view before her. Unquestionably, this view had been the deciding factor when she had been searching for a townhome one year ago. From where she now sat, she could smell the large pine trees that drooped over to shade the patio. Behind the trees, there was a small pond approximately one-fourth of a mile away that the realtor had told her teamed with ducks at this time each year. As she looked out at the pond now, she thought that *teamed* had not even begun to describe the large population of birds that floated gracefully across the water. Just watching them drift and then dip their heads beneath the surface in search of small fish and insects was quite fascinating and serene.

Serene. The word hung in her mind like some murky cloud. For the past few months, the mere idea of serenity had been a foreign concept in her world. Cassie felt more akin to words like caution, confusion, fear, and pain. Why was that? Why was her life more likely to be so much more volatile when a man was in the picture? And then calmer, more settled when she was alone. The fact was that Cassie was happier when she was alone because the questions surrounding a man's intentions were not an issue. She wasn't concerned with appearing considerate, interested, or attentive like an ideal partner should be. At least that was Cassie's idea of an ideal partner. She didn't worry about being used, mistreated, or disrespected. She didn't have to guard her feelings, her reactions, her wants. So why bother at all with men and relationships when they seemed to add only strife? Maybe Dana had a point after all that Cassie should not be so determined to forge a solid relationship with Johnson or anyone else right now. But Cassie didn't want to dwell on these things today.

She picked up the book she planned to read, *Along Came a Spider* by James Patterson. As Cassie became engrossed in the novel, a breeze came from across the yard near the pond. Before long, a drizzle began to fall and she was forced to stop reading long enough to pull her chair further back so the rain wouldn't spatter her legs. Just as she was settling back into the book, the phone rang. *I really don't feel like talking to anyone today.* Cassie glanced at the caller ID screen on the cordless phone beside the chair. Unfortunately, the caller's phone number was private so no useful information appeared on the unit. "Damn." She considered answering the call, but then changed her mind. If the call was important, whoever it was could leave a message on the answering machine. She again held her book back to her face, but stared at the phone and waited to hear a voice on the answering machine speaker in the bedroom. Unfortunately, when the machine finally picked up the call, the person hung up. Mildly disappointed, she clucked before continuing to read. Fifteen minutes later, the phone rang again and Cassie again glanced at the caller ID. Another private number. She debated whether or not to answer, but curiosity got the better of her this time.

"I knew you were at home. Why didn't you pick up a little while ago?" Todd's question was obviously provoked by caution in the event that Cassie had male company.

She had almost hoped the caller would be a telemarketer, someone she could rush off the phone. Too bad that it was Todd. She still felt sorry for him and, thus, could not bring herself to be abrupt or rude with the man. "I was reading a book and I didn't want to be interrupted." She inserted a bookmark and set the book down on the table as she talked.

"Oh. Well, if I caught you at a bad time, I can call back later."

"No, that's okay. We can talk for a few minutes." *I'm not staying on the phone with you for an hour or two.* The rain was now coming down in drops the size of ping-pong balls and Cassie looked over to the pond to see the ducks still swimming as though the sun was bright overhead. A little bit of rain didn't bother them. "So to what purpose do I owe this call?"

Todd laughed lightly. "Why does there have to be a purpose? Can't I just call to say hello and to see how you're doing?"

"Sure you can. I'm doing fine. How about you?"

"I'm hanging in there, keeping busy as usual."

"Me, too. But today I'm just relaxing. I don't feel like going anywhere or doing anything." Cassie stretched out on her chair and spread her toes. She really needed to touch up the polish on her toenails.

"Hey, you deserve a day to yourself. I'm glad you're taking advantage of it." Pause. "So, Miss Project Lead, how are things going on the job? Are you ready for Puerto Rico?"

"Yeah, I'm ready. We've got the whole trip mapped out with just enough time to tour San Juan. One of my coworkers was telling me to check out the glass bottom boats so I can see all the different fish and plants in the water along the coast. I heard that it's breathtaking."

"Yes, it *is*. I'd say that just about the whole island is beautiful. There are colorful tropical plants like ferns and orchids and also *huge* barracudas in the water. I think you're really going to love all the mountains around the place. It's like visiting another planet compared to Atlanta or Dallas. Make sure you take a camera so you can get plenty of pictures."

"You've been to Puerto Rico before?" Cassie was surprised that Todd seemed to know the island so well.

"Uh huh. I was there in February this year on business." He chuckled in that velvety voice. "When I left Atlanta for the trip, the temperature here was around thirty degrees, which was *freezing* to me, so I was wearing my trench coat and winter socks when I boarded the plane. Then I got to Puerto Rico, where the weather was extremely warm, and started sweating bullets in the heat. It was crazy. By the time I got to my hotel from the airport, my clothes were drenched."

"Wow! Thanks for the warning. I guess I'd better take a lot of cotton slacks so I don't have to wear pantyhose. At least that would help me a little."

"You'll be fine. It's hotter in Texas right now than it ever gets in Puerto Rico so you won't need to adjust to a large temperature change like I had to."

Cassie considered his comments. "Okay, but I think I'll pack a lot of light clothes just to be safe." She began to mentally organize the wardrobe she would take on the trip.

"Other than your trip to Puerto Rico, what else is going on?"

"Not too much. Like I said, I'm relaxing today so that's really the long and the short of it. What's happening with you?" *Let's get this subject off me.*

"Oh, 'bout the same as you, only I'm not relaxing today. After we hang up, I'm heading to the office. I get more work done when no one else is there."

"I can understand that." Cassie walked inside and got both nail polish remover and dark red nail polish. She may as well start on her toes while she talked. As she sat down once more on the patio, another call came in on her other line. To her disdain, however, it was yet another private phone number. "Can you hold on, Todd? I've got another call."

"Sure." His tone was suddenly flat.

Cassie clicked over to the other line hoping she wouldn't be sorry for doing so. "Hello?"

"Cassie! Girl, why haven't you called me back?" Her sister, Maven, sounded both cheerful and anxious. "I've been waiting to hear from you before booking a flight out there."

Cassie shook her head and scorned herself for being so forgetful. "I completely forgot to call you. Hold on a minute while I get off the other line." Cassie clicked back over to Todd. "Todd, that's my sister so I need to go."

"I remember Maven." He seemed relieved at learning the identity of the other caller and a chipper quality returned to his voice. "Tell her hello for me, okay?"

"Okay." They exchanged goodbyes and Cassie clicked over to Maven again. "I don't want to make excuses, but I got your message late last night and it slipped my mind. You know you can come here, Mave."

"I figured you'd say that, but I still needed to check. You know how I am."

The sisters quickly moved on to the latest happenings in their lives with Cassie providing her sister with only a brief lowdown of Johnson's insolent behavior. Predictably, Maven gawked and guffawed indignantly before eventually shifting the conversation to her own personal life, which was also quite dramatic at the moment. Maven was currently dating three men and saw no reason to choose one.

"Why *should* I choose one? I like all three of them for different reasons so, unless I can combine them all, I'm going to continue *dating* them all. Men do it all the time so I don't feel bad about it."

She and Cassie laughed about the role reversals that were becoming more common nowadays.

"I certainly agree with you and I wouldn't feel bad either. I wish there were three guys around Dallas that interest me enough to go out with them all at once. Maybe I need to move back to Chicago."

"Come on back, girl. We can be players together. *And* we can teach these men a thing or two while we're at it."

For nearly an hour, Maven and Cassie conversed animatedly until Cassie received another call on her second line. She glanced at the caller ID for good measure, but saw what she was learning to expect—a private number message was displayed on the phone. "Hold on, Mave. Someone is calling on my other line."

Still laughing at Cassie's comments, Maven declined to hold. "Girl, I've got to get off the phone. I'm going to the eleven thirty church service and I need to get dressed."

"Alright." Cassie was disappointed to end the conversation with her sister. "Don't forget I'll be in Puerto Rico next week and then Atlanta after that."

"Woohoo! We're going to have some *juicy* stuff to talk about when I get there."

Cassie giggled as she and Maven ended their call and she answered the other line. "Hello?"

"Hello, Cass." Johnson's voice seared Cassie's ears and she abruptly stopped laughing as her heart dropped. Why hadn't his name and number appeared on the caller ID?

Cassie rolled her eyes and smacked her lips disgustedly. "Hello," she responded coolly.

"How are you doing?"

She smacked her lips again before, "I'm doing fine." Opting not to inquire about Johnson's own health, Cassie dumped nail polish remover onto a cotton ball and began to wipe off the polish on her toenails.

"That's good, that's good."

Silence. Johnson seemed to be waiting for Cassie to become her normal talkative self, but his wait was in vain. She instead continued working on her toenails, unconcerned with thinking of something interesting to say.

"So what have you been up to this past week? I've tried calling you a few times, but you haven't been at home."

"I've been busy." *A few times?*

"Oh. You were working more long hours?"

As soon as he completed the question, Cassie was overcome with extreme perturbation and stopped working on her toenails. "Johnson, why are you calling me? What do you want?"

"I just want to see how you're doing. We haven't talked in a little while so..." He seemed uncomfortable with the bold manner in which Cassie had ruined his attempt at normality.

"We haven't talked because I've been waiting until I could calm down and talk like I have some sense, to use your precise words." Cassie was getting angrier by the second just thinking about Johnson's arrogant language and his apathetic exit last week.

"Aw, come off it Cassie. You know you got carried away that day." His tone sought a middle ground between placating her while also holding his position.

"*Carried away.* You call my asking you about our relationship getting *carried away*. Tell me, Johnson, what do you call sleeping around with women? *Platonic friendship?*"

"We have never done anything you didn't want to do. And I've never lied to you about where I stand on commitment."

"In my book, omitting the truth is the same as lying."

"I haven't omitted the truth, Cass."

"You never told me that you didn't want a relationship."

"You never asked."

"I *did* ask you."

"You asked me last week for the first time and I told you the same thing I'm telling you now. I do *not* want a girlfriend right now. However, I *would* like to continue seeing you because I enjoy your company."

"Johnson, I don't understand your problem with commitment. I mean, we already *act* like we're committed anyway." Cassie kicked herself again for not having raised the questions months ago.

"I'm just not ready, Cass. It hasn't even been a year since my last serious relationship ended and I don't want to jump into another one so soon."

"Is that because you're seeing other women?"

For a long second, Johnson was quiet. "No, I'm not seeing other women."

Cassie released her breath, not realizing that she had instinctively held it while awaiting his answer. She was relieved to know that he had been monogamous, but the crucial question remained unsatisfied. "Then I still don't understand your problem. If you haven't been seeing other women, why do you insist that we've been *dating* for all these months? It just doesn't make any sense to me."

"Because...How can I put this?"

"Johnson, just say it."

"Because in my last relationship, the woman was very insecure. She wanted to know where I was and what I was doing at all times. And if she couldn't reach me at any given time, all hell broke loose. She would grill me for hours, sometimes days, because she was so suspicious that I was seeing other women even though I wasn't. It's like she thought I answered to her and I was supposed to check in every few hours when we weren't together."

"Really? You never told me that."

"Yeah, and when we broke up, I felt like I had been paroled from prison or something. It was crazy and I just don't want to go through that again."

"I can understand that, but I've never treated you like you answer to me. And I certainly haven't worried about what you're doing when you're not with me."

"No, you haven't. I agree with that, but I think it would all change if we were in a committed relationship. Women are just like that. You expect us to call twenty-four seven and to spend every waking moment with you when we're not at work. And I don't want anyone expecting that from me right now. At least this way while you and I are dating, you're not pressuring me to call you and to spend time with you. I can do those things for the sole reason that I *want* to."

Cassie bristled at Johnson's stereotypical comments about women, but made a conscience decision not to take them personally. She would be painfully remiss, however, if she failed to set the record straight. "First of all, Johnson, nothing about the way I've treated you would change if we were in a serious relationship. If you don't know anything else, you *should* know that what you've seen is what you would get. Second of all, I've had some bad experiences, too. You're not the only one of us with emotional scars, but I don't hold other men's mistakes against you."

"I believe you. I really do, but I just can't, Cassie. I can't commit myself yet. I'm sorry, but I need more time."

The finality of Johnson's position began to sink in and Cassie wrestled with feelings of futility. He didn't want a relationship so what *did* he want? *Bed buddies*. The words haunted her and she knew she couldn't be satisfied with such an arbitrary involvement. She *wouldn't* be satisfied, particularly since she was being denied an active role in defining their relationship. If she went along with Johnson at this point, he would be pulling all the strings. In a way, the situation was reminiscent of the events that had ultimately led to the collapse of her relationship with Todd, only now the conflict was commitment rather than time.

"So, Cass, can we keep seeing each other?"

Johnson's desire to do so was quite evident in his voice, but Cassie wasn't willing to agree to his terms. She looked over at the flock of ducks still swimming undisturbed on the pond despite the torrential downpour. *Water off a duck's back.* She remembered her father saying that whenever he was confronted with difficult dilemmas.

"Cass?"

"I don't know, Johnson. Let me think about it." She honestly didn't know how she should handle this situation, but one thing was for sure—she didn't have to rush to make decisions any more than he had to agree to a more formal relationship.

"Okay, that's fair. Can we see each other while you think about it?" He laughed as though trying to lighten the mood.

"Maybe, but not today."

"What about sometime this evening?"

"No, that won't work either."

"Do you already have plans?" No more laughter.

"Yep." *I'm painting my toenails and reading a good book.*

Once again, Johnson was slow to respond as though waiting for Cassie to elaborate on her plans. It wasn't long before he realized that *Yep* was as good as it was going to get.

"Alright. Well, I won't hold you. Call me tomorrow if you want to meet for lunch."

"Okay. I'll talk to you later." *More later than sooner.*

When Cassie and Johnson ended their conversation, she folded her legs beneath her and settled into a more relaxed position on the patio chair. However she decided to handle Johnson, he definitely would not have his cake and eat it, too, which was essentially what he was asking of her. The best and most logical decision would be to cut Johnson loose and to spare herself any additional grief.

Cassie glanced over to the pond and thought that the wind seemed to be pushing the ducks across the water. Along the way, they continued dipping their heads in, sometimes resurfacing with small fish in their beaks. They were probably using the wind to make their meals more attainable. If they stopped paddling, perhaps more fish swam closer, not realizing that a predator was waiting on the surface. The fish could see sideways, but not upward. They didn't stand a chance.

Although the sky remained deeply overcast, the rain was finally letting up a little and, along with it, the tension Cassie felt slowly dissipated. She concentrated on the smoky heavens and wondered where the sun must be at the moment. *Burning brightly somewhere else in the world, that's for sure. I'd like to have more sunlight in my world. Is that asking for too much?*

Ah, Puerto Rico. Her friends' descriptions had fulfilled their promises of beauty. The skyline was more beautiful than any Cassie had seen and just the change she had craved a week ago. It was currently approaching midnight and the evening sky was not black, but instead a color more similar to a rich navy blue. And the moon was quite luminescent such that it appeared to have a halo that swallowed several surrounding stars. To say the least, the view was unparalleled to any other that Cassie knew of.

She and her group had now been in San Juan for a little more than one day, which was long enough to be awestruck by both the colorful plants as well as the lively buildings. In Old San Juan, there were lavender, yellow, green and red buildings, many of which were renovated and maintained as celebrated reminders of the island's history and culture. Cassie enjoyed imagining what the residents must have been like who had originally populated this city and how it may have looked a few hundred years ago. How had the now cobblestone roads looked when horseback was the mode of transportation? What were the original building colors before age and weather had faded them? Who were the men who had designed and built these buildings? It was all so fascinating!

Upon crossing over to New San Juan, a more modern city had been built, possessing all the normal amenities to which big city dwellers like Cassie were accustomed. Although the buildings were still uniquely colorful, the construction was much more contemporary and less inspiring to Cassie, who was immediately disappointed that she and her group would not be housed in Old San Juan. She wanted to learn more about the old city and be able to walk the streets. She longed to escape the confusion of her life and to instead immerse herself in a time before her own. Of course, there was little time for frolicking and touring, particularly since she would be flying out on Friday and it was already, as of midnight, Tuesday. There was much work to do before then. *C'est la vie,* she mourned inwardly.

While alone on her hotel patio, Cassie had poured over and organized several pages of meeting notes before succumbing to weariness. It had been a very busy day. She and her team had started off with a brief meeting with the BookMart order processing manager and then been given a tour of the large facility. Following lunch with the manager and several of his direct reports, the group had then met with the senior managers for the remainder of the afternoon. At the end of the workday, Cassie and her team went out for dinner and sightseeing. When they returned to the hotel, Cassie was sure she would be asleep before her head hit the pillow, but to her surprise sleep refused to come. She, therefore, collected her project meeting notes and organized the managers' comments by needs, current problems and issues, outcome desires, and areas considered efficient. Although the apparently productive areas weren't high on her team's priority list, they would still be surveyed at some point for improvement possibilities. Cassie decided to assemble a meticulous outline of the main issues to ensure her group was correctly focused while she was in Atlanta. Already she was realizing that the BookMart project was going to be bigger than the "whopper" she had spoken of with Mitchell.

After a few hours, Cassie was finally exhausted and so decided to memorize the superb patio view, but before long her mind wandered to Johnson. Since their conversation last Sunday, he had called nearly every day wanting to see her. However, despite his unrelenting pursuit, Cassie had only become more despondent and evasive. In the back her of her mind, she knew she had already decided to stop seeing him. They were on entirely different wavelengths and there simply was no point to delaying the inevitable. *Bed buddies.* The mere idea was repulsive to her and no matter how he framed his interests in her, the bottom line remained unchanged. She was once again confronted with the fact that she really wasn't losing anything.

And then there was Todd, who was relentless in his pursuit of something he could no longer have. Both men were clearly enticed by the unattainable. For Johnson, it was milk and cake. For Todd, it was love and redemption. Cassie would satisfy neither man.

When she was again in bed, sleep descended like a soft blanket and her slumber was heavy and dreamless. Not once did she stir or awaken with restless concerns. The road she must travel was as clear as the Puerto Rican skies and the march forward had already begun.

Chapter 10

THE FLIGHT TO ATLANTA the next Monday was unpleasantly turbulent. As Cassie reviewed a synopsis of Pilot Software, the plane rocked and bumped as though riding an ocean rather than moving through air. Nevertheless, the sky was a perfect blue, for which Cassie was grateful. In fact, she was actually looking forward to arriving in Atlanta and seeing how the city had changed since her departure. When she had moved over a year ago, there had been several sites under construction: new malls, new residential areas, an expanded railway system. It would be interesting to see how everything had turned out.

Once at the Hartsfield-Jackson Atlanta International Airport, Cassie disembarked the plane and entered the waiting area in search of a sign with her name on it. It was roughly 10:00 a.m. and her instructions were to go directly to the Pilot Software office where she would meet with the CEO to discuss his process concerns. As a convenience, the CEO had ordered a limousine and driver to fetch her and her luggage as expeditiously as possible. Pilot Software was also assuming all expenses for her hotel up front as opposed to awaiting the bill from Pinnacle Consulting. After Cassie was safely delivered to the company's location, the driver would transport her bags to the Embassy Suites near the office and ensure they were taken to her room there. Such first class treatment had worked to change Cassie's attitude about the last minute project.

The driver was extremely courteous at the airport as he carried her luggage and escorted her to the black Lincoln Town Car limousine. As they now cruised smoothly along highway 685, which formed a perfect loop around the city, Cassie's eyes never left the view beyond the darkly tinted windows. From the highway, she couldn't see much that had changed, but she knew that a drive deeper into the suburbs would reveal several modifications to the city's infrastructure. She would do some exploring that evening after securing a rental car.

Shortly before 11:30 a.m., the limousine pulled into the Peachtree Tower I and II office driveway. They were in the Perimeter area of Atlanta, a wealthy section of the city that lured both corporations and affluent homebuyers alike because of its convenient location between downtown Atlanta and the suburbs located on the city's outskirts. As usual for Atlanta, the rainbow of flowers planted in every direction created a sea of color that added yet more beauty to the surroundings and Cassie realized that she missed being able to regularly indulge her senses in the scenery. Office buildings, hotels, condominiums, and expensive apartment homes intermingled easily along the roadway because the building designs and landscaping were appealingly similar. Of course, the towers definitely stood out and had once been one of Cassie's favorite sights in the city when she lived there. When viewed from the freeway, the grayish, glass buildings appeared to be around thirty stories high and had white, arching beams that crisscrossed over each building top. In the evenings, these arches were one of the highlights of the Perimeter area's skyline because they lit up the buildings like well-controlled spotlights. Cassie had been awestruck the first time she witnessed the buildings' evening magnificence. And when she learned that Pilot Software was located in one of the towers, she was pleased that a reason to venture inside had been presented.

"Good morning, Ms. Stewart." The Pilot Software receptionist warmly greeted Cassie when she was escorted into the corporate lobby. According to the nameplate set on an eyelevel panel, her name was Sharon Tate. "I trust that your travel was pleasant."

"Good morning and, yes, the trip was very pleasant. And I really do appreciate the assistance at the airport." Cassie looked over her shoulder to thank her escort, the driver, but he had already exited the lobby and was probably on his way back to the car.

"I'm glad to hear that. If you would kindly have a seat, I will let Mr. Brody know you're here."

"Mr. Brody?"

"Yes, our CEO. He should be with you shortly."

Agape, Cassie watched Sharon lift the phone to her ear, dial four numbers on the keypad, and announce Cassie's arrival to someone, probably a secretary. When she completed the call and looked up, she was surprised to see Cassie still standing in front of the large, black marble desk.

"I'm sorry, Ms. Stewart, is there a problem?"

"Uh, no, no. Thank you. Um..." Cassie struggled for the right words to nonchalantly phrase the question, but the words eluded her as the receptionist waited expectantly.

"Yes?" Sharon continued to smile as a call came in. "Excuse me one moment." Once again she lifted the phone to her ear. "Pilot Software. May I help you?" Silence as she listened to the caller. "Well, good morning, Mr. Marshall. How are you doing today?" Sharon was clearly pleased with the identity of the caller.

Meanwhile, Cassie continued to stand in front of the woman and wished she would get off the phone so Cassie could ask the burning question.

"That's wonderful. I always enjoy hearing good news." Sharon averted her eyes upward and back to Cassie as she spoke. "Mr. Marshall, would you please hold for a brief moment?" Pause. "Thank you." Sharon focused on Cassie again. "Ms. Stewart, the CEO will be out shortly. Did you need something while you wait?"

Finally! "No, thank you. I was just wondering about Mr. Brody. That wouldn't be *Todd* Brody, would it?"

"Yes, it is. He should be with you in a few moments."

The rage immediately overtook Cassie, but she refrained from unleashing it on the innocent receptionist. If she had a car outside, she would walk right out the building and never look back, job or no job. "Thank you." Her smile was stiff, but professionalism prevented her from displaying her true emotions. She was going to *kill* Todd for this!

With murderous thoughts running through her mind, Cassie walked over to one of the large, comfortable chairs in the lobby and took a seat. She stared blindly around the lobby, furious and waiting for Todd to show himself. She imagined punching him in the gut so that he crumpled onto the black, marble floor. She considered knuckling him in his nose so hard that blood spattered his pricey suit. That would teach him. Just what did the man think he would accomplish with this big game? More than anything else, Cassie did not like to be manipulated, which was exactly what Todd had done with the help of Mitchell. Did Mitchell know what was *really* going on? She would get to the bottom of it as soon as she got to the hotel. And with any luck, she would catch a flight back to Dallas tonight.

As Cassie brainstormed various methods for inflicting harm on Todd, he entered the lobby looking better than she could remember. It seemed that the man was impervious to any form of disrepair and for a few seconds Cassie experienced her unfailing bout with conflicting emotions.

"So what do you think?" He stood smiling proudly in the center of the lobby and spread his arms out to his sides.

Fury returned in full force as Cassie stood up and walked over to face him. "What do I think? I think you've got a lot of nerve, Todd." she hissed. "Just who do you think you are to use my work to manipulate me? What did you think I would do when I got here, huh? Fall into your lap? Because you've got another thing coming." She pointed a finger at his face. "You are lucky that there's a witness in the room because otherwise I would really do you some serious damage."

Cassie spoke in a near whisper so Sharon couldn't overhear her, but her body language gave away the intensity of the exchange. Saying that she was thirsty, the receptionist excused herself from the room. Todd, however, never flinched and the smirk remained fixed his face.

"Well, the witness that you're so concerned about is gone. Here's your chance for payback."

"Don't tempt me, Todd. Don't tempt me."

"Hey, I know I deserve it. I knew you would be angry when you discovered that I was behind all this."

"Then why did you do it? How could you?"

"I did it because it was the only way to get you here. I wanted to show you what I haven't told you." He again spread his arms out to his sides. "Look at what I've done, Cass. Stop hating me for one minute and just look around you. This is all mine—this business, the furniture, the bills. I own it. *Me*. Todd Brody."

Cassie squinted her eyes at Todd to say, *You are not off the hook*, before allowing them to wander meaningfully around the room. Now she was actually noticing the area and all its effects, the plush yet professional décor. She had already noted the black, marble floors, but now she also took in the expensive multi-color rug beneath the black lacquer table, which was set in the center of a ring of leather chairs and sofas. On the other side of the lobby were large, matching leather chairs for individuals along with pewter lamps and a broad selection of technical magazines for waiting visitors to read. Behind the receptionist desk, the wall consisted entirely of glass and from where Cassie stood she could see that highway 685 was cluttered with the normal lunch hour traffic. She also had a terrific view of the cluster of shops and restaurants located on the other side of the highway, establishments that Cassie had frequently patronized while an Atlanta resident. Though angry with Todd for his duplicity, she was also glad to be back in the city she had known so well.

Perhaps sensing the shift in Cassie's mood, Todd excitedly took her hand and pulled her to a hallway. "Come with me. I want to show you the rest of the place." Cassie was willingly led through a hall that ended in a series of offices. "These offices are for the programmers on staff. At the moment we have eight, but we'll be hiring more very soon because we continue to get more projects than we can accommodate. I've actually been turning down clients, can you believe it? We just don't have the manpower right now. But we will."

They strolled past the occupied offices within which the programmers worked diligently. Not one person looked up from his or her computer screen as Cassie and Todd walked by their doorways.

"Everyone is so grim." Cassie wasn't accustomed to such an unfriendly work environment.

"Oh no, they're not grim. They're ambitious. Every single person here has a vested interest in the success of Pilot Software because they all were given stock in their contracts."

"Your company is already publicly traded?"

"No, but we will be, Cass. We will be. Like I said, we're growing faster than I can hire people! I can hardly believe how far we've come in a year."

They walked back through the lobby area and then through another hallway that led to the administrative staff.

"I want to introduce you to my office manager. She will be meeting with you about the administrative improvements we need before the business really explodes."

"So there actually is work you expect me to do?" Cassie had already mentally planned her flight out of town at the earliest available time.

Todd seemed surprised by Cassie's question. "Of course! I'm not paying two-hundred-thousand dollars for nothing."

"*Two-hundred-thousand dollars?*" Cassie grabbed his arm and yanked him around to face her. "Are you out of your mind? One person for two weeks of work is not worth two-hundred-thousand dollars."

"That's where you're wrong. I'm not paying for just any person on staff at Pinnacle Consulting. I'm paying for the cream of the crop and you're worth every dime." They continued to head for the office manager's work area. "The way I figure it, I'll save at least two million dollars next year alone by taking advantage of your expertise now. And I'm looking forward to receiving your suggestions because I know they will be top notch."

After passing several offices, they reached the end of the hall and Todd used his knuckles to rap on one of the office doors. "Ericka, I'd like you to meet Cassie Stewart. She's the Pinnacle consultant I told you about who will be helping to streamline some of our administrative processes." As he spoke, Todd motioned Cassie into the office.

"Hello, Eri—Hey, don't I know you?" Cassie walked toward the woman with her hand extended. Ordinarily, she maintained a purely professional posture with clients, but she would hardly call today's events ordinary. She and Ericka both smiled broadly as they shook hands.

"Yes, I do think we've met before, but I can't place the where and when."

"You two met at the Technet company party a few years ago. I brought Cassie with me that evening."

"Ohhh." Both women reacted in unison before laughing.

"It's good to see you again, Cassie. I'm glad you're here to help us get everything more organized." She then scolded Todd playfully. "Now, Todd, you know we have to take good care of Cassie while she's here since she's an old friend."

"Rest assured, Ericka, that I have every intention of taking care of Ms. Stewart."

To Ericka, Todd's response was exceptionally gracious and she smiled fondly at her boss. To Cassie, however, it was exceedingly ominous and she began counting the reasons she should leave Atlanta before discovering what Todd had in store.

"So why did you decide to start your own business?" Cassie and Todd were at Houlihan's, a popular restaurant that had always been one of her favorites, eating lunch. Although she was still miffed with Todd's manipulations, she was also impressed with what he had accomplished in such a short period of time.

Todd used his napkin to dab his lips before speaking. "It was time, Cass. I had spent the first eight years of my professional life working for other people and getting nowhere."

"I wouldn't call being a manager at Technet getting nowhere." She spooned some potato soup into her mouth while continuing to gaze intently at Todd.

"It's getting nowhere when you imagine yourself having control over your time. I was tired of allowing someone else to call all the shots. Plus, I was automatically forfeiting ownership of my greatest software creations because I was working for a corporation I didn't own. When I think of the millions of dollars I made that company! And I wasn't even earning one percent of the profits I generated so I decided to bail. Seemed like the most logical thing to do."

"You've taken on quite a heavy load with your own company. How do you feel about it? You must be working some serious hours." *No wonder you've been working nearly every weekend.*

"Cass, I would challenge that statement with the fact that you work just as many hours as I do and you don't even own your business."

"That's true. I hadn't thought about that."

"I know. And the truth is that you, not Pinnacle Consulting, should be receiving the two-hundred grand that I'm paying for your services here. I mean, think about it, what is your boss doing right now while you're traveling and juggling projects? I'll tell you what he's doing. He's busy planning your next trip somewhere else while he relaxes in his cozy office and reads e-mail." Todd sliced the huge steak he had been neglecting while talking. It looked delicious, fresh off the grill.

As he sliced the steak, Cassie pondered his statements, which were undoubtedly true.

"Anyway, that's why I opened my own business. I have more control over my time, I set my own prices and determine my well-deserved wages, and the best part is that I answer to no one. You can't beat all that with a stick." He placed a large piece of steak in his mouth and rolled his eyes with delight. "Man, this is good. You can't beat this steak either."

Cassie smiled. "I'm really glad that so much has been working out for you. The changes were obviously what you needed because you're much happier now than you were over a year ago."

"No kidding. I was definitely not the happiest guy in town. I'm sorry I put you through so much when you were here. I should have handled things much differently."

"Would you please stop apologizing? It's all in the past now and we have to let it go." It seemed like Todd apologized nearly every time they spoke and Cassie wished he would stop bringing up old news. "I've been wondering how Ericka came to work for you. Did you steal her when you left Technet?"

"Damn right." Todd laughed loudly. "She was my secretary at Technet and I knew she was smart enough to take on more challenging responsibilities than she would ever have there. Once I got Pilot going, I gave her a call and she came on board. In fact, she was my first employee. All the programmers and other administrative staff came along around six months ago when we moved into the Peachtree Towers. I'm telling you, business just took off faster than I expected and things have not slowed down for one minute. It's pretty exciting."

"I'm sure it is. I understand that you developed a firewall software that set everything in motion."

"That's right. Once word of the software got out, everyone wanted it. I thank God every day that a head honcho at IBM gave us a chance and then told some of his clients about us. That was a huge thumbs up."

Cassie and Todd polished off their lunches and then headed back to the office. While in the car, Todd reached for Cassie's hand, squeezed it quickly, and then let go. It all happened before Cassie could react to his touch.

"I know you're upset with me for tricking you into this job, but I hope now you can understand why I did it. How else was I going to show you what I've been doing? And I wanted you to see it with your own eyes because you are the inspiration behind it all." He smiled warmly at her before restoring his eyes to the road.

"I'm the inspiration? I don't understand." Cassie was quite surprised by this last revelation.

"If you had not told me where to get off on that fateful day, I don't think I would ever have left Technet. One of the reasons I started up Pilot is because I needed something to get my mind off of you. And it helped a lot that I was so pissed off with all the things you said. I used that energy to keep me motivated. I figured you'd be sorry for dumping me when you saw the empire I created." He smiled to himself as he reflected on his past intentions. "I guess that in the end, I learned that the only person who was sorry was me. It took me a while to get that. After the swift kick you gave me, I spent several months just licking my wounds, but eventually the light came on and I saw your message like writing on the wall. Anyway, the bottom line is that I'm glad you're here, even if you're mad at me. I'm loving every minute of your company."

Cassie could not get over how much Todd had changed. If she wasn't witnessing it firsthand, she would never have believed it possible. Never in their past had he so candidly expressed his emotions and he certainly did not criticize himself. *Ever.* And yet here he was today talking about his feelings, exposing his weaknesses, and allowing Cassie to see inside Todd the actual man, underbelly and all. While she had always found his external good looks extremely appealing, his internal workings had never seemed to match and so she had long ago accepted that he was only eye candy. Now, however, Cassie found herself reassessing her established conclusions about the man and she admitted to herself that she was beginning to like the sweetness that had surfaced in Todd. And yet Cassie was nevertheless mindful of their hard history and decided it would be wise to keep their interactions to a minimum. The infamous butterflies would not be taking flight along with her senses while she was in Atlanta. This was a working trip and a working relationship. Working. End of story.

Chapter 11

Luscious. Against her will, it was the word that crept into Cassie's mind when she looked at Todd from across the meeting room table. To ensure that everyone was aware of her presence and purpose at the office, Todd had called a meeting with all the Pilot employees. Cassie admired the way he commanded everyone's attention and their obvious respect. He did not condescend to his employees as though he held their fates in his hands. Rather, he addressed them as equals and was clearly receptive to their ideas and even to their disagreements. Todd openly invited everyone to share their thoughts before closing the meeting with a resounding greeting to Cassie. She would be treated as part of the family and team while at the office.

Todd had clearly selected a bright group to help launch his company and Cassie knew she would enjoy working with them. She was especially glad for Ericka's presence since they had already fallen into a very comfortable relationship. Cassie guessed that Ericka was in her late forties although the woman was as spunky as a teenager.

Cassie and Ericka left the meeting together so Cassie could begin learning about the administrative processes in place. The twinkle in Ericka's eyes as they walked toward her office gave away the question before it was asked.

"Okay, Cassie, I see the way my boss is looking at you. What's the scoop?" She smiled and leaned back in her chair, signaling that work could wait.

"I don't know what you mean, Ericka." Cassie took a seat across from her and shrugged. "Nothing's up."

"If you don't want to talk about it, I understand. It's none of my business so I won't pry." Ericka's facial expression, however, spoke volumes. *I'm not buying what you're selling,* her eyes said. But despite Cassie's aloofness, the twinkle was still quite bright. She folded her hands together and shifted her position so that she was leaning toward Cassie. "On to work we go then."

Cassie nodded agreeably and produced a notepad from her briefcase. "Great."

At around five thirty that evening, Todd stopped by the office that Cassie would occupy while at Pilot Software. Ericka had left for the day nearly an hour ago and Cassie was now typing the notes she had taken during their meeting while the information was still fresh on her mind.

"Hey, I was hoping you hadn't left yet. Do you have plans this evening?"

Cassie hardly glanced up from the computer. "I'm going to finish these notes and then call it a night earlier than usual. I think jetlag is setting in."

"Yeah, you've had a long day. I'll take you to the hotel when you're ready to go."

"Actually, I need to get a rental car. Would you mind taking me to the nearest Hertz? We have a contract with them so they will give me the best rental rates." She kept typing while talking, adding the finishing touches to the document and then selecting the save option.

"Sure. We should've had a car delivered today so it would be here when you needed it. I wish we had thought about that." He was truly disappointed about neglecting the small detail.

Cassie detached her USB flash drive from the computer and began shutting it down. "Todd, you've already done more than most clients, more than we ask. I can get my own rental car. I always do." She dropped the flash drive into her briefcase and stood up.

"Yes, I know, but I'm not just a client. I want to be sure you're safe."

As with in the lobby so many months ago, Cassie found herself weakened by the man. She could see the raw emotions in his face, the ardor, and for a moment she wanted to respond, but somehow managed to restrain herself. Their history, the rocky road she had spoken of with Monique…It was just too much to overcome.

"Don't worry about me. I'll be fine." She moved toward the door and walked past him. *Be cool. Take it slowly.* "Are you ready to go?"

He hesitated for a brief moment before walking toward her. "I'm ready if you are."

The following day passed at a mad pace. Cassie spent the morning with Ericka discussing the efficiency goals required to accommodate the rapid growth of Pilot. Afterward, she met with Stephanie Wilder, Todd's secretary. She was a very dishy Caucasian woman, a brunette with all the curves of an hour glass. Stephanie possessed Todd's vintage body type, although Cassie knew he was not inclined to sleep with her. He had reserved himself for the sistahs only. Still, Cassie was certain Todd was enjoying the view immensely.

"Ericka tells me that you are responsible for typing proposals, managing Todd's calendar, filing, and other administrative needs that arise." Cassie ticked off the bullets on the notes she had typed yesterday.

"Uh huh, that's right."

Stephanie was chewing gum and the smacking sound was already irritating Cassie.

"Good. I'd like for you to take a look at this task list and tell me if anything you do is not listed. We need to be sure that all your functions are identified."

"Do you need that right now? I've got a last minute deadline to meet. Mr. Brody has a new client coming in this afternoon and the pamphlet he plans to distribute isn't completed yet."

"Oh, Ericka didn't mention that you would have anything pressing to do this morning. She thought this was a good time to meet with you."

"Well, Ericka can't know everything, can she? Mr. Brody came to me, not to her, since this is my job."

"I understand." *What's her problem?* "Tell you what, I'll just leave this list with you and you can get back with me this afternoon on anything that needs to be added."

"I can't make any promises, but I'll try to find time to look at it today. I'm very busy, ya know." *Smack. Smack. Smack.* She turned her back to Cassie and began typing.

Cassie had dealt with women like Stephanie before and was quick to dismiss her sassy attitude. *I'm just here to do a job, lady. You don't need to prove your importance to me.* She walked back down the hall toward to Ericka's office to apprise her of Stephanie's busyness.

"Yeah, yeah, sure, sure. I know what that's all about." Ericka seemed unsurprised by Stephanie's haughtiness. "I'll have a talk with her."

"You have my attention. What's it about? All I asked her to do was tell me if any tasks she performs were missing from our list."

Ericka clucked under her breath but was obviously humored. "Her problem has nothing to do with any tasks you need identified. Her problem is that she doesn't like having competition hanging around, especially someone as pretty as you are."

"What do I have to do with anything?"

"Girl, you can't be that dense. I refuse to believe it."

"I'm sorry, Ericka, but I just don't understand how I can be perceived as competition. I definitely don't want Stephanie's job if that's what you mean."

Ericka stood up, walked around her desk to stand directly in front of Cassie, and then leaned backward against the desk corner. "Close my door. I don't want anyone walking by to hear what I'm about to say."

Cassie obediently shut the door with a puzzled expression.

"Now let's get down to the nitty gritty. I'm sure you've noticed that Stephanie is a very pretty girl."

Cassie nodded.

"I'm sure you've also noticed the way she dresses. Everything she wears draws attention to her body, which looks to be perfect from what I can see."

Cassie considered this statement before nodding again.

"So why do you think she dresses that way?"

"I have no clue and frankly I couldn't care less."

"Of course. You're just here for a couple of weeks to help straighten things out so you shouldn't care. Really, I don't care either. But whether or not we care is not the issue. You asked why Stephanie had such an attitude with you and I'm trying to answer your question."

"Okay, so what's her problem?"

"Stephanie wants Todd and you are distracting him from her feminine wiles. She's been after that man since the day she got hired and within two days you have put her back in her place. That's her problem." Ericka crossed her arms and pursed her lips.

"What have I done? There's nothing between me and Todd."

"What have you done? You showed up, that's what you did. Lord, girl, open your eyes and see what everyone else sees. That man has it *bad* for you. A blind person could see that."

"Ericka, even if that's true, Todd would never want Stephanie. She's not his type."

"She's his type, just not his preferred color. For a while, though, she was thinking he could get over that. Then you show up, pretty, smart, a sistah, obviously one-hundred percent Todd's taste and she's hating your guts for it. She knows she doesn't stand a chance now that she's met you."

Cassie silently absorbed Ericka's statements and was very quickly able to sum up her opinion in two words: *So what.*

Ericka must have read Cassie's facial expression because she unfolded her arms and walked back around her desk to take a seat.

"As I said earlier, I will have a talk with Stephanie about her sudden attack of workhorse and make sure her priorities are straight. We should be able to schedule tomorrow morning for the two of you to go over her tasks." Ericka hit a key on her computer to refresh the spreadsheet she had been updating when Cassie walked in.

"That will be fine. Meanwhile, I'll begin collecting some accounting data from the software y'all use so we can determine the current accounts payable volume, the rate of volume increase, and accounts receivable needs. We'll want to consider all these things when deciding on a software that allows Pilot to grow without problems."

"Knowing Todd, he will want to create his own accounting software." Ericka chuckled at the thought, which was not a dim reality. She knew her boss.

"I wouldn't recommend it since Pilot is growing so quickly, but it would certainly be his decision." Cassie smiled and opened the office door.

"One more thing, Cassie. I don't know what's going on between you and Todd, but I'd appreciate it if you take it easy on my boss. We sort of like the guy around here."

Unable to think of an appropriate response, Cassie simply left the office as quickly as her feet could carry her.

Once again at precisely five thirty in the afternoon, Todd poked his head in Cassie's temporary office. "What do you think about hanging out with an old friend tonight?"

Cassie heaved a long sigh. "I really have too much to get done, Todd. I'm trying to wrap up this project early next week so I can focus on the project in Puerto Rico."

"You mean the project that's carrying on without you?"

"Yeah, the one I'd be working right now if you hadn't been such a sneaky scoundrel."

"Ouch. Touché. Do you think you can ever forgive me?"

"Do you think you will ever change?"

"Alright, we'll call this one a draw. In any event, I'm not going to help you leave early. I'm paying for two full weeks of your time and I won't settle for less."

"You're paying for my work, not my time."

"Same difference. And as your client, I'm commanding you to stop working right now and to come with me. I have something to show you."

"Todd, really, I can't. Not tonight." *I don't trust myself to be alone with you. I haven't figured out how I feel about you and I don't think I want to.*

"Trust me, it will all be here tomorrow. Now get up so we can get out of here." He walked behind her chair and pulled it away from the desk. "Up, woman, up."

Cassie couldn't suppress the laughter. "Alright already. I'm getting up. Just let me save my work and shut down the computer." She rolled the chair back to the desk and began typing again as though he had disappeared. When Todd attempted to touch the computer power button, she slapped his hand mercilessly. "One more sentence and then I'll be ready."

Now it was Todd who burst into laughter. "Go ahead. You're just doing what you're paid to do." He rubbed his hand. "You didn't have to hit me so hard, though."

"I didn't hit you nearly as hard as I'd like to so count your lucky stars."

"I'll keep that in mind." He smiled while watching her fingers fly on the keyboard.

He was standing close enough for Cassie to feel his body heat and she willed her fingers to move faster so they could leave. More importantly, she needed to increase the proximity between them. The man did things to her constitution that she would never be able to handle as well as she would like. *But he will never know so help me God.*

Cassie finally saved the document and shut down the computer. "Okay, let's go."

"Cool. And let's take my car."

"I'd rather follow you in the rental." *I'm not getting trapped somewhere with you.*

Todd seemed reluctant, but quickly relented. "Okay, just make sure you don't fall too far behind. I don't want you to get lost. Do you have my cell number just in case?"

"Yes, I have your cell. You haven't told me where we're going."

"It's a surprise."

"I think I've had enough surprises this week. Where are we going? Tell me or I'm going back to the hotel." Cassie meant it.

"Aw, you're such a wet towel. We're going to my house."

"No thanks, I'll pass." *You think you're slick, but you ain't gettin' none of this, my friend.*

"See, that's why I didn't want to tell you. I knew you would get the wrong idea, but it's not even like that. I'm not trying to get you into bed, Cassie. I don't need you for sex."

"I'm sure you don't."

"So just come with me, okay? You won't be sorry."

"Todd, I'm not in the mood for any games. I came here to do a job, that's all. This whole trip has turned into way more than I bargained for."

"I'm not playing any games with you. And I'm not interested in controlling you, trapping you, or hurting you. Got it?"

"I hear you talking."

"Would you please just come to my home, grace my doorstep with your fine presence, and tell me what you think of the place? I picked it out by myself and I could really use a woman's opinion, especially for decorating. You know how terrible I am at that. Come on and help out a brothuh."

Cassie squinted her eyes at him before collecting her briefcase. "Okay, I'll go, but you'd better not try any funny stuff, Todd. One false move and I'm outta there, understand?"

"Understood. You're running the show."

As they exited the office, Cassie remembered when Johnson had shared his news about being promoted and claimed that he was now running the show. Her response had been that he was running his mouth. *Now I'm the one running my mouth.* "How the tables do turn," she muttered under her breath.

"What was that, Cass?"

"Nothing. Just thinking out loud." *I'm walking straight into a trap with my eyes wide open. I'm a fly being dragged to the spider's web. We both know that if he tries to seduce me, I won't put up much of a fight. I never could before and some things never change.* She was tempted to feel sorry for herself, but then decided against it. If she was going to be stupid, she may as well accept her stupidity with as much intelligence and accountability as possible. *I'm a deer heading directly to the hunter, a mouse being lured to the trap. I give up. I feel sorry for myself. Wouldn't Monique be thrilled to know where I'm going tonight. And she would be celebrating, not expressing sympathy. I just hope I'm stronger than I think I am. I hope, I hope, I hope.*

Simply stated, Todd's home was perfectly gorgeous. And huge. He had purchased a two-story, eight-bedroom house in Buckhead, one of the most expensive neighborhoods in the entire city. When he walked Cassie through the rooms, she felt as if she were touring a small palace. The windows practically lined the walls from floor to ceiling in all but the bedrooms and bathrooms. And she guessed that sunlight must cascade into the house and light up everything on clear days. But Cassie's favorite part of the house was the hardwood floors. Just about anyone could decorate a room that wasn't limited by colorful carpets. As far as Cassie could tell, Todd had a blank pallet to work with. Actually, empty was more like it. There wasn't a single piece of furniture in the place.

"Have you moved in yet?"

"Of course. I moved in a month ago. I just haven't decorated yet."

Cassie stood in the center of the living room and placed her hands on her hips as she looked around. "Why not? You have enough money now to hire a professional decorator. There's no reason you should be living in an empty house like this."

Todd came to stand before her and placed his hands in his pockets. "You're right, but I don't want a professional decorator. I want you."

Cassie dropped eye contact and began walking around the room. She pretended not to have heard his statement. "I know a few people I could put you in touch with. You could choose one of them or use all of them to spice up the rooms. They're all fabulous decorators."

Now Todd walked up behind her and spoke softly into her ear. "Did you hear me? I don't want anyone else but you to decorate this house. I'm hoping that one day this will be *our* house so, you see, it just wouldn't do for anyone but you to decide what goes where and which colors work."

Cassie remained stationary and closed her eyes. She had anticipated a ploy of some sort, but not the sweetness with which it would be revealed. She felt Todd's arms encircle her waist and draw their bodies closer together as he continued standing behind her.

"Cassie, everything I've done in the last year I did for you. The company, this house, everything. I love you."

Although deeply moved emotionally, Cassie was unable to move physically. Tears began to stream down her face as she grappled with the feelings that Todd's words evoked in her, feelings that she had believed were dormant, but that had obviously been lying in wait for a new occasion to be revived. All at once, Cassie was confused, delighted, and frightened.

Without removing his arms from her waist, Todd came around to face Cassie. Upon seeing the tears, he raised his hands to her face and began wiping them away.

Cassie finally opened her eyes and looked into his. The concern she saw in his eyes caused even more tears to fall.

"Baby, why are you crying?"

Cassie sniffed and reached into her purse for a tissue. "I don't know. I guess I'm just confused."

"Don't be confused, Cass. I don't want to confuse you." He pulled her against him and held her while stroking her hair. "I'll back off. I promise. I'll let you call the shots. You tell me what you want."

"If I knew what I wanted, I would tell you, but I just can't right now."

"It's that other guy, huh?" He pulled away so he could see her face again. "Is it serious?"

"I don't want to talk about him. Anyway, it's not about him, it's about you. How am I supposed to forget about everything that happened between us? I was messed up for a long time after all that drama. You couldn't see it or hear about it since I had moved away, but the truth is that I really went through it. And now you seem to think we can lightly dismiss all that and pick up where we left off." The tears were still falling freely, but the flow was slowing down. Cassie reached for a new tissue and broke away from Todd's hold.

"I'm not asking you to forget, just to forgive. I know you're still angry with me. It's all over your face every time you look at me, but do you think you can ever stop being angry and give me another chance?"

"I already told you I don't know." Cassie had turned her back on Todd while pacing the room and was surprised to glance up and find him standing in front of her.

"Then let me tell you what I know." Once again, his arms circled Cassie's waist as he peered into her eyes. "I know that you're the only woman who's ever made me feel like I can conquer the world. You're the only woman I've ever loved for exactly the way she is. And you're the only woman who has ever made me feel like magic when we do this." He slowly brushed his lips against hers and drew back for a moment before succumbing to a more urgent kiss.

Without thinking, Cassie responded and wrapped her arms around him, allowing the kiss to burn through and into her.

They continued kissing like lovestruck teenagers for several minutes before Todd pulled away. He then leaned forward just enough for his nose to touch Cassie's. Afterward, he kissed her nose and forehead. The two held each other silently for what seemed like hours before Todd spoke again.

"I love you, Cassie. Regardless of what you feel for me, I love you. And I want to make love to you so badly, more than you could possibly know. Bu I don't want you like this. I don't want you unless you *know* you want me. That's where I am now. I want your love, Cass. I want all of you or nothing."

Cassie had no response and so looked away and eventually down at the hardwood floors she had admired a few short moments ago.

Realizing she was not going to respond, Todd reached for her hands and clasped them. "Come on, baby. Let me walk you to your car while I'm still able to let you leave unsullied."

They walked outside and once again held each other before Cassie got into the rental car. She practically melted into the car seat and started the engine as Todd shut the car door.

"You think about what I said, Cassie, and let me know when you have an answer. Take your time. I won't pressure you, but don't make me wait forever." He leaned into the car and kissed her cheek.

"Todd, I just don't know what to say. If I think of something, I'll tell you, okay?"

"Okay, just make sure you're thinking about it. Now get outta here. Drive safely and call me when you get to the hotel."

"I will." She backed out of the driveway as tears began to fall again. Cassie was more confused than she had ever been in her life. She didn't know whether she'd be able to tell Todd what he wanted to hear, now or in the future. Why did she suddenly feel obligated to tell him *anything?* owHoNothing was making sense anymore.

Chapter 12

"I KNEW I LIKED that Todd!" Monique could not have been more thrilled with the developments Cassie shared over margaritas at Soho jazz club that Saturday night.

Thankfully, Pinnacle allowed consultants to fly home on weekends when performing projects in other cities. As soon as Cassie had reached a reasonable stopping point at Pilot, she had practically fled Atlanta and the suffocation she was feeling. In many ways, it was like déjà vu.

"Todd loves you, girl. Men don't act like that unless they're in love. He bought a house for you! Ooh, girl!"

"He did not buy the house for me." Cassie shook her head as though the idea was preposterous and then turned her attention to the music filling the club and bouncing nicely off the walls. The sound was so soothing to her. A saxophone was crooning a soft melody that caused something inside her to float and she was relieved for the opportunity to unravel. The tension she had been feeling all week was being lifted and carried away into the air. "Where's Dana? I thought she was coming with us tonight."

"She'll be here later. She wanted the baby to be asleep before leaving the house."

"Why? Alan can handle the baby for one night. I see what she means about being trapped by children."

"I don't think she really feels trapped. Frustrated sometimes, but not trapped. She'll be alright." Monique sucked some salt from the edge of the glass and then took a drink. "You're really good at changing the subject, you know that?"

Cassie only smiled and stared straight ahead at the band on stage. The drummer was kind of cute. He caught Cassie's eye and winked at her.

"So what's the deal with Johnson these days? Is he still in hot pursuit?" Monique moved her head and neck to the beat while talking.

"Oh, I don't know. I haven't been in town enough to be pursued."

"But he's still calling you every day, right?"

"Yeah, he leaves messages on my cell phone, but I haven't had time to call him back."

"You mean you haven't *felt* like calling him back. Payback is always a mothuh."

"I'm not trying to get back at him, though. I honestly have not had time to call him. I've got so much on my plate at work." Cassie exhaled deeply as she thought about all the work awaiting her in Atlanta and Puerto Rico. "It's just unreal how busy I am, girl."

"Uh huh. Well, we make time for the things we want to do. Who do you think you're kidding?"

"Monie, Cassie, I finally made it." Dana was pulling a chair out from the table and sitting down as she announced her arrival.

"What's up, girl?" Excited to see her friend, Cassie walked around to Dana and leaned down to hug her. "It's so good to see you! How are you?"

"I'm fine. What about you? I hear you've got two men nipping at your heels."

Cassie looked at Monique and rolled her eyes. "Can't you let me tell my own business? My goodness." Cassie returned to her seat and playfully scolded Monique. "I don't need your help to discuss my life."

"What's a little gossip between friends?" Monique took another sip of the margarita as Cassie nudged her and smiled.

"Excuse me, ladies."

They all looked up to find a waiter standing at the table with a large bottle of champagne.

"The gentleman on stage has asked me to deliver this champagne to you on the house." He set three chilled glasses on the table and poured champagne into each one.

The women looked toward the stage and the drummer once again caught Cassie's eye and winked. When the waiter was gone, Dana and Monique pounced on their friend.

"What's up with the drummer? Why is he winking at you?" Dana tossed her hair and rested her hand on her face.

"He's been winking at her since we got here, girl. She didn't think I noticed." Monique giggled.

"No he hasn't," Cassie objected to the exaggeration.

"Jees, Cassie, aren't two men enough for you?" Dana was getting in on the jabs now.

"Hey, hey, enough already. Why are y'all picking on me tonight?"

"We're not picking on you." Monique elbowed Cassie. "We're just sharing the love, that's all."

"Please, no more love!" Cassie clenched her hair in her hands as though fighting off a fit of madness. "I can't take it anymore. Augh!"

Dana and Monique could only laugh at the melodrama.

"I'm serious, y'all. I've got too much love going on right now. First I can't *buy* love and now the love has gotten out of control! What's up?"

"That's what Monique has been telling me. You have two exceptional men wrapped around your fingers."

"I didn't say all that. Don't go putting words in my mouth."

Dana flapped her hand at Monique as her usual silent retort. "Anyway, you seem to have a delicious problem on your hands. I'm envious."

"Girl, don't be because I'm not having fun."

"Oh, but you *should* be."

"See, that's what I keep telling her. For once, Dana and I agree." Monique was obviously pleased to have Dana on her side.

"How can I have fun with two men driving me insane?"

"Stop looking at it that way and enjoy the *power*!" Monique clenched a fist and raised it in the air. "Do it for all the women in the world who would kill to be in your shoes."

A trumpet blared as if on cue and then the music halted briefly as the band left the stage for a break. Seconds later, a beautiful cello solo was playing along with snare drums from speakers around the club.

"Ah, Monique, only you can outdo yourself." Dana drank some champagne and then pulled her hair back from her face in a single dramatic gesture. "How do you think I would look with a really short haircut?"

Taken aback by the question, Cassie and Monique exchanged glances before answering.

"You would look great."

"Without a doubt."

"You could wear your hair in any style and look good."

"Uh huh."

"Why? You're not actually thinking about cutting it off, are you?" Monique appeared stunned.

"Yes, actually, I am. I'm thinking about it."

"But why? Your hair is so gorgeous. And you can do so much with it. Why would you cut if off?" Like Monique, Cassie simply could not believe her ears.

"Because I need a change. I'm tired of the status quo. It's just hair. It can't bear children or bring home the bacon." She released her locks and they fell back around her shoulders to frame her face. "It's cumbersome and it gets in my way all day. I should have cut if off a long time ago."

"Boy, I'll bet Alan doesn't want you to cut that hair. You know how dumb men are about it. You'd swear it was spun gold or something."

"I know that's right," Cassie agreed with Monique. "What brought all this up, though? You're talking about hair, but I get the feeling that there's more to it than that."

Dana nodded her head. The expression on her face was somewhat strained. "I suppose I just want control of something. Right now, the external forces in my life seem to dictate everything, but the other day I had an epiphany. I *can* control my hair. I can choose to cut it all off and no one can stop me. If I cut it off, I can wake up every day and not spend an hour blow-drying hair, which means I have more time to do something else. I can get to work earlier and leave earlier if that one hour is added back into my day. Or I can sleep later, maybe make love to my husband, whatever. It would be my decision, my time, my hair. And then I think, why not? Why shouldn't I cut it?"

"Cut your hair, girl!" Monique was definitely in the mood to celebrate woman power tonight. "You go!"

Cassie only shrugged. "Do what you gotta do. If you want to cut your hair, then go for it. Since you're the one who has to comb it every day, it's really not up to anyone else." Cassie sympathized for Dana, who was still struggling against the demands of a new baby. Hair was not the real issue, but maybe cutting it would help her friend to feel better. Sometimes the smallest changes could make life a little more manageable.

So what sort of changes do I need to make my own life more bearable? It was quite dumbfounding how Johnson had abruptly turned up the heat once Cassie stopped paying attention to him. The combination of his and Todd's affections had become disconcerting over the past few weeks. Then again, it shouldn't be surprising since their behavior matched the trends about which her mother had lectured for as long as Cassie could remember. Men didn't like easy women so as long as Cassie was hard to get, both men were equally enamored with her. Okay, Todd was definitely more enamored since he'd had more time to stew over his rejection. *Something has to give.*

Monique tapped Cassie on her arm. "What zone are you in? You're staring at the wall as if it's a good-looking man."

Cassie smiled weakly and rubbed her arm. "Sorry, I guess I got lost in my own thoughts for a minute."

As usual, Dana tossed her hair back elegantly and Cassie knew she would never cut it off. "Wouldn't it be nice if life just came together without us working so hard to smooth out the edges? I mean, it seems like society places so many pressures on us to be so many different things and we feel obligated to make ourselves fit into those square holes. It's just not fair sometimes."

"Hmm, I don't think I'm trying to live up to social expectations." Cassie weighed her thoughts carefully. "I just think I've moved beyond all the games that go into making a relationship work. Other than that, I have no complaints."

"When you're with the right man, you don't have to play any games. Things just sort of work themselves out." Monique was bubbly about life and love for obvious reasons. "Rodney and I keep it real, even if reality isn't the way we'd want it. But you know, that's what makes our relationship so exciting. There's no pretense between us."

"Yes, I know what you mean. You two would be surprised at some of the things that Alan and I talk about."

"Have you ever told him how you feel about having a second baby?" The question flew out of Cassie's mouth before she could stop herself. She had been wanting to ask since Dana made the comment about needing control over something in her life.

Dana was nodding before she spoke. "Believe it or not, yes, I've told Alan about my feelings. Now he's worried about me. He thinks I may be suffering from postpartum depression."

"Really? What do you think?" The wispy smile fled Monique's face in exchange for a concerned frown and she stopped swaying to the slow instrumental emanating from the ceiling speakers.

"Oh, I don't know. He may be right. We've made an appointment for me to get examined Monday morning. It can't hurt."

"Good. I'm glad you're going to get a checkup. I'm sure everything will be alright." Monique patted Dana's hand as a sign of sympathy and support.

The band returned to the stage and began playing an upbeat version of *On Broadway* and the crowd practically screamed with excitement. All at once, the dance floor was packed with couples moving their hips and twisting in unison with the beat and Cassie got caught up in the jam that heated the air.

"Hey, let's go dance!" She stood up and grabbed Dana's and Monique's hands and pulled them to the dance floor.

The women found a spot in the center, threw their arms up, and moved with the music and the crowd. When Cassie looked at Dana, her friend was laughing, gleeful as a gorgeous, much younger man tapped her shoulder and began dancing with her. There was no visible depression that Cassie could see. The girl just needed to get out and to have fun more often. Cassie and Monique continued dancing together, shoulder-to-shoulder, showing off in rhythm as if the night would never end.

Cassie was becoming increasingly perplexed about how to handle Todd upon returning to Atlanta. To help work off some energy, she decided to go on a power walk at the first sign of daylight that Sunday morning. As she strode briskly down the neighborhood sidewalk, she pumped her arms to help maintain the pace. Already her calves were aching as she walked up a small incline. She was *really* out of shape!

The walk was good because her mind was able to drift to various issues without her stomach knotting. There was Johnson, who had become exceedingly persistent in his attempts to see Cassie. Todd, of course, was on the brink of proposing marriage despite Cassie's efforts to keep him at arm's length. Her work projects were at critical phases, both in Atlanta and in Puerto Rico. When she had spoken with one of the senior consultants still in Puerto Rico over the weekend, she had learned that the BookMart job had become impossibly complicated. Apparently, the order processing center had been performing most of its functions using excessively manual methods, which answered the questions about why so many orders were either late in being filled or altogether erroneous. To make matters worse, the BookMart management group didn't have a budget large enough to accommodate the software improvements that would help the business run more smoothly. Cassie and her team would need to be extremely creative with the solutions they eventually recommended. And finding those solutions would be like searching for needles in a haystack.

Cassie rounded the corner heading back to her townhouse. Just as she approached the driveway, a navy blue Toyota 4Runner turned in and the engine was shut off. It was Johnson. Cassie smacked her lips, displeased with his unexpected arrival.

Johnson got out of his car and waited for Cassie's approach. Surprisingly, he was smiling broadly, obviously happy to see her.

"So you *are* still alive. I almost thought you must have died and no one told me about the funeral. I thought I'd better come check up on you." He removed the sunshades he was wearing and made a big to-do about looking her over. "Nah, you are obviously alive and kicking. You just don't have time for a brothuh anymore." He smiled to show he was only joking.

Cassie was nonplussed. She placed her hands on her hips and faced him head on. "Johnson, you know I don't like it when people just drop by my place without calling first. What are you doing here?" She was sweaty, her hair was pulled back into a frizzy ponytail, and she was stressed out. This was not the best time for his antics.

"I just wanted to see you." He put his shades back on. "You haven't returned any of my calls in three weeks and there was no other way for me to catch up with you."

"I was going to call you back, Johnson, but I've been busy. That doesn't give you permission to just come over here as if I owe you something. You didn't want a commitment, remember?" She held her ground, hands on hips and eyes like spears.

Without realizing it, Johnson backed up a few steps. "I didn't say you *owed* me. And, yes, I remember what I said about a commitment. What's the big deal? All I did was come by to see you. Friends do that, ya know. And I can remember a time not too long ago when you would have been thrilled."

"Well, that's all over. From now on you cannot come here unless you're invited." Cassie rolled her eyes and began walking to her door. She really was pissed off with Johnson. He wouldn't have come by like this if he didn't think the gesture would be well received. It was her own fault, though, for treating him like a king for six months without a commitment to speak of.

"Cass, can we talk?" He was following her to the door.

"Talk about what?" Still annoyed, Cassie removed a key from her pocket and unlocked the door. She walked inside and left Johnson to close the door after also entering.

"I don't know. I guess we could start with how you're doing." He again removed his shades and this time hung them from a pocket on his t-shirt. "How are things at work?"

"Johnson, I do not feel like talking about my job with you." Cassie was now in the kitchen getting a glass of water, but they could still see each other through the bar area in front of the kitchen sink.

"Since when?"

"Since I hadn't planned on talking to you at all today." She began drinking water while eyeballing him.

"Oh, so you were just never going to call me back. Alright then, I see how it is now."

"It *is* the way you wanted it."

"I never said I wanted things to be this way. There you go again getting carried away."

"And there you go again belittling my feelings." She walked back through the living room area and into her bedroom as Johnson walked behind her. "You can't have your cake and eat it, too."

"I'm not trying to have my cake and eat it, too. And, anyway, if this is the way you felt, why didn't you tell me that a few weeks ago when we talked?"

"I guess you didn't ask me three weeks ago." Cassie went into her large closet, pulled down an empty suitcase, and lugged it over to her bed so she could begin packing for her return to Atlanta.

"I did ask you. Why are you being like this?" Johnson's frustration was clearly mounting and the pitch of his voice was getting higher.

"Obviously you didn't ask the right question so you misinterpreted my intentions. Doesn't feel too great when the shoe is on the other foot, does it?"

Without looking at him, Cassie began to throw various clothes into the suitcase—underwear, bras, stockings, shorts, and matching shirts.

"Ohhhhh, so *that's* what this is all about. Revenge. I should have known, but I expected more from you."

"I wouldn't waste my time trying to get revenge on you, Johnson. You overestimate yourself." Cassie returned to the closet and then exited with another suitcase and a red evening dress.

"What's with the dress? Who are you trying to impress?"

"Don't worry about that." She hung the dress from a doorknob to ensure she didn't forget to pack it later. "You really have some nerve asking about anything I do."

Johnson removed his car keys from his pocket and grabbed his shades. "This was obviously a bad idea so I'm leaving."

"Fine. You can show yourself out." She went back into the closet as Johnson toyed with his keys. When Cassie emerged from the closet again, she was surprised to see that he had not budged. "I thought you were leaving."

"I am leaving, but before I go, I want to know what your problem is. First you say we can still see each other, but then you don't return my calls. Then you say I can't have my cake and eat it, too, which was never my intention. What exactly is going on?"

Exasperated, Cassie sighed heavily. "Johnson, I don't have time for this right now. I have a business trip to prepare for and errands to run before the flight. Really, I think you need to leave. We can have this conversation some other time."

As before, Johnson did not budge, only now he was speechless. After staring at Cassie for a few long moments, he finally put on his shades and walked out the bedroom.

Cassie was relieved when she heard the front door open and close behind him. *Thank God.* She went to the door and locked it, glad to be alone. Johnson would be better off with some bimbo that was happy to be just a bed buddy. He shouldn't have any problems finding that somewhere else.

Chapter 13

"My girl is back!" Todd hugged Cassie after she set down her briefcase in the office. "How was the trip?"

"It was okay." She removed herself from his embrace. "You'd better stop doing that. Someone is going to see us."

"I don't care. I own this joint." He hugged her again. "I'm glad you're back. I missed you."

"I was only gone for two days." *And I'm already feeling suffocated again.*

"I know, but two days is too long. We'll have to do something about that." He smiled that beautiful smile that always made Cassie's knees weaken.

"I thought you said you were going to back off."

Todd pulled his arms away and stepped backward. "You're right. I did say that and I'm a man of my word."

Somewhat flustered, Cassie walked around the desk and sat down. While the computer booted up, she removed her notepad and the Pilot Software synopsis from her briefcase. "So how's Stephanie doing today?"

Todd shrugged his shoulders. "She's fine I guess." He sat on the front edge of her desk, picked up her notepad, and began scanning the pages. "Ericka tells me that she's been giving you a hard time. Do I need to get involved or is everything under control?"

"Don't worry about it. I can handle her."

"I know you can, but I won't tolerate insolence in my office. I've hired you to help us and Stephanie had better get a grip on herself."

"I think she'd rather get a grip on you." Cassie connected a USB flash drive to the computer and looked at Todd sideways to see his reaction.

"Yeah, well…" He set the notepad back down on the desk. "She's not the woman for me. I like women that can use my comb, if you catch my drift."

"I know." Cassie smiled and pulled up a flowchart she had started over the weekend. It would eventually give Todd and Ericka a visual demonstration of the processes that Cassie was considering as recommendations.

"Cassie, welcome back." Ericka entered the office with a large smile. "Are you ready to get started on the staffing forecasts?"

"Good morning, Ericka. Yes, I've put everything together so we can pretty easily project a reasonable headcount that corresponds to Pilot's growth and the process streamlining I have in mind. Wanna meet in your office?"

"That will be great. Give me five minutes. I want to get a cup of coffee."

"Sure thing."

When Ericka was gone, Todd beamed at Cassie proudly. "You are a tough sistah, you know that?"

Cassie pursed her lips while now pulling up a headcount spreadsheet. "You're biased."

"Maybe so, but I still know tough when I see it. How did I let you slip through my fingers?" He shook his head as though marveling at himself as Cassie reviewed the spreadsheet without responding. Finally, he stood up and placed his hands in his pockets.

Once again, Cassie was forced to acknowledge that the man was extremely well built. *Um, um, um. He is just too fine for words.*

"I wanted to let you know that I will be offsite all day for a conference at the Ritz Carlton downtown. If you need to reach me, just use my cell number."

"Okay, thanks." *Thanks for the breathing space.* She now stood up as well and collected a printout for her meeting with Ericka. "We should meet tomorrow morning so I can begin going over my recommendations with you. I'm sure you'll have some changes that need to be considered before we wrap everything up."

"That'll work." Todd went to the door. "See ya later?"

"See ya tomorrow."

He smiled that smile. "Alright, I hear you. Tomorrow it is."

When Todd was gone, Cassie released a deep breath and rubbed her temples. Todd. Johnson. Todd. Johnson. Her head ached from all the tension that was freely dispersing itself throughout her body. She hated feeling as though she had no control over her emotions. While Dana battled with external elements, Cassie fought with internal feelings, flip-flopping within herself and hiding it all from everyone. She didn't want the power that Monique spoke of. Nor did she want the freedom that Dana felt she should relish. Not really. Certainly, independence was important to Cassie, but she had never felt as though Johnson wanted to control her and so independence had lost its salience as an issue. Because of Johnson, Cassie had learned that she could have both companionship and freedom without the two conflicting. And power? She had nothing to prove. Power over what? Or who? She wasn't interested in leading Todd on or playing with his mind. That wasn't the sort of power she sought. So then what did she want? What? And who?

The waterfalls were breathtaking. After taking her on a drive around the city Thursday evening, Todd had treated Cassie to dinner at the Cheesecake Factory and now they were walking through a small park, one of the new attractions constructed after Cassie moved to Dallas. As they headed toward a gazebo, they had passed the waterfalls and she stopped to look into the pale blue pool of water. There were lights at the bottom as well as around the spray that shot up into the air from the jets placed at the center.

"Can we sit here? I love looking at the waterfall."

"Whatever you want, baby."

Todd's voice was husky and Cassie knew where his mind had wandered.

They sat on the low-set concrete wall surrounding the pool and Cassie continued looking at the falls.

"Do you want my coat? It's a little cool out here."

"No, I'm fine. Thanks."

"You sure are. That dress is really doing justice to your body."

He whistled as she blushed. She was wearing the red evening dress that Johnson had balked over and she knew it looked good on her.

"Thanks."

They sat in silence for a few moments. Todd dipped his hand into the water and moved it back and forth to make small waves.

"So have you been thinking about what I said last week?" He continued moving his hand in the water without looking at her.

"Yes, I've been thinking about it." The statement was a breath as Cassie's eyes moved from the waterfall to Todd's profile. Luscious.

"And?" Todd removed his hand from the water and dried it on a handkerchief that had been folded inside his coat pocket. He still didn't look at Cassie, but rather watched his hands move around the handkerchief.

"And I still don't know. I don't know what I want right now. I wish I did, but..." She again stared at the waterfall, but her gaze now went through the waters.

He continued moving his hands through the handkerchief although there was no longer a need. He seemed to be pondering a response. "I know I caught you at a bad time. That guy you're seeing in Dallas must be handling his business the way I should have."

"No, actually he's not. We broke up." Cassie subconsciously used her hands to rub warmth into her arms. In an immediate reaction, Todd removed his suit coat and wrapped it around her shoulders.

"I told you it was cool out here." His smile reached out to her and his eyes spoke the words he knew Cassie didn't want to hear at the moment. "So why did you break up?" The hope he had suppressed was now evident in his voice.

"In a nutshell, we wanted different things."

"Umph. That's too bad. Too bad for him, that is. Good for me."

"Stop." Cassie laughed lightly at Todd's selfish perspective.

"Hey, I'm just being honest here. That's what you want, isn't it?"

"Of course."

"Okay, then you have to take the good and the bad that goes with it." He neatly folded the handkerchief, placed it in his pants pocket, and grabbed Cassie hand. When he looked into her eyes, she thought she could drown in the adoration she saw. "I meant what I said about not pressuring you, but I want you to know that it's not easy. It's not my nature to leave things to chance."

Cassie squeezed Todd's hand and smiled. "I know. But if you *really* want an answer tonight—"

"No, no, that's alright. I can wait." He laughed half-heartedly. He knew not to rush Cassie and to thereby provoke the very answer he didn't want.

"Are you sure?"

"Oh yeah. I'm sure. I'm a big boy."

"Alright."

Once again they sat in silence and Cassie's eyes drifted back to the beautiful waterfall, which was trapped inside the concrete walls but free to go as far upward as the jet beneath could launch it.

"When you get back to Dallas, can I come see you sometime?"

"I don't see why not." She huffed dispassionately. "Man, this weekend is going to be hectic. Both my mother and Maven are coming to visit for the Labor Day holiday." *Hard to believe that Mama will be in town for three whole days. Why did I agree to that? She's going to drive me crazy.*

"For real? Mrs. Stewart is going to be in town? Aw man, I would love to see her."

Another couple passed by and sat on the other side of the falls.

"Would you mind if I fly down for a day or two while she's there?"

Cassie didn't like the idea at all. "Maybe some other time. Maven and I already have more plans than we'll have time for. We'll be keeping Mama veeery busy."

"But you know she would be happy to see me. She used to think of me as a son."

"Yes, I remember that all too well." *And I am not trying to hear about you for another three years if she sees you again. If only she knew what I had put up with from you.*

"Then don't be that way. Look, I don't have any plans for the weekend. To be honest, I was hoping you would stay here a little longer."

"That ain't gonna happen!"

"I know, but what's the harm in me coming to Dallas? I'll come on Sunday morning and leave that same evening. What do ya say?"

"Why are you so desperate to see my mother? What's up your sleeve?"

"Nothing, baby! I just happen to think a lot of her. I always have."

Cassie knew that was true. Todd and her mother had liked each other from day one. And Mama still defended him if Cassie spoke disparagingly of the man. Could she tolerate the two of them together in one room after all this time? Probably not. "Let me think about it and I'll let you know."

"Uh-uh. Not this time. If I wait on you, she'll be back in New Orleans before you call. I'm coming to see Mrs. Stewart this weekend. She was like a second mother to me and that's the least I can do." He stood up and held his hand out for Cassie's.

Annoyed, she looked up at his face and ignored his hand. "You would come even if I don't want you to?"

"I sure would."

"But you said you would respect my feelings about needing space. You're breaking your word, which shouldn't surprise me."

"Cassie, this isn't about you. I happen to like your mother. You should be happy that a man who wants to marry you has a good relationship with your family. Stop being so stubborn." He lowered his hand and then squatted down before her. "Don't you know by now that I would do anything for you? Don't you understand how I feel? Mrs. Stewart raised the woman that I want to spend the rest of my life with so, yes, I'm coming to Dallas even if you don't want me to. I'm coming because I love your family, Cassie. And the reason I love your family is because—whether you like it or not—I love you." He placed his hands on her knees as she remained motionless. "I'm sorry if that offends you because it's the last thing I want to do. I'm just telling you how I feel."

Still silent, Cassie set her hands on top of Todd's and then moved her fingers beneath his. What was she doing? Why was she so willing to let the past destroy a possible future with this man? Cassie touched Todd's face and ran her fingers along the lines—the lips, the eyebrows, the eyes—as he allowed her touch to move undisturbed. When he stood up again, he pulled her gently with him and then kissed her with the full impact of his emotions. She felt his hands glide across her back, her neck, and her waist and she remembered the lover he was. She remembered how much she had missed the feel of his body and she gripped his back as they continued to kiss.

"I want you to love me, Cassie." The statement was urgent and breathless.

Cassie's eyes remained closed and they kissed again. She began to yearn for him, for the physical connection, the lovemaking. When she finally opened her eyes, he was looking down at her, studying her face closely.

"You are so beautiful. I want to memorize everything about you tonight. This dress, your hair, your face—and the way you're looking at me right now. You haven't looked at me that way in a long time."

Embarrassed, Cassie cast her eyes downward. Suddenly, she was more acutely aware of the breeze blowing through the park and she began to shiver.

Todd pulled the coat more closely around her body and then used his fingers to raise her chin and lips back up. Softly once more, he kissed her. "Will you really be upset if I come to Dallas this weekend?" He held her now and rested his chin on top of her head.

Cassie laid her head against his chest and clung more tightly to him before speaking what she knew was the truth. "No, I would love it if you came."

Chapter 14

WAS IT LOVE? AND, if not, what was it? Once back in Dallas, Cassie found herself thinking about Todd incessantly. Saturday morning, she began cleaning her home from top to bottom in preparation for Maven's and Mama's arrival later that day. As she made her bed, she wondered how Todd would look sleeping on the sheets. As she washed her bathtub, she fantasized about sharing a bath with him. When she scrubbed the kitchen stove, she thought about cooking a meal for him and letting him taste it. Somewhere along the line, he had managed to part the seas in which her heart had been submerged and she felt her defenses beginning to crumble. She hummed as she vacuumed, no longer dreading her mother's visit.

Cassie didn't hear the doorbell ringing until she turned off the vacuum. "I'm coming," she called as she trotted to the door and opened it.

"Good morning, ma'am. Are you Ms. Cassie Stewart?" He was a short, clean-cut deliveryman of some kind.

"Yes."

"I have a delivery for you. Would you please sign here, ma'am?" The man presented a pen and a receipt for her and then went to his truck parked in the driveway. The words "Flora's Flowers" were painted on the side.

Cassie watched him swing open the two back doors and collect two large arrangements of flowers that included tulips, roses, and gardenias.

"Where would you like these, ma'am?"

"Um, over here will be fine." She walked into the living room and pointed to the display table behind her sofa. The flowers' fragrance rapidly began to fill the room.

The deliveryman held his hand out for the signed receipt. "Thank you, ma'am."

"Oh, let you me get a tip for you." Cassie moved to locate her purse.

"No thank you, ma'am. Everything's been taken care of." He went to the door. "Have a good day."

"Thank you. You, too." He was gone as quickly as he had come.

Cassie closed the door and then went to stand in front of the flowers. Both arrangements were very different, creative and exotic. She smelled the blooms and eventually found a card in the vase containing every imaginable color of rose. *For my beautiful lady. Thinking of you with love, Todd.* Cassie smiled and thought of the evening in the park. They should have made love that night, but Todd wanted to hear the words that Cassie had learned not to speak anymore. In fact, she had not uttered *I love you* since moving from Atlanta. God knew she could never have expressed such emotions to Johnson. But maybe, just maybe she would tell Todd again one day soon. He was certainly doing all the right things to stir the emotions within her. A year ago, she would not have believed it possible.

She called him and left a message on his voicemail service to thank him for the flowers. That afternoon, she was still gushing when she arrived at the airport to meet Maven's flight.

"Girl, what's got you cheesing so hard?" Maven laughed as she hugged her sister. "Are you *that* happy to see me?"

"You know I'm glad you're here." Cassie kissed Maven's cheek and grabbed her hands. "Let me get a closer look atcha'. Wow! I love your hair! You've got that Halle Berry thing going on."

"I know. It was an accident. I went to the beautician for a trim and the next thing I know, half my hair was on the floor. That heifer! I'm not going back to her again. I think I ought to sue her." She pouted as she ran her fingers through her hair, which was no more than two inches long on top and even less in back. "Do you really like it?"

"Uh huh. It looks good on you. I wouldn't say so if I didn't think it. Now I know how *I* would look with a short do." The sisters were nearly identical twins.

"Thanks. I knew I could count on you to be honest. I'll be glad when it grows back, though."

"Well, one thing's for certain. It will definitely grow back. I should introduce you to my friend, Dana. She's been thinking about cutting her hair and you may be the inspiration she needs."

Cassie tousled Maven's hair before pulling her through the airport to the gate through which their mother would emerge in less than an hour. After verifying that the flight was on schedule, they found a Chili's restaurant near the gate and decided to share an order of chili fries while waiting.

"Okay, girl, I know you like the back of my hand. You have been smiling nonstop since I got here and I know it's a man. All I need to know is which one it is. Todd or Johnson?" Maven placed a French fry drenched with chili in her mouth.

"I should be asking the same about you. What's with the glow on your face?"

Both sisters looked sheepish as they continued eating. Who was going to spill the beans first? An unspoken dare stymied their talk before Maven caved.

"Alright, I'll go first. Darren, girl."

"Darren? Who's that? I don't remember you mentioning him."

"That's because we're only friends. At least, we *were* only friends until a couple of weeks ago." Maven used a fork to pick up more French fries. "Then, I don't know, things just sort of escalated and..."

"And?"

"And I think he may be the one." She began chewing the fries and intently watching Cassie's face.

"*Excuse me!* What happened to being a playa? Did you kick the three other guys to the curb?"

"Yeah." The sheepish look again. "After all that talk, I got rid of every one of them. I don't have any backup now."

"Well, you're doing the right thing if you really care about Darren." Cassie thoughtfully sipped her Dr. Pepper from a straw. "So why this Darren guy? What makes him so special?"

To Cassie's surprise, Maven blushed at the question.

She's got it bad. Cassie smiled to encourage Maven to talk openly.

"I just like the way he treats me. He's not the most handsome guy in the world, but he's extremely smart and we can talk about anything. It's like I'm dating my best friend or something."

The Monique comment again. "Do you think you're soul mates?"

"I don't know if I believe in that, but if soul mates exist, he's mine." Maven blushed again at the admission.

Cassie had never seen her sister behave in such a shy manner.

"What about you? Which guy has made you so happy? It must be Johnson!"

"No, no quite."

"Get out! Todd? Oh my God!"

This time, Cassie blushed. "I guess I'm the one who's crazy." She shrugged as though the situation was really not important.

"There's nothing established between us. I'm taking it one day at a time."

"I knew we were going to have some juicy stuff to talk about when I got here. That man got a hold of you in Atlanta, didn't he?"

"Hold up, now. There was no hanky-panky. Nothing serious anyway."

"Nothing *yet*. You'd better not tell Mama. She'll never let you live it down if you and Todd get back together and then split up again."

"That's the tricky part. Todd is coming to town tomorrow and he wants to see Mama."

"No way! Girl! No way! Mama is going to fall out when she sees him." She forked more fries into her mouth. "Is he going to ask for Mama's permission to marry you?"

"No, of course not. He just wants to see her, that's all."

"He's flying *allll* the way to Dallas just to see our Mama? Girl, please." She waved her fork in the air. "Todd is after something and I don't believe for one minute that it's a conversation with Mama."

"Cassie, stop driving so fast. Why are you rushing up to red lights? You're going to cause an accident." Mrs. Stewart sat stiffly in the passenger seat and patted her chest for effect. "I hope I don't have a heart attack."

"Just chill out, Mama. We're almost to my house." Cassie looked in the rearview mirror and saw Maven shaking with silent laughter. "And just what are you laughing at, Miss Perfect?"

Maven's laughter abruptly filled the car. "You and Mama will never change. It's just hilarious how alike you are."

Mama turned her head to see Maven in the back seat. "You know she doesn't want to hear that." She smiled and turned back to face the road. "You really do drive too fast, Cassie. You drive like your father."

"Cassie, Dallas is nicer than I thought it would be. I like all the flowers around the city. It reminds me of *Atlanta*." Maven stifled a giggle.

"There are a few similarities, but not very many." Cassie cut her eyes to the rearview mirror again and waited for Maven to look into the mirror as well. Cassie let her eyes do the talking. *You'd better be quiet back there, girl. Don't say a word about Todd.*

After an eternity on the road, they pulled into Cassie's driveway whereupon Mama and Maven besieged the townhouse with compliments. The exterior was painted a pale taupe shade and the landscaping was largely composed of a rich mixture of lavender, red, yellow, and white flowers reminiscent of Atlanta's typical foliage. The best features, however, were the large windows, which were arched rather than square in shape.

Once inside the townhouse, Mama and Maven were even more impressed with the furnishings and décor. They complimented the African carvings, the pottery, and the unique art pieces placed strategically around the rooms, things that Cassie had long since found customary and borderline nondescript. They admired the contrast of purples, blues, reds, and creams that composed the primary color schemes in her living room and bedroom. Over the years and between apartments, Cassie had accumulated a host of odds and ends to bring her home to life, but had eventually overlooked how uniquely beautiful those things were and so it was weird for her to now see her home through other people's eyes. She had never thought of it as being nicely decorated. Rather, she was always looking for something else to help spiff up the place.

In Cassie's opinion, the location of her townhouse was the greatest prize because it provided easy access to three major freeways in the city. She also had a great selection of shops in every direction since, as with in Atlanta, she had opted to live near the Galleria mall.

"Oh, Cassie, this dining room table is really nice." Mama ran her fingers along the smooth wooden surface that was polished to a high gleam. "Do you ever have company over and serve dinner on it?"

Maven jumped in before Cassie could reply. "Is this the table you bought a month ago? It *is* nice."

"Thanks." *Thanks for sparing me Mama's nosy question.*

The sisters shared a knowing look. They would work together all weekend to keep Mama out of their personal business.

Todd's impending visit, however, would certainly inflict some damage to these plans.

"Cassie, who gave you all these beautiful flowers?" Mama walked over to the roses and began pressing her nose into the blooms. She then moved on to the gardenias. "Did Johnson give these to you? They must have cost him a pretty penny."

"No, Johnson and I aren't seeing each other anymore. A friend of mine sent those." Cassie was determined to be as ambiguous as possible for the time being.

"He must be some friend! What's his name?"

"Um, Cassie, do you need some help with Mama's luggage?" Maven was again trying to rescue her sister, who was quickly getting cornered by Mama's questions.

"No, thanks. I've got it." Without answering Mama's last question, Cassie carried her luggage into the guest room and set it down. "Mama, you will sleep in the guest room and Maven will sleep with me since my bed is bigger."

Although obviously disappointed that Cassie had avoided her question, Mama continued to follow Maven into the remaining rooms, complimenting both the layout of the townhouse and Cassie's décor. In the process, she also changed the subject. "Well now, Cassie, you sure have become quite the decorator. I think I could use some of these ideas in my own house." Mama finally sat on the living room sofa.

"Thanks, Mama." Cassie leaned down and kissed her mother's cheek before walking into the kitchen. "I was thinking about making some chicken and dumplings for dinner. How does that sound?"

Maven was now seated beside Mama and using the remote control to scan the cable channels. "Sounds good, but I don't feel like staying in tonight. Can't we have dinner at Houston's or something? It's so nice outside. The weather is perfect for eating outdoors and Houston's restaurants usually have nice decks."

"That *does* sound nice. Cassie, let's eat at Houston's tonight. Can you make those chicken and dumplings tomorrow?"

"Yeah, I can make dinner tomorrow. Houston's works for me."

Mama looked over at Maven, who was still scanning channels. "Must you keep switching channels like that, chile?"

Before Maven saw it coming, Mama yanked the remote control from her and began watching the station that Maven had last selected.

"See, this is just fine. What's wrong with this show?"

It was a gourmet cooking show and Maven could not have been less interested. She stood up and went into the kitchen.

"Cassie, I don't think I can put up with Mama for three days, girl." Maven was now standing beside Cassie and whispering as Cassie began running water to wash a few dishes.

"What could be wrong already? Y'all just got here." Cassie plugged one of the sinks with a stopper and added dishwashing liquid.

"She's just getting on my nerves. She always has to control everything."

"I know." Cassie shook her head sympathetically. "But that's Mama. It's the only way she knows how to be, which is why I was so glad to move out when I was old enough. I'm telling you, I'm still surprised that you wanted to visit at the same time as Mama would be here."

"Hey, I thought you could use the help." Maven laughed and patted her sister's back. "In the future, I won't be so generous with my time and energy. I'm already zapped and it's only been a few hours. The woman just sucks me dry, right down to my bone marrow." She rounded her lips into an "O" and began to loudly suck in air as Cassie laughed.

"What's so funny in there?" Mama was still watching the cooking show and her eyes never left the screen even as she turned her head sideways to ask the question.

"Nothing," the sisters responded in unison although continuing to laugh.

"Mama, would you like something to drink? I can make you some tea if you want." Already knowing the answer, Cassie opened the refrigerator and retrieved the filtered water container.

"Yes, honey, that would be just fine. Make sure you add ice and two packets of sugar the way I like it."

"Okay."

Cassie and Maven looked at each other and for a moment they were teenagers again, eager to find ways to divert Mama's attention away from them. They had long ago figured out the two main strategies that never failed—tea and shopping. And so the sisters had devised a three-day visit that would consist primarily of shopping while tea would be the weapon to pacify Mama. The combination had worked when they were younger and it would work now. It had to. If it didn't, the sisters would certainly suffer throughout the visit.

"Cassie, while you're in there, would you bring me some of that cake I saw on the counter? It sure does look good. What kind of cake is that?"

"It's orange cake, the same recipe that Grandma used."

"Really? How'd you get that recipe?" Mama stood up and walked into the kitchen. As she entered, Maven returned to the living room, grabbed the TV remote control, and began scanning the channels again.

"I got it from Grandma's cookbook. When she passed away, I took it from the house since I knew Grandpa wouldn't be using it. Everybody knew he wasn't *about* to cook anything for himself." As Cassie spoke, she went to a kitchen pantry and pulled out the book. "See? Here's her book." It was actually an old scrapbook that had been converted into a cookbook. The years of use were obvious as the book cover and several pages were stained with various gravies, marmalades, and oil.

Mama gently took the book and stared at it as though it was a magical object. She then carefully turned back the cover and began reading the recipe on the first page. Her fingers moved slowly down the page as though touching precious jewels and marveling at their beauty. After several moments, Mama ran her fingers along the edges of the book and then turned several more pages. "These are the very recipes my mama used when I was a little girl. She's the one who taught me everything I know about cookin', ya know. Mama sure could cook! If you could name it, she could cook it."

"I remember." Cassie was unsure of how to react to her mother's emotions and sentimentality. It was a rare display. "Grandma used to make homemade doughnuts and all kinds of pies when we visited in the summers. It seems like she was always cooking something. There were times when I could smell chicken frying at midnight and I would get up and go into the kitchen only to find Grandma turning the chicken over with a fork. I think cooking helped her to relax back then."

"Yes, cooking was her way of dealing with things. That's why your grandfather got so fat." Mama closed the book and pressed it against her chest. "I still miss my mother. She was so good to me, to all of us when we were growing up. I can't even count how many times Mama would do without things just so we would have enough money for a particular prom dress or school clothes. And I never heard her complain, not once. She was content just seeing her children happy." Mama chuckled under her breath. "She was a good woman and I have always felt blessed to have known her and to have been loved by her."

"I miss her, too. She was just as good to me and Maven as she was to her own children."

"Yes, she was. She loved you and Maven very much." Mama ran her fingers around the book cover once more before handing the book back to Cassie. "And I'm sure she's thrilled that you have her book and continue to use her recipes. In some ways, you are keeping her alive. She's right here with us at this moment."

Cassie restored the book to its place in the pantry as Mama continued talking.

"Cassie, I know that I haven't been the best mother to you and Maven."

Surprised at her mother's statement, Cassie's first reaction was to deny its accuracy. "That's not true, Mama. Why would you say something like that?"

"Because it *is* true. I know it and so do you."

Cassie continued denying the statement. "No, Mama. Maven and I could always count on you. You were good to us."

"Now, now, baby, you don't have to say that. I want us to have an honest conversation about this. Yes, I was a reliable mother, but I don't think I gave you and Maven the kind of love that you needed."

"We know you love us, Mama." Cassie was feeling extremely awkward with her mother's emotional candor. Once again, she wasn't sure of how to react.

"Of course you know I love you, but I don't think I've always *shown* it the right way. I think that I've loved you both too hard, been too protective at times. I'm afraid sometimes that I'll drive you away from me. I worry that you don't confide in me the way I talked to my mother."

At this, Cassie could no longer meet her mother's eyes.

"I'm right, aren't I?"

"It's just that…" Cassie picked at her fingernails the way she had done as a little girl. She didn't really pick at the nails, but used her fingernails to push the cuticles back on each finger.

"It's just that what, baby?"

"Well, Mama, sometimes you're just too judgmental and bossy. You don't seem to realize that Maven and I are grown women now with normal adult needs. We don't always want your advice, but you don't know how to listen without putting us down for making mistakes. The only way we can protect ourselves is by not telling you anything."

Mama leaned back against the kitchen counter and pondered Cassie's words.

As Cassie looked at her, she admitted to herself that they shared many of the same facial features. Cassie had always known that she had her mother's smile, but now she could also see that she shared her mother's eyes and chin. Funny how she had never noticed—or had subconsciously blocked—these similarities before today.

"Is that why you've always been closer to your father?" Mama was still seeking an understanding of where her relationship had taken a wrong turn with her daughters.

"I guess so. Daddy doesn't try to give me orders or make me feel bad when I screw up. It's easier to talk to him."

"I'm sorry for making you feel that way. I do know that you and Maven are women now, but you are still my little girls. It's important to me that you two are happy. Obviously, I've been overzealous in my attempts to guide you. It's so hard to let you go."

"But, see, that's just it, Mama. You *can't* guide us. You can't make our decisions for us. The best thing you can do for us is to listen when we need you to and tell us how great we are when life is kicking us around. You've done your job, you've raised your little girls. Now it's time for you to let us go, accept that we will make mistakes, and love us anyway."

The expression on Mama's face was so sad that Cassie walked over and hugged her. "Stop looking like that, Mama. It breaks my heart."

"I can't help it, baby. Someday you'll have your own children and you'll understand."

"I don't know, Mama. At the rate I'm going, I don't think I'll *ever* have kids. I don't even have a man, remember?"

Mama released Cassie, but continued holding her daughter's hands. "You'll meet the right man when you least expect it. And he's going to be some kind of special to be worthy of my baby."

"Since when do you think that?" Mama was full of surprises today.

"Since always. That's why you're not married. You're waiting for that uncommon man that will bring you uncommon happiness. You and Maven both." She rubbed Cassie's arms and then placed a hand beneath Cassie's chin as her daughter smiled. "You will always be my little girl, but I will make more efforts to respect the fact you're also a woman now, okay?"

"Okay, Mama." Cassie hugged her mother once again, this time with a huge smile. "I love you."

"I love you, too, baby. I love you, too."

Just then, Maven appeared in the kitchen. "I think I'll have some of that orange cake, too. Why are you two all hugged up?"

"Come here, baby, and give your mother a hug."

Mama and Cassie each freed an arm to welcome a reluctant Maven into the circle.

"Oh, alright. But for what?" She slowly approached them and Cassie pulled her in. The women all laughed together and shared kisses.

"For no reason other than the fact that I love you two. Is that good enough for you?"

"Sure, Mama." Maven gave Cassie a look that asked, *Is Mama okay?*

"From now on," Mama said as she looked at her daughters, "we're turning over a new leaf. And I promise to treat you both like the beautiful, intelligent women that you are, *but...*"

"I knew there had to be a 'but' somewhere." Cassie rolled her eyes while continuing to smile.

"*But* that doesn't mean you won't still be my babies in my heart."

The three hugged again and both Cassie and Maven kissed their mother's forehead affectionately. As if an omnipotent hand moved across their lives and touched their souls, the barriers between them began to disintegrate. For the first time in many years, mother and daughters were mutually bound and

Cassie's heart swelled with happiness that she might finally have the mother she needed now.

Chapter 15

THE FOLLOWING MORNING, CASSIE awakened earlier than usual to prepare breakfast for Mama and Maven. She decided to make the basics—grits, bacon, eggs, and toast—since the combination was fast and easy.

"Good morning, Cassie." Mama yawned as she entered the dining room area and took a seat at the table where she could easily see and talk to her daughter. She was wrapped in a powder blue bathrobe that covered her body entirely from her neck to her ankles. "Got any coffee in there?"

"Good morning, Mama." Cassie went to the coffeemaker and poured a large mug of coffee for her mother. "Of course. I was even sure to buy Folgers the other day since I remember how much you like it." She carried the coffee to Mama and handed it to her.

"Thank you, baby." Mama took a sip of the black brew as Cassie went back into the kitchen. "That sure smells good in there. I wish I had more of an appetite, but the truth is that I'm still full from dinner last night."

"That's okay. I'm sure Maven will eat plenty. You know how greedy she is." Cassie flipped the bacon over in the skillet and then began beating some eggs. Within the next ten minutes, the entire breakfast was ready to serve. Like Mama, however, Cassie discovered she didn't have an appetite at the moment so she covered all the food to keep it warm until Maven got up. Afterward, she poured a second cup of coffee, this time for herself, and sat at the dining room table with Mama.

"You know, you never told me who gave you those flowers in there. Is it someone special?" Mama sipped her coffee and eyed her daughter knowingly.

I may as well tell her now and get it over with. Cassie delayed her response long enough to drink more coffee. Before she continued, she set the mug down and clutched it as though for dear life. "Mama, there's something I need to tell you, but before I do I want you to promise to remain calm."

"Oh no! You're pregnant, aren't you?" Mama raised her hand to cover her mouth, clearly expecting the dreaded confirmation.

"No, Mama, it's nothing like that." Cassie shook her head, displeased with her mother's immediate assumption.

"Oh." Now she smiled and leaned forward. "Has someone asked you to marry him?"

"No! Gosh!" Cassie considered not telling her mother and instead diverting Todd somewhere other than to her home when he arrived later that day.

"I'm sorry, baby. I promised to stop doing that to you. Old habits die hard." Her eyes continued to apologize as she added, "Go ahead, Cassie. What is it you want to tell me?"

Cassie remained quiet for a few long seconds, still clutching her coffee mug and debating whether or not to tell Mama about Todd. In the end, she really had no choice since Todd was so determined to see her. "Mama, do you remember Todd Brody, the guy I dated in Atlanta?"

"Why, of course I remember Todd. He was such a nice young man. Have you spoken to him since you moved to Dallas?"

"Uh, yeah, I've spoken to him very recently, in fact."

"And how is he doing these days?"

"He's doing fine. Actually, he owns a software company now that has become pretty successful."

"Really? Oh, that is just wonderful! I love to hear about you all succeeding. And since Todd was like the son I never had, that makes his accomplishments even nicer to learn about. How long has he had the company?"

"Around a year now. But, Mama, that's not what I wanted to tell you."

"Okay." She swallowed more coffee. "I'm listening."

"Todd and I are seeing each other again."

Mama clapped her hands together in a single stroke. "That's even better news! I knew the two of you should never have broken up."

"No, Mama, I didn't say that we're a couple again. We're just sort of, I don't know, hanging out sometimes, no strings attached, and seeing how things work out."

"Chile, who do you think you're talking to? I wasn't born yesterday. Hanging out, my dear Aunt Susan. Please." Mama huffed as though Cassie were treating her like a fool. "Is he the one who gave you all those flowers?"

As usual when Cassie felt awkward with her mother, she began pushing the cuticles back on her fingers. "Well, yeah." Cassie sighed and looked up once more at her mother, who waited with silent expectation. "Anyway, I need to tell you that Todd is coming to visit us today and he'll be here for dinner."

"Todd is coming here?"

Cassie nodded.

"From Atlanta?"

Cassie nodded again.

"Why?"

Cassie shrugged. "No reason in particular. He just wanted to stop by when he heard you would be in town, that's all."

"So he's coming by to see me for no particular reason?" Mama obviously was not buying Cassie's explanation. "And all the way from Atlanta?" Now she clucked and drank more coffee without looking at her daughter. "What time is he supposed to be here?"

"At around noon."

Just then, Maven shuffled into the room rubbing sleep from her eyes. "Is there still some breakfast left? I'm starving."

"Yeah, help yourself. Mama and I weren't hungry so eat as much as you want."

"Okay." Maven yawned loudly and stretched while walking into the kitchen.

"Maven, did your sister tell you that Todd is coming to visit us today?"

Cassie cut her eyes to Maven and hoped she didn't answer truthfully. Unfortunately, she could only see Maven's back and hear silverware lightly striking a glass plate as food was piled on.

"Todd who?" Maven must have read Cassie's mind or sensed her sister's tension. She would give nothing away to Mama.

"Todd Brody. From Atlanta."

Maven walked to the table with a plate heaped with food and sat down to eat. "Oh, I remember Todd. He was pretty nice. He's coming *here*?" She used a spoon to scoop up some grits and began eating.

"Uh huh, that's right. All the way from Atlanta and for no particular reason."

"I was telling Mama that Todd was excited about seeing her when he learned she would be in town." Cassie looked at Maven uneasily, unsure of how to free herself from Mama's questions. "He's supposed to be here this afternoon and he's staying for dinner."

Maven reacted with perfect nonchalance. "That's nice. So I guess we're not going to the outlet shops today." She stuffed a fork full of eggs into her mouth.

"Probably not since he'll be here before they even open. Maybe we can rent some movies or something like that."

"I didn't fly down here to watch movies. I can do that in New Orleans whenever I want to." Mama seemed nonplussed as she stood up with her coffee still in hand. "I'm going to take a shower and get dressed." Mama turned her back on her daughters, who immediately shared a conspiratorial look. "Oh, one more thing." She turned back around, but both Cassie and Maven were again the picture of innocence before Mama's eyes met theirs. "While I do think it will be nice to see Todd after all this time, I'm not fooled for one minute by your explanation for his visit. And if he actually told you that he's coming here just to see me and you believe that reason, then you're more naïve than I realized." She turned back around and left the room as Cassie and Maven once again shared looks.

Maven pointed her fork at Cassie. "I told you, girl, that Todd isn't coming here to see Mama. Even Mama doesn't believe that."

"Well..." Cassie threw her hands up. "I don't know. I don't know what to believe. He said he wanted to see her and I don't have time to analyze everything the man says and does." She now also stood up, went into the kitchen, and vigorously washed her coffee mug, focusing on making sure every square inch was covered with soap suds.

"I'm not saying that you need to analyze anything. I'm just *wondering* if he's really coming here to get permission to marry you."

"I already told you *no*. Todd wouldn't do that. He knows I'm not ready to go to that level with him. And anyway, he would need to speak with Dad about that."

"Yeah, he would eventually need to speak to Dad, but there's no reason he couldn't start with Mama." Maven continued eating.

Cassie finished washing the mug and set it on a dish rack on top of the kitchen counter. "Whatever. I'm not going to even think about it." She walked past Maven and headed toward her bedroom.

"I wouldn't think about it either. I would just sit back and get ready for the ride."

Todd arrived that afternoon at around 12:15 p.m. looking as crisp as if he had simply driven a few minutes from home as opposed to flown a thousand miles. When Cassie answered the door wearing a lavender sundress, neither her smile nor her excitement could be suppressed and she was glad to embrace him tightly for the few seconds they were alone.

"Hey, baby." Todd pecked Cassie's lips quickly, grabbed one of her hands and stepped into the townhouse. "Where is everybody?"

"Todd! How are you doing?" Maven stepped around the corner to give Todd a quick, friendly hug. Without releasing Cassie's hand, he responded with as much friendly familiarity.

"Mave, it's good to see you after all this time. I'm doing fine. How about yourself?"

"I'm doing fine, thanks." She smiled at her sister, who was grinning from ear to ear. "Mama's in the living room. Come on. She's waiting to see you."

They all walked into the living room, where Mama was sitting on the sofa watching television.

"Is that Todd?" She turned her head to see him and then stood up with a large smile.

"Hello, Mrs. Stewart."

"Hello, baby." They hugged each other tightly like a mother and son being reunited after several years of separation as both Cassie and Maven looked on with smiles still pasted on their faces.

It was obvious that Mama and Todd still had some form of connection that transcended blood ties, a phenomenon that Cassie had never completely understood about them, but had quickly learned to dislike once she and Todd had broken up. As of now, she still wasn't sure of how she felt about their uncanny bond since it tended to work against her when Todd was out of the picture.

"Mrs. Stewart, you still look good." Todd stepped back and resumed a position closer to Cassie.

"So do you, young man." Mama gestured to the sofa. "Have a seat so we can catch up. I want to hear all about this company that Cassie tells me you started up. I'm so proud of you."

"Yes, sit down, Todd. Do you want something to drink? We have some tea if you'd like some." Cassie had prepared a pitcher of cold tea that was ready to serve. Of course, Mama already had a glass resting on a coaster on the coffee table before her.

"Sure, tea sounds good. Thanks." Todd walked to an empty spot on the sofa, sat down, and looked up at Cassie with that golden smile.

"I'll help you." Maven was clearly eager to get Cassie alone. Based on her facial expression, she was bursting with something to say.

The sisters disappeared into the kitchen, where Maven immediately unleashed her excitement. "Todd is *sooo fine.* Girl, I forgot he looked that good!" She fanned herself playfully with her hands. "He is definitely a tall drink of water, my sistah."

As Maven talked, Cassie opened the refrigerator, removed the tea, and got a glass from the cabinet. "That he is. I still get weak in the knees whenever I see him." She began pouring tea into the glass. "I've never told anyone this, but..." Cassie filled the glass and moved to replace the pitcher in the refrigerator.

"But what, girl? You *know* I want to know."

Cassie closed the refrigerator and leaned against it heavily. "Todd has the most perfect body I've ever seen. I mean, from head to toe, the man has everything necessary for a woman's complete satisfaction."

Maven screamed under her breath so no one beyond the kitchen would hear. "And when you say everything, I trust that you do mean *everything.*"

"Uh huh. *Everything*."

Now they both screamed under their breaths. They may as well have been youngsters again.

"Girl, I believe you because he carries himself like he knows he's the total package. He's very confident."

"And he has every reason to be." Cassie rolled her eyes suggestively, retrieved the glass of tea, and walked back into the living room with Maven following closely behind. "Here you go, Todd. Would you like anything else?"

Todd took the tea and again smiled that wonderful smile that melted Cassie every time. "No, this is fine. I'm saving my appetite for dinner."

"Oh, okay." Todd scooted over so that Cassie could sit beside him and Maven walked over to a love seat placed closer to the television.

"Cassie, did you know that Todd's company will be expanding to Canada next year?"

"No, this is the first I've heard of it. When did you make that decision, Todd?"

"It's been in the works for a couple of months now. That's why I need to make sure everything in Atlanta is running smoothly. I can't possibly start up another office in Canada unless headquarters is up to par and, thanks to you, I think it's all going to work out. I was telling Mrs. Stewart that I'll be spending large amounts of time in Canada starting in November. We've got to find a building and start advertising the positions we'll need to fill."

"Wow, that's great." Although Cassie was certainly impressed, her reaction was only halfhearted. Only now did she realize how much she had been looking forward to spending more time with Todd in Atlanta. And she had simply assumed in error that his thoughts were along the same lines.

"That's awesome, Todd!" Maven's enthusiasm made up for Cassie's shortfall. "One of these days, your photo is going to be on the cover of Forbes magazine and I'll be able to say 'I know that guy.' How exciting for you!"

"Thanks, Mave." Todd took Cassie's hand and folded his fingers between hers as he looked into her eyes. "I was also hoping that your sister would be willing to help me with all the work on the expansion."

"What?" Cassie was completely surprised with this development.

"You sure couldn't do better." Mama looked at Cassie with an 'I told you so' expression. "Cassie is not only good at her work, but she works hard and you know you can trust her."

"That's right, Mrs. Stewart. I know I can trust her."

"But I can't do that. I have a job that demands too much of my time to get involved with outside projects."

"So quit the job. You won't need it because you'll be working for me."

Cassie was shaking her head. "No, it's not that simple."

"Why not? You'll have more authority, more freedom, and more money than you have now. And I can personally guaranty that you'll have any and all the challenges you want. I know how important that is to you."

"Maybe you should think about it, baby," Mama cut in. "I know it's a big decision, but it sounds like the opportunity of a lifetime." Once again, Mama's facial expression was quite transparent: *This man is going to be your husband.*

Cassie decided not to get into it any further with both Mama and Maven present. She would speak with Todd later when they were alone so she could remind him that she was happy with her life in Dallas and was not willing to make a giant leap into unknown territory, especially when the leap placed her squarely at his disposal. "Well, I'm going to get dinner started. Will y'all be okay while I'm in the kitchen?"

"Oh yes, we'll be just fine. Don't worry about us." Mama clasped Todd's free hand and allowed her exuberance to be freely transmitted to him. "Todd and I still have plenty of catching up to do."

"Let me know if you need help with anything, Cass." Maven had now found a movie on television and so was not especially interested in parting with the screen.

Cassie knew that she would be better off leaving all three to their own devices. "That's cool." She returned to the kitchen and began removing all the ingredients she would need for this evening's meal. With Todd visiting, chicken and dumplings had been ruled out as an option. Instead, Cassie had decided to prepare a roast, fresh green beans, pasta salad, yams, and a peach cobbler. She expected to have at least two hours to herself—away from Todd and Mama—during which time she would be spared the reminiscing and bonding session currently going on. Now she also needed the time to decide whether or not to scorn Todd for cornering her in front of Mama with a job offer. *God! Did he really expect me to chomp at that bit? Or was he thinking that Mama would persuade me on his behalf?* Cassie would set everything and everyone straight before the evening concluded.

Chapter 16

Late that afternoon, the townhouse was filled with the various aromas of food and everyone was seated at the dining room table awaiting the pre-meal prayer. Everything except the cobbler, which was in the oven, was placed in large dishes at the center of the table and Cassie admitted to herself that she had done a good job. As she looked around the table, she could see that all her guests agreed.

"Cassie, your dinner looks marvelous." Mama turned to Todd, who was seated immediately to her right side. "I taught her everything she knows about cooking."

Todd chuckled. "So then we *know* it's all good."

"That's right, baby." Mama laughed at her own vanity. "Now, Todd, I want you to lead the prayer for us before we eat this good food that Cassie has prepared."

"Yes, ma'am." Everyone linked their hands together around the table and bowed their heads as Todd recited a prayer that thanked God for the food as well as for everyone's health and presence at the table. "Amen."

"That was beautiful, Todd, just beautiful. Now pass me those yams!"

Mama was ready to dig in and everyone now laughed at how forcibly she demanded the commencement of dinner.

Todd handed the bowl of yams to Mama while Cassie and Maven went for the green beans and pasta salad. Before long, all the bowls had been passed around the table and everyone had more food on their plates than they could eat.

"Umm, Cass, this is really good, girl. You outdid yourself." Maven had no sooner stopped talking before she inserted more food into her mouth.

"You sure did. You are a woman with many talents." Like Maven, Todd quickly placed more food into his mouth, clearly savoring the taste of it.

Cassie smiled graciously, ate some of the roast, and then dabbed the corners of her mouth with a napkin. Before she could take another bite, however, the doorbell rang. "I wonder who that is."

"Do you want me to get it?" Maven was closer to the door than Cassie and was already scooting her chair back from the table.

"No, thanks." Cassie stood up and placed her napkin on the table. "It's probably just some kid selling cookies or something. I'll be right back."

Everyone continued eating without interruption as Cassie went to the front door and opened it. Had she been able to fall safely backward without the risk of injury, she certainly would have done so when she saw who her visitor was. To Cassie's shock and surprise, it was Johnson.

"Hey, Cass. How are you?" His demeanor was mellow and even to some degree cautious.

Cassie stepped outside the door and pulled it closed behind her. "What are you doing here?" she hissed. "I just told you last week that I don't want you coming over unannounced like this." She subconsciously looked over her shoulder at the door, expecting to see Todd appear at any minute.

"I know what you said, but you leave me no choice since you won't return my calls." Johnson walked toward the door. "Can we go in? It's hot out here."

"No, we cannot go in." Cassie grabbed his arm and pulled him back in her direction, which was away from the door. "My family is here for the weekend and I don't want you causing a scene in there."

"A scene? You know me better than that." He pointed at the door with a curious expression. "When you say 'family', do you mean your parents are in there? I'd love to meet them."

"It's just my mother and my sister, but you can't go in, Johnson. We were all eating dinner when you showed up."

"That's even better. Got enough for one more?"

"No! Now come on." Cassie again grabbed his arm and pulled him this time toward his car. "You have to leave."

"Okay, okay." Johnson dislodged his arm from Cassie's grip and walked toward the car without her strong-arm assistance. "But I'm not leaving until I've said what I came to say."

Will it never end? Cassie was so tired of these battles with Johnson. She placed her hands on her hips and stood near the front of his car. "Fine, just make it fast."

He came to stand a few feet in front of her, looked at the ground for a brief moment as though gathering courage and collecting his thoughts before allowing his gaze to meet Cassie's once more. "I've had a lot of time lately to think about what you said a few weeks ago. Remember when you were asking me what I wanted from you?"

Cassie's response was to now cross her arms as the impatience mounted within her. "Yeah, so?"

"So I think I know now. I know how I feel about you and I had to tell you before..."

"Before what?"

"Before it was too late." Johnson reached out and gently touched Cassie's face and hair.

"Johnson, don't. Don't do this. Just go." Cassie was ready to flee the scene so she wouldn't have to respond to whatever Johnson was going to say, but she was forced to stand there and to listen to him or risk being followed back inside her home.

"I want you to know that these last few weeks have been an eyeopener for me. I realized that I have been taking you for granted all these months and just assuming you would always be there when I wanted you to be. What I failed to see was that

I didn't just assume you would be there. I *wanted* you to be there."

"And what made you realize that after all this time?"

"Well, something happened at work this week. I closed a really big deal with Pfizer, the biggest our firm has ever had, and the first thing I wanted to do was call you and share the news. I knew you would be happy for me and you would want to celebrate with me just like when I got the promotion. You know what I'm saying? *We* were supposed to celebrate this Pfizer deal together. But I could never reach you and I was disappointed because I couldn't think of anyone else who I would want to celebrate with." He reached for Cassie's hand and carefully, delicately placed it between his own. "And I realized something even more important. I realized that I love you, Cass. I don't think I knew it before. Or maybe I did, but I didn't know how much until—." He shook his head as though in disbelief with himself. "Baby, you're my best friend, did you know that?"

Cassie looked deeply into Johnson's eyes, her emotions suddenly rising to the surface and spinning as uncontrollably as whirlpools. His last statement was affecting her most. "Your best friend?"

"Yes, my best friend." He used his thumb to trace her lips and then leaned down to kiss her.

Before their lips met, however, the townhouse door swung open and Cassie reflexively jumped backward and away from Johnson, restoring a platonic distance between them.

"Cassie."

It was Todd's voice and she turned around just in time to see the displeasure on his face at seeing another man in the driveway. While his initial intention seemed to be merely calling her back in from the doorway, he was soon instead striding toward her and Johnson.

Upon seeing Todd's approach, the confusion on Johnson's face became obvious and he looked at Cassie for an explanation with his mouth slightly agape.

"That's a friend of mine named Todd. He's visiting from Atlanta."

Cassie turned to tell Todd to go back inside, but he was already upon them and wrapping his arms around Cassie's waist. He then kissed her cheek as Johnson continued to watch, his confusion having turned to anger.

"How are you doing, man?" Todd extended a hand to Johnson, who accepted and shook the hand stiffly. "I'm Todd. And you are?"

"This is Johnson." Cassie attempted to gain control of the introductions. "He just dropped by to say 'hello' since we haven't seen each other in a while, right Johnson?"

Johnson looked from Todd to Cassie, the disgust emanating from his eyes targeted solely at Cassie. "Yeah, sure." He turned and walked to his car door. "Cassie tells me that I came at a bad time so I'll be leaving now." He opened the door and climbed into the car.

Meanwhile, Todd began to run his hands over Cassie's hips and waist in some display of possession.

"Stop it, Todd." Annoyed, she slapped his hands and threw his arms off of her to walk toward Johnson, who had already started the engine. "Call me, okay? Maybe we can get together next week or something." She was talking through his window, but she knew he could hear her.

Johnson only glared at Cassie, put his car in reverse, and backed out of the driveway as Cassie helplessly and miserably watched.

"Is that the guy you were seeing until a couple of weeks ago?" Todd had once again come from behind and circled her waist with his arms, but Cassie stepped out of his reach again, angry at the way he had behaved while Johnson was there. She reeled to face him once Johnson's car was heading down the street.

"How *dare* you do that!"

"Do what, baby? What?" Todd fixed a baffled expression on his face.

"How dare you paw me like that in front of my friend. Why would you *do* something like that? Oh, wait a minute. I forgot who I'm talking to because I already know why you did it. You had to make sure he *knew* that you're here and that I belong to you. Well, guess what! I *don't* belong to you! I'm not your chattel or some other *thing* that you can claim as your property."

"Hold up, why are you so angry? If the guy was just a friend, who cares what he thinks? And, more importantly, you *do* belong to me. We belong to each other."

"*Why*, Todd? *Why* must you always try to control every-thing and everyone? You didn't need to come out here to check on me. You didn't need to give Johnson a show. *Why* couldn't you just continue eating dinner and wait for me to come back inside? Have I ever been dishonest with you? Have I ever misled you or mistreated you? *What* did you think you were protecting by coming out here? *What?* I'm not yours, Todd. I'm not yours or anyone else's." With that, Cassie released a fiery huff and charged angrily back into the townhouse. Rather than immediately returning to the dinner table, however, she went into the bathroom to wash her face with cold water.

"Cassie, I put your plate on the stove to keep the food warm," Mama called from the dining room.

"Thanks, Mama. I'll be back in there shortly." Cassie closed the bathroom door and splashed water over her eyes before looking at herself in the mirror. "What are you doing?" She shook her head at the image peering back at her and repeated the question. "What are you doing?" Johnson had said she was his best friend. *Best friend.* Hadn't he once been hers as well? In many ways, yes, he had been, but then he had sorely disappointed her with his emotional distance, which had caused Cassie to feel cheap and used. Now as a result of Cassie's emotional and physical inaccessibility, Johnson had turned over a new leaf and decided that he loved her. *Augh.* And Todd's ridiculous display in the driveway had been unacceptable. *How dare he do that!* Just thinking about it and the look on Johnson's face was making her angry all over again.

But why should she be angry with Todd and sympathetic for Johnson? If Johnson had realized how much he cared a month ago, none of them would be in this situation. Cassie splashed more water on her face and then used a clean towel to pat her skin dry. After one more glance in the mirror, she exited the bathroom and retrieved her dinner from the stovetop.

Once resituated at the table, Cassie observed Todd's pensive silence. Although he dutifully ate his meal, his jovial disposition had all but disintegrated, reappearing only when Mama drew him into a conversation that called for him to smile and laugh for her benefit.

Mama didn't seem to notice the change in Todd, but Maven had clearly discerned the shift and her eyes frequently darted between Cassie and Todd as she vainly sought to determine the problem. The minutes drug slowly by and seemed more like hours as far as Cassie was concerned.

After dinner was finished, Cassie and Maven cleared the table while Mama and Todd went into the living room and continued to talk.

Maven couldn't wait to ask the obvious question. "What happened outside, girl?" She turned on the kitchen faucet and began running water into a sink filled with dishes.

Cassie's face flushed immediately and her skin felt hot again. Todd. Johnson. Todd. Johnson. After a solitary deep breath, she struggled to collect herself and then told her sister about Johnson's unexpected visit, what he had said, and how Todd had behaved before Johnson angrily departed. In the meantime, she used a dampened paper towel to wipe her face as she confided in

Maven, who could only react with amazement throughout the story.

"I'm sorry, Cass. Everything is just so messed up with these two men. Why do they always wait until you've moved on to figure out how great you are? It's like they're brain damaged and frankly it really pisses me off. To hell with both of them."

Cassie smiled despite herself. "I know. I just can't take it anymore. I really can't. I feel like I'm going to crack up inside."

"Well, don't do that. It will get better." Maven rubbed Cassie's back as she spoke.

"I know it will. The question is *when*?"

"When men sprout breasts and have periods, that's when."

"What?" Cassie burst into surprised laughter at her sister's unexpected response. "What do you mean?"

"Well, how else are they going to learn to think with a different head? If they had breasts, they would understand how we get tired of them gawking at ours and acting as if *our* breasts are *their* property. One of the reasons that men like Johnson fear commitment is because they hate to commit themselves to one set of breasts for the rest of their lives. I mean, what if a bigger, softer pair comes along? Then they'll have mammary regrets."

By now, Cassie was laughing hard enough for her stomach to hurt. Nevertheless, Maven continued with her parapsychology analysis.

"And if breasts aren't enough to make them rethink their caveman antics, then at least the menstrual cramps would knock them out for the count and spare us all the insanity for a few days out of the month. Then men like Todd, for example, wouldn't be around to bother anyone with their stupid B.S."

Cassie began to shed tears borne from laughter and held her stomach in a futile effort to ease the accompanying pain. "Mave, have you ever considered becoming a standup comedienne because I think that's your calling."

"Hey, I'm just calling it like I see it, that's all." She also laughed at her own farfetched solutions to Cassie's man problems. "When is Todd leaving Dallas?"

"I think he's flying out tomorrow morning. He booked a hotel room for one night at the Hampton Inn down the street from here."

"Oh. So he can stay and talk to Mama tonight for as long as she can stay awake, huh? That's a positive and a negative."

"Yep."

As they talked, Cassie washed and rinsed the dishes while Maven dried and stacked them.

"We can't win for losing tonight, can we?"

"Nope."

They finished the dishes in silence and then wiped clean all the kitchen counters as well as the stove.

"Mave, would you please go find out if either Mama or Todd wants some cobbler?"

"Okay." She walked out of the kitchen and returned a few seconds later with a dubious look on her face. "Neither of them wants any pie."

"Okay, thanks." Cassie pulled out a pan in which to place the entire cobbler for storage in the refrigerator.

"And, Cass, I think you should know that Mama has already gone to bed for the night."

"Really? It's only eight o'clock." Cassie wheeled around to face her sister.

"So you know it's a setup. She's trying to get you and Todd alone. You should see him in there all by his lonesome. He looks so pitiful."

"Pitiful my butt." Cassie inhaled deeply. "Those two are dangerous."

"Do you want me to stay in the room with you?"

"No, that's okay. I need to talk to Todd about a few things anyway." She resumed transferring the cobbler to the storage pan. The process calmed her nerves.

"Alright. I'll be in the bedroom so just holler if you need me to come back."

"Okay. Thanks."

When Cassie finally entered the living room, Todd was sitting on the sofa with his hands folded together. His tension was betrayed only by the fact that he leaned forward in a hunched position and continually rubbed his hands as though in deep thought.

"Hey." Cassie walked around the sofa and sat beside him.

"Hey." As he spoke, his hands stopped moving and he leaned backward to sink into the sofa. "So do you wanna tell me what that was all about in the driveway earlier?"

"Todd, I'm sorry." Cassie paused to search for the best way to communicate her decision.

"Sorry for what?"

Cassie dismally looked away, the right words having failed to come to mind.

"You don't have to say it. I already know."

"How could you?"

"Because I could see it when I went outside." His earnest disappointment and hurt could not have been more evident. He paused briefly before posing the obvious accusation as a question. "Do you still want this Johnson guy that came over here today?"

"No...I don't know. No. Maybe. Anyway," she dismissed the question by waving her hand through the air, "whatever I decide about Johnson has nothing to do with you and me." She paused again to find the right words as Todd maintained an unnerving silence. "When you and I first met, I loved the way you took charge of everything. It was one of the reasons I was so drawn to you. I felt safe, as if I didn't need to worry about anything because you were so sure and strong. But eventually, I started to feel like you were controlling me and my life. I felt like I had to look a certain way, dress a certain way, be something I wasn't just to make you happy. And then I resented you for manipulating everything and everybody, including me." She sighed long and hard. "But now I realize that the things about you that drive me crazy are the exact things that have made you so successful, and I wouldn't dream of asking you to change. What I mean is that your personality benefits you, but at the same time it brings me down."

"I never knew you felt that way." Todd was visibly stung. "I'll admit that I probably do manipulate certain things in my work to ensure positive outcomes, but I would *never* try to manipulate you, Cass. Never."

"That's not true and I don't believe you even think it is."

"It *is* true, Cassie. Okay, tell me what I've done to make you think I want to manipulate you. Give me just one example."

"That's easy. I'll even give you three examples. For one thing, you used my job to get me to Atlanta."

"Oh, come on. That was different. I was trying to show you how much I've changed and accomplished because of you."

"Since you've been here today, you tried to use my mother's affection for you to influence my decision about taking a job in Canada with your company."

"It's a golden opportunity. I knew you wouldn't listen to me. Of course, now I know you won't listen to her either."

Cassie continued without responding to any of Todd's defensive comments. "You practically felt me up outside so Johnson would think that we're a couple despite the fact that nothing had been decided yet."

"Now, Cassie, you know you're exaggerating. I only touched your hips like I always do. Why is that suddenly a crime?"

"Because it was disrespectful. You wouldn't have done that in front of my mother so you shouldn't have done it in front of Johnson."

"You know, I think that you're just looking for reasons to stop seeing me."

"If that's true, I certainly don't have to look very hard or very far, Todd."

He began rubbing his hands together again, but Cassie was strangely calm. She knew she had made the right decision.

"I'm sorry that you have such a poor impression of my intentions, Cass, but you couldn't be more wrong about me."

"I'm sorry, too, Todd. And if I am wrong, I apologize for that as well. Either way, the bottom line is that we don't belong together."

"Well, I'm not giving up that easily." Todd reached into his pocket, removed a small black jewelry box, and held it out to Cassie. "I told you a few months ago that I came to Dallas for you. Since I'm still hoping that we can work this out, I'd like for you to have this."

Cassie stared at the box without moving. "Whatever it is, Todd, I can't accept it. You know that."

He withdrew his hand long enough to open the lid and hold the box back out. It was a perfectly cut, very large diamond engagement ring. "Won't you even think about it?"

Although certainly impressed with the ring, Cassie was still not interested in accepting it. "I'm sorry, Todd, but no. You should save that ring for the right woman."

"Like I've said before, I don't want any other woman." He set the open ring case down on the coffee table and the diamond literally reflected all the lights in the room. It was like having a tiny star on the table. "Cass, the truth is that I was hoping you would help me with my work in Canada as more than an employee. I was thinking more along the lines of a partnership. The marital kind."

"Todd, it would never work. Maybe we'd be happy for a little while, but then things would go back to the way they were before in Atlanta and I would feel like I was settling for less than I deserve in a relationship. And I don't want you to feel put down because I know you're a good person and you have good intentions. I *know* that. But you and I just don't have what it takes to have a lasting relationship. In fact, I think the only reason that you want me is because you can't have me and that's not love."

Throughout Cassie's response, Todd had closely watched her face, perhaps in search of the love that had continually remained unrequited despite his best efforts. "I hear you, Cassie, and I know without any doubt that you're wrong." He turned his head to again look at the ring, the symbol of a rejected promise. "I also know that you've made up your mind so nothing I say is going to make a difference with you." He exhaled before finally standing up and gesturing toward the ring. "I won't be giving that ring to anyone else so if you don't want it, do with it as you please."

Overwhelmed with guilt, Cassie barely heard him. "I'm sorry, Todd."

"Stop apologizing, Cassie. It's not your fault." He stood before her and looked into her eyes. Everything he couldn't say with words was stated beautifully through his soulful brown eyes. "I'll never give up on you in here." He patted the area near his heart. "No matter what you say. Thirty years and five grandchildren later I will still love you."

Moved by Todd's strong emotions, Cassie now also stood up and stepped into his arms. When he pulled her tightly against him, Cassie responded in kind, enjoying the feel of his body for what she knew would be the last time. *He feels so good. Why couldn't we ever make this work?* And then her mind strayed to Johnson once more, to the look on his face when Todd had appeared in the doorway. Johnson had only seconds earlier confessed his love for Cassie as well as told her she was his best friend. *Best friend.* The very words that Monique, Maven, and Dana had used to describe their own partners. The very kind of romance and relationship that Cassie had thought would forever elude her. She and Todd had never had the types of conversations and closeness that she and Johnson had once shared. And although it was probably too late to salvage any form of friendship with Johnson, that was no reason for Cassie to get locked into a dissatisfying relationship and future with Todd. Despite Todd's feelings for her, he could never be the man with whom she could be happy on a permanent basis.

They continued holding each other for several long moments before Todd kissed Cassie's forehead and released her. "I guess I'll reschedule my flight and head back to Atlanta tonight. There's no reason for me to stay in Dallas."

Once again feeling guilty for disappointing Todd, Cassie broke eye contact briefly. "Do you want a ride to the hotel?"

"No, there's a cab waiting for me outside."

"What?" Cassie was bewildered that he had already prepared for an early exit. "When did you call a cab?"

"As soon as your mother went into her bedroom. When I saw the way you looked at Johnson today...well, I knew...but I still had to hear your decision with my own ears."

"But there's nothing between me and Johnson."

"Maybe that's true, Cass, but I think you still have feelings for the guy. Damn! Why does it have to be this way? Why can't you love me instead of him?" Todd studied Cassie's face for the answers before smiling weakly and resigning himself to a situation he could not change. "Well, Ms. Stewart, you have all my phone numbers. Use them whenever you like." He walked to the door and turned to look at her once more.

"I will." Cassie smiled and also went toward the door as Todd stepped outside and strode toward the waiting taxi. She watched him get into the car and then waved when he peered out the window. He merely nodded his head and signaled the driver to go. Once he turned his eyes forward, he didn't look at Cassie again and something inside her knew that Todd had just bid her a permanent farewell.

Chapter 17

With Todd gone, Cassie decided to sit outside on her patio with a cool glass of tea. She couldn't see much at this time of night, but she could still smell the fragrant pine, which relieved some of her tension. As the night wind blew through her hair, she allowed her head to fall backward against the patio chair as a heavy breath escaped her body. In a surprising turn of events, Cassie could not get Johnson off of her mind. She didn't know which set of circumstances had made her feel worse today—Todd's untimely marriage proposal or Johnson's confusion and anger over Todd. The day had certainly turned out to be the wild ride that Maven had predicted that morning.

"Is it really that bad, honey?"

Cassie looked up to see Mama standing in the doorway with her own glass of tea. Without waiting for Cassie's response, Mama walked over to the only other chair on the patio and sat down.

"Oh, yeah. This is the life, isn't it? You've got a fresh breeze, the scent of pine in the air." Mama inhaled deeply to enjoy the scent. "The sky is beautiful and clear tonight. The conditions are perfect for you to sit out here and feel sorry for yourself, huh?"

"Mama, please, not tonight. I think I've had enough for one day." Cassie sat up a little straighter and sipped her tea.

"I'm sure you have, I'm sure you have."

Mother and daughter sat in silence for a few minutes, peering out into the black night and allowing the wind to have its way with their hair. They could hear the leaves rustling, rebelling against that same wind, while somewhere in the distance an owl beckoned to his mate.

Cassie felt that the untamed breeze mirrored her emotional state and she wished the night air would relieve her of the turmoil swirling too freely inside.

"I remember when I met your father so many years ago." Mama was still peering somewhere into the night as she spoke. "You wouldn't know it today, but he was actually a very shy man, sort of a nerd back then." Now she turned to look at Cassie and smiled.

"Really?" Cassie attempted to envision her father as a nerd. She had seen pictures of his more youthful days, but Cassie had always been struck by how handsome he had been. It had never occurred to her that his personality had been anything other than what is was today—sweet, fun-loving, and gentle.

"Yes, chile, yes. To this day, I don't think he realizes that *I* actually asked *him* out on our first date. That's how shy he was." She laughed gaily and threw her head back so that the breeze caressed her neck.

Mama was obviously feeling extremely relaxed and Cassie thought about asking what might be mixed in with her tea.

When Mama restored her eyes to her daughter's face, the tenderness she felt reached across the space between them. "He had no real understanding of how special and outstanding he was. You remind me of him that way."

"I do? Why do you say that?"

"Oh, because you've always been reluctant to go after the things you want. It's almost as if you don't think you deserve what you need to be happy, especially when it comes to men."

"I don't think that's entirely true. I think it would be more accurate to say that I haven't always *known* what would make me happy, but I'm figuring it out. Don't worry about me."

"I can't help but worry about you because I carried you for nine months, but that's beside the point." She drank some tea and allowed a moment of silence to descend before, "That young man who came by earlier today...Was that Johnson?"

"You saw him?"

"I took a quick peek when Todd went outside to check on you. It looked like a pretty intense situation."

"Yes, it was."

Mama nodded her head. "How do you feel about Johnson? Do you love him?"

"I really don't know."

"Hmph. I think you do. Love him, that is. I could tell by the way you moved around him. I couldn't see your face since your back was to the window, but your body language was a dead giveaway. Must have scared poor Todd to death since he was hoping he'd get you to marry him. But anyone with eyes could see that just wasn't going to happen."

"So you *did* know that he was going to propose."

"Of course I knew! I knew that the instant you told me he was coming here. Coming to see me indeed!"

Cassie now laughed. "I guess everyone could see through him except for me."

"That's because you didn't *want* to see through him. You've known all along that you have no interest in marrying Todd. And why? Because you really love Johnson and there's not enough room in either your head or your heart for both of them."

"Well, everything is certainly a mess now." Cassie ran her hands over her hair and looked at her mother. "Johnson was so angry when he saw Todd...I'm sure he never wants to talk to me again."

"I thought you and Johnson had broken up."

"We did. Around four weeks ago."

"And when did you start seeing Todd again?"

"Um, maybe two weeks ago."

"Then Johnson doesn't have a leg to stand on if he's angry about Todd being here."

He wouldn't have had a leg to stand on before we stopped seeing each other since there was no commitment to speak of. "Yeah, you're right, Mama. I just don't know what to do at this point."

"In my opinion, baby, the *first* thing you need to do is figure out how you feel about Johnson. Once you do *that*, you'll know what to do."

"Maybe."

"No, not maybe. You *will*. You'll know just like I knew what to do if I was ever going to have a date with your father. Sometimes, Cassie, you just have to go after what you want. And don't be ashamed to do it either." Mama paused long enough to take another swallow of the tea. "I'm going to make this one point and then go to bed. If you love Johnson and if you want to work things out with him, you're going to have to take some initiative in the matter. But, of course, that's *only* if you love him because if you don't, you should just let it be." Mama rose from the chair, walked over to Cassie, and gently rubbed her hair. "Dear daughter, pride has no place in love." She leaned down and kissed the top of Cassie's head. "Try to get some rest, okay?"

"Okay, Mama. I'll see you in the morning."

"Yes, and I think that *I'll* make breakfast this time. How do you feel about some of my famous blueberry pancakes?"

"Ooh, that sounds good! Thanks, Mama."

"Of course. Goodnight."

"Goodnight."

The patio door closed and Cassie was once again alone to ponder everything that had transpired that day as well as

Mama's parting words. Pride and love. Was Cassie being proud? She didn't think that was entirely the case now. In truth, she was afraid. Afraid of her feelings for Johnson—afraid of fully unveiling the emotions that she had experienced earlier in the driveway when he said she was his best friend; afraid to expect and to openly want his love; afraid to give him her own love. In fact, throughout her involvement with Johnson, fear had been her primary motivator. Fear had prevented her from asking about his feelings early in the relationship and fear now prevented her from calling him. Fear.

It seemed impossible, but a full circle had somehow evolved. Around six weeks ago, she had needed to know whether Johnson loved her and, after today's events, she was again wondering the same thing. Within that same timeframe, she had gone from despising Todd to yearning for him and then back to despising him. Okay, maybe she didn't actually despise Todd, but she certainly did not like many of his controlling behaviors. In the end, Todd was history once more and Cassie was back at square one—entirely, indisputably alone.

But being alone was not the most distressing thing on her mind. Rather, Cassie was more bothered by the hurt on Johnson's face, the image of which remained steadfastly before her eyes. Mama was right that he had no legitimate reason to be upset, but Cassie imagined how she would have felt if she had seen him with another woman. It would not have been pretty. So did that mean she loved him? Because of the nature of their relationship, she had always been unwilling to really evaluate her emotions for Johnson. Instead, she had focused her attention on getting *him* to tell *her* how *he* felt. But would it really have mattered so much if she hadn't loved him? *No. It wouldn't have mattered at all. Who am I kidding here? I have loved Johnson since the day we met. I have loved everything about him and shared as much with him as I would Monique and Dana. Of course, Johnson and I shared much more and I guess I can finally admit to myself that he was my best friend, too. Yes, I do love Johnson. For what it's worth, I really do.*

A very noticeable chill began to intermingle with the night air and Cassie was compelled to go inside. Before doing so, she stood at the balcony, rested her hands on the smooth wooden boarding, and turned her face upward to the sky. "God, I really don't know what to do right now. I'm so confused." She rubbed her arms to generate heat and bowed her head. "I don't know how I'm going to make it through this and I could really use Your help. Otherwise, I'm afraid that whatever I do won't solve anything. I'm afraid, God, that if it's possible, I'll just make things worse than they already are."

By 4:00 p.m. the next day, both Mama and Maven were on their flights back to their homes and Cassie was left to stare at her phone and wonder if it would ring. She found herself pacing back and forth around the townhouse, watching the phone remain silent and trying to ignore her fervent desire for Johnson

to call. Between her pacing sessions, she packed her luggage for tomorrow's return to Puerto Rico, she called Monique and Dana to tell them about Todd's proposal and Johnson's surprise visit, she called her father to learn how he had fared without Mama at home, and she read the *Oprah Magazine* for some uplifting words. Periodically, she also couldn't help picking up the phone and placing it against her ear to ensure it was actually working. Was the ringer turned on? Was the dial tone there? Was the jack securely attached to the wall? *Why won't you ring? Ring. Please! And let it be Johnson.* But nothing happened.

Finally at around nine thirty that evening, Cassie's pride had entirely eroded away and she picked up the phone to call Johnson. Surprisingly, her hands trembled as she dialed his number and placed the phone up to her ear. When she got his voicemail, Cassie was almost relieved, but then she thought, "Where is he?" *Oh well.* She set down the phone and stood staring at it, immobile, trying to decide if she should call back and leave a message. *Of course I should leave a message. After everything he said yesterday, that's the least I can do.* Cassie picked up the phone again and dialed Johnson's phone number, this time finding the courage to speak when the voicemail greeting ended. "Hi, Johnson. It's Cassie. Um…Listen, I'm really sorry about what happened yesterday and…Well, I was hoping we could finish talking about some of the things you said. Would you please call me? Or come by? Oh, that's right. I'll be in Puerto Rico on a project for the next week so I won't be here. Um…Well, would you call me when you get this message tonight? I'll probably be up late, okay?" Pause. "Okay, well, I hope to speak with you soon. Bye." Cassie dropped the connection and cringed. *Oooh, I sounded like such an idiot! Lord!*

She started pacing around the phone again and staring at the inanimate, non-ringing object. Suddenly, the phone had become an enemy and Cassie briefly considered shutting it off all night so she wouldn't know whether or not it rang. *Can't do that, though, since Mama and Maven are supposed to call when they get home.*

She flopped onto the sofa and looked sideways at the phone while tapping her fingers on the sofa arm. It wasn't ringing. In fact, except for Mama's and Maven's calls late that night, the phone never rang.

Thoroughly disappointed, Cassie went to bed and stared at the ceiling. She wasn't sleepy at all, but she also could not continue watching the phone. At the very least, the ceiling provided a change of scenery. *I guess Johnson hates me now. There's no way to fix it and I can't change what happened. I'm going to have to accept that it's over for good. It's over, it's over, it's over. There's no going back and I have to move on. Accept it. It's over. Accept it. It's over.* The entire time Cassie lectured herself, she still hoped that the phone would prove her wrong and ring. But it never did.

Chapter 18

FEBRUARY ARRIVED WITH THE usual icy weather that Cassie dreaded each year, but she was prepared. She had purchased a charcoal, wool trench coat that thankfully spared her legs the freezing rain that was now covering the streets and turning into black ice. Motorists were creeping past the church in which Monique and Rodney would soon be married, taking good care to maintain speeds below ten miles per hour since the hazardous ice patches were frequently too difficult to see. Meanwhile, the guests attending the wedding, which numbered around three-hundred, had for the most part already arrived and been seated within the warm confines of the church. Cassie would be one of the few who couldn't seem to get there on time. She ducked her head and practically scurried the distance from her car to the chapel, hoping that she had not missed a second of the ceremony. When she finally walked in and realized that the service had not yet started, she exhaled relief as she removed her coat and was ushered to an empty seat.

For the occasion, Cassie had worn a light wool, cranberry-colored dress that fell just below her knees and an off-white scarf dotted with the same cranberry shade. It was simple, understated, and nevertheless flattering.

Cassie had never been inside this church, but she knew that Monique and Rodney had become members specifically because they wanted to be married here in the beautiful, awe-inspiring sanctuary. There were thick, solid white pillars lining the walls and at least thirty stained glass windows with religious images presented in an artistic style that was reminiscent of Leonardo Da Vinci's paintings. However, perhaps the most impressive feature was the high, domed ceiling that gave the chapel a feeling of omnipotence. Cassie felt that the height of the ceiling alone served to remind everyone who visited the church of God's greatness as well as the humbleness they should feel in His presence.

It had been over five months since Mama and Maven had visited and the time could not have flown at a swifter pace. Cassie had been overjoyed to wrap up the Puerto Rico project, which had been extended several times until last month. Finally, she had moved on to other types of clients and challenges. In the meantime, she had never heard from Johnson and Todd's calls had dwindled to a consistent minimum. *It's just as well*, she learned to tell herself. *If Johnson and I were meant to be together, we wouldn't have had to work so hard at just getting our feelings on the table.* Monique, on the other hand, was not interested in hearing Cassie's resignation speech.

"Call him, girl. Stop being so stubborn!" Monique urged at every opportunity.

"I can't, Monique. I've already tried to reach him a few times and he doesn't return my calls so it's pointless."

"Have you ever told him how you feel?"

"You mean have I told the voicemail? No and I'm not going to. If Johnson wanted to know, he would have called me back by now."

"But he's hurting. That's why he hasn't called you back. I don't think he's trying to be mean or anything."

"Well, I'm not a mind reader so I don't know if you're right about that. Anyway, life goes on. There will eventually be someone else."

At this, Monique would invariably smack her lips and cross her arms, but at least the subject would be dropped, for which Cassie was grateful.

Now as Cassie looked around the church, she caught Dana's eye a few aisles in front of hers and waved. The two friends shared a silent greeting and then Dana pointed a gloved finger forward with a sly wink. Cassie's eyes followed the direction in which Dana pointed and very soon fell on Johnson, who was seated a few aisles up and to the left of Dana. Without realizing it, Cassie sank down slightly to hide herself, not that he had seen her. When she looked at Dana again, Cassie's face bore the frantic state she had entered as Dana continued to smile and faced forward once again.

What is Johnson doing here? He and Monique don't know each very well. But as quickly as the questions came, so did the obvious answer: Monique. She was a grand schemer indeed and her objective was all too transparent. Cassie should have been suspicious that Monique was up to something since she had constantly interrogated Cassie about her work schedule in the weeks leading up to the wedding. There had been a chance that the Puerto Rico job would be extended again and Monique had been especially alarmed that Cassie may not even be in Dallas for the ceremony. At the time, Cassie had chalked up Monique's concern to both nervousness and friendship, but now she knew better. *Uh huh. You are a slick one, my friend.* But what Monique could not have factored in was the fact that Cassie could be equally as crafty and was already making up her mind to avoid Johnson at all cost. There would be no awkward reunion today if Cassie had anything to do with it. Undoubtedly, Monique's ploy was going to prove a futile one and Cassie would emerge emotionally unscathed from the dubious predicament. She already had the situation under control. With her firm resolve intact, Cassie's confidence began to return and she slowly eased back up into a comfortable sitting position. *Cool. Be cool. You can handle this.* But the troublesome question insisted on resurfacing in her mind: *Are you sure?*

When the wedding song, "Here Comes the Bride," finally signaled the appearance of Monique, everyone in the chapel stood up at once and smiled as an especially radiant bride slowly sauntered very sexily down the aisle. In keeping with her previous conversations with Cassie, it was obvious that Monique wanted Rodney to drool as she walked toward him and, judging from his face, the mission was certainly being accomplished. From her seat, Cassie could see the energy the two exchanged as they connected on sight. And she didn't need to see Monique's face to know that Monique was smiling a promise of evening ecstasy for her husband-to-be, a promise that Rodney was very clearly thrilled to accept on a forever basis.

Just look at them. They really have something special. That's what Cassie wanted, a soul connection like Monique's and Rodney's. From the beginning, they had been intertwined on every imaginable level: spiritual, mental, physical. It was all there and they were best friends on top of it all. *Best friends.*

Once Monique was standing beside Rodney exchanging vows, Cassie's eyes found Johnson again. As far as she knew, he had never looked in any direction except forward. Curious of whether or not he had brought a date, she looked to his side and noticed a very beautiful woman that had escaped her attention earlier. As Cassie checked her out, the woman leaned over and whispered something into Johnson's ear and they both smiled while continuing to watch the wedding. *The jerk actually brought another woman knowing that I would be here! He's trying to get back at me, but he will leave without that satisfaction. Cool. Be cool.*

The woman sitting with Johnson was definitely a looker with long, straight, dark hair that was pulled into a soft bun at the nape of her neck. Her skin was slightly lighter than Cassie's and she had an air of elegance that was obviously natural for her.

Where did he find her? No matter how she fought back the jealousy, Cassie was very soon consumed in its bitter grip. She eventually forced her eyes back to Monique and Rodney, now more than ever determined that Johnson's path would not cross hers at any point that day. Her heart rate and breathing accelerated at the idea of bumping into Johnson and his date. While she would certainly be polite, she would also be completely humiliated. But then she reminded herself that over three-hundred people were attending the wedding, which meant that avoiding such an encounter was an entirely plausible reality. She would somehow remain lost among this crowd for an appropriate amount of time and then leave. Of course, there was the reception that followed, but she would simply dine at her assigned table, congratulate Monique and Rodney, and then go home. *And I'm definitely going to need a strong drink after all this.* It was all very possible and Cassie relaxed somewhat as she imagined the events playing themselves out accordingly. Mingle, eat, and go home. Nothing very hard about that. Nothing very hard at all.

"Cassie, you look beautiful. You should wear cranberry colors more often because they really bring out your eyes and skin." Dana had found Cassie before everyone was seated at the reception and she now hugged Cassie warmly.

"Thanks." She gave Dana a quick once over. "You look like you've lost weight!"

"Yes, I finally got rid of all that baby fat. Thank God. I can fit into clothes I haven't worn in nearly two years."

"Well, you look really good, girl. I'm still trying to lose a few pounds so I could use any tips you have."

"Oh, Cassie. Where would you lose it? You're perfect just the way you are."

"I know that's not true, but thanks again. By the way, did you know that Johnson was going to be here?"

"Not until I saw him walk into the church. Isn't it exciting? You two may finally have a chance to straighten everything out." Dana reached out to touch Cassie's shoulder as her husband, Alan, appeared at her side.

"Cassie, it's good to see you." He smiled as he placed his arm around Dana's waist.

"Hi, Alan. How have you been?"

"Fantastic. And yourself?

"Great. Just great." *Even greater in around an hour when I can get out of here.*

Alan's eyes brightened as they fell on Dana. "This brings back memories, doesn't it?"

"Yes. The best kind."

Alan leaned down and kissed Dana's cheek and she blushed like a schoolgirl. After being married for nearly ten years, the two were still obviously smitten with each other.

"Everyone is sitting down now so we should find our table. Do you remember which one we've been assigned?" Alan reached into his coat pocket in search of the wedding reception information.

"I think we're at table twenty-two over that way." Dana pointed in an eastern direction before asking Cassie, "Which table were you assigned? I hope you're dining with us."

"I think I'm supposed to be at table eighty or something like that." The table was located on an entirely different side of the room.

"Now why would Monique do that? She knows we don't know anyone else here." Dana was truly dismayed.

"Honey, aren't some of your other coworkers here?"

"Yes, I suppose a few are, but only a handful." Dana sighed and looked at Cassie disappointedly. "I guess we'll see you later, Cass."

"Okay. It was nice to see you, Alan."

"Likewise, Cassie. You take care."

They all went in opposite directions in the crowded room.

For the reception, Monique had chosen a large banquet hall that had a dance floor at the center. Round dining tables had been arranged close to the dance floor and a live band was playing various jazz instrumentals as waiters and hosts began to disperse throughout the room.

When Cassie finally reached her table, she looked at the placement cards with everyone's names in search of her own. As she read the cards, she circled the table until she found her seating assignment and sat down. So far she had successfully managed not to bump into Johnson and his date. She was relieved to have safely arrived at her table. Out of habit, Cassie reached for the tablecloth and unfolded it in her lap.

"So...we meet again under happier circumstances."

Cassie didn't need to look up to see the man behind the voice. She cringed inwardly before turning her head to see Johnson standing beside her. He was alone. "Hi. How are you?" *Be cool. Cool.*

"I'm fine. And," he pointed at the name card set to the right of Cassie's, "it appears that I'm one of your dining mates this evening."

Cassie glanced over at the card, which listed his name, and kicked herself for not having noticed sooner. Here she had been congratulating herself on dodging the man so expertly throughout the affair! Obviously, Monique had been even more clever than Cassie had anticipated.

Johnson pulled out his chair and sat down, after which time an uncomfortable silence ensued. As he looked around the room at the guests, Cassie either fidgeted with the napkin in her lap or stared blindly in any direction but his. This continued for several minutes before Cassie broke the silence.

"Did you come here with anyone?" *Why did you ask him that? Why didn't you ask something like 'How's the job?' or some-*

thing else impersonal. Now he will think you care since it was the first question out of your mouth.

"Uh, no, actually, I came alone."

Cassie experienced a brief moment of relief as Johnson continued.

"How about you? Is your friend here?" His eyes were vacant of any emotion. It was a casual question.

"What friend?"

"That guy I met at your house a few months ago. What was his name? Thomas, I think."

"Oh." Cassie was all at once depressed and she looked down at her hands. "You mean Todd. No, he's not here."

A few more guests took their seats at the table, but they were not close enough to overhear Cassie's and Johnson's conversation. She smiled lamely across the table at them as Johnson once again began looking around the room.

"Johnson, I've been wanting to tell you how sorry I am about what happened the last time we saw each other. I have felt terrible about it ever since that day."

"Hey, no apology necessary. You didn't do anything wrong."

"Yeah, well, I just want to apologize if I did anything to hurt you."

He adjusted his tie and then set his hands palm down on his knees. Meanwhile, Cassie could hardly look at him and so returned her attention to the guests, most of which were now seated at their respective tables and enjoying animated conversations. The room was increasingly becoming filled with their voices as people endeavored to be heard across their tables and over the music.

"Cass, I know you're not to blame for what happened between us. You did everything right when we were seeing each other. I was the one who couldn't figure out what I wanted so *I'm* the one who should be apologizing for any hurt, not you."

Cassie was stunned, appreciative, and left speechless by Johnson's words. Remarkably, she felt something ordinarily knotted tightly inside her stomach begin to unwind, to soften as Johnson looked her squarely in the eyes.

For the first time, Cassie realized how much she had missed him. She hesitated for mere seconds before deciding that it was time for her walls, all the emotional barriers, to come down. It was time for her to be more willing to take risks and to express her feelings when life presented those rare, special opportunities. This meant that she needed to learn how to allow relationships and emotions to naturally unfold, grow, wither, whatever. And Cassie would also need to stop being frightened of the withering or *whatever* possibilities. After all, everything converged into the ingredients necessary for a full life, right? And who was Cassie cheating by shutting off her feelings or trying to hide them from the men she loved? No one except herself.

Pride and love. Mama had been right that pride and love could not successfully coexist. But neither could fear and love. Pride coupled with fear could only hinder her chances for a devoted, meaningful relationship and happiness.

Without further hesitation, Cassie finally told Johnson, "I've really missed you."

He smiled. "I've missed you, too. And I must say that you're looking very nice tonight."

"Thanks. You're looking pretty dapper yourself." He had always looked good in his suits.

"Well, you know, I've got it like that."

They laughed at Johnson's unusual self-flattery and the ice was suddenly, entirely broken. And as they laughed, the past just didn't seem important anymore.

"I trust that you'll save at least one dance for me before you leave."

"It would be my honor, Mr. Hughes. I would like that very much."

He grabbed her hand and squeezed it as they continued smiling at each other. "No, Miss Stewart, the honor will be all mine. You can believe that."

About the Author

I have a passion for books, both as a reader and a writer. The countless novels that I've read throughout my life are my inspiration for creating my own plots and characters. I feel very fortunate to have an active imagination that I can allow to run free while writing novels.

I'm a native Texan and have three four-legged kiddos who I absolutely adore. Because of them, I am daily reminded that the simple things in life are what matter the most.

For information about my other novels, please visit my website: www.krysbatts.com.

www.ingramcontent.com/pod-product-compliance
Lightning Source LLC
Chambersburg PA
CBHW071311170626

46809CB00001B/402